For friends and colleagues who were so generous

with their encouragement and good counsel

Praise for
The Blitz Business

"*The Blitz Business* is a tale of resilience during World War II through the eyes of Jamie, a teenager with intellectual disabilities. D.A. Spruzen's narrative will make readers rethink their perceptions of the challenges facing people with such challenges, a bold and progressive perspective even in today's modern world."

—**Betsy Schatz,** Executive Director
Langley Residential Support Services,
a residential and community support provider for adults with
intellectual disabilities

"*The Blitz Business* is a fine book, with characters you come to care about and root for; Jamie, the 15 year old main character is memorable and well drawn—an unconventional lead in a story of not only survival but redemption. This historical novel is a winner."

—**Robert Bausch**
Author of *Far as the Eye Can See* and
The Legend of Jesse Smoke

"*The Blitz Business* is an extremely ambitious novel, about big issues and big events, with a large and compelling cast of characters and a complexity that evolves to a wonderfully satisfying resolution. This is an outstanding debut that gives us a whole new angle on the last great war while offering richly imagined characters who are real from the first page to the last."

—Fred Leebron
Author of *Christiania* and
In the Middle of All This

"Deeply moving and endlessly surprising, *The Blitz Business* brings heart and unexpected light to the darkest corners of war-torn London. In Spruzen's capable hands, a vulnerable young man's search for a forever home becomes an irresistible journey filled with indelible characters and real danger. A novel of striking wisdom limned with a gritty historical edge."

—Laura Benedict,
Author of the *Bliss House* trilogy

The Blitz Business
by D.A. Spruzen

© Copyright 2016 D.A. Spruzen

ISBN 978-1-63393-268-5

All rights reserved. No part of this publication may be reproduced, stored in a retrieval system, or transmitted in any form or by any means – electronic, mechanical, photocopy, recording, or any other – except for brief quotations in printed reviews, without the prior written permission of the author.

This is a work of fiction. The characters are both actual and fictitious. With the exception of verified historical events and persons, all incidents, descriptions, dialogue and opinions expressed are the products of the author's imagination and are not to be construed as real.

Cover image of St. Pauls Cathedral during the Battle of Britain
courtesy of The National Archives (archives.gov)

Published by

210 60th Street
Virginia Beach, VA 23451
800-435-4811
www.koehlerbooks.com

I hope you enjoy Jamie's journey —

For Brd~

The Blitz Business

D.A. SPRUZEN

VIRGINIA BEACH
CAPE CHARLES

PROLOGUE

The swell rode high, breaking hard enough near the shoreline for freezing water to slurp into his rubber boots. When a stealthy current pulled him under, his cry died in a salty mouthful as he struggled to keep hold of his heavy burden. Rivulets coursed down his body, keening wind shuddering them into every crease of his sodden clothing as he headed for shelter under the cliffs. He stumbled and twisted an ankle, swearing in clipped whispers. He'd expected a sandy cove, not this god-forsaken stony beach. To think that only yesterday he had been in Deauville among the decadent French, slaves to their stomachs. Even in wartime those in the right circles ate well. British food was bad enough at the best of times.

Oars splashed behind him. The young man turned to catch the hazy outline of a face bobbing under the diffident light of a waning moon. Strong arms pulled away, back to the Isle of Wight.

Shivering, he cursed again as his stiff fingers—blue by now—fumbled the string that bound his oilskin package. One more hard yank broke it open. He unstrapped the canvas bag inside where he found a rough towel. He took a deep breath and stripped then rubbed himself down feverishly to reawaken a sluggish circulation and stop his teeth from rapping like a woodpecker. He scrambled into scratchy underwear, shirt, sweater, the tweed jacket with slightly modified identity papers secreted in its inner pocket, woolly socks, and heavy shoes with thick rubber soles. The towel went back into the bag, as did the wet clothes and boots.

He limped up a steep path to the road, staying close to its gorse-spiked edge. That ramshackle contraption must be the old shop they'd described, unused now, even in summer. No chocolate, no ice cream, no toys anymore, everywhere the same. He leaned against the wall farthest away from the road, sank down on his haunches, and bowed his head, struggling to order his thoughts, reaffirm the commitment and courage he would need to succeed in this, his first mission. He was dead tired.

A braking car startled him awake. He pushed to his feet, flattening himself against the splintery planking. A mocking voice, too loud and strangely cheerful, recited, "I hope you had a pleasant crossing. I'm told this is the best time of the year for fishing."

"No, the fishing is better in March, they say."

Thank God. He didn't know how long he'd been waiting, only that it seemed like hours and must be dangerously close to dawn. He sidled around the corner to show himself. Shock rendered his legs oaken. A stocky man leaned against a police car, legs crossed and hands in pockets. *A weapon?* Puffs of breath, too fast from his own slack mouth, slow and steady from the other's, hazed the air between them. All for nothing, then. And not even a hero's death.

The fledgling spy forced his voice to a low, raspy register. "Who are you?"

The man started to laugh, then cut it off. "Don't worry, I am Rooster. I'm going to drive you to friends now for food and rest. We have already found you the perfect job. You'll be in action in no time."

Fear dissolved into relief then hardened to contempt. *A traitor.*

"Thank you very much," he said. "You are most kind."

1

Something smashed far away, making Jamie jump and cry out. One of Mr. Hitler's bombs, probably. *Thirty-six, thirty-one—what?* Oh botheration, he'd lost count. So hard to fill up a day, so boring to keep walking round and round counting his steps. Into the kitchen, back to the lounge, into his bedroom—he wouldn't dare open Roy's door. It must be quite late, almost lunchtime, but his cousin still wasn't up. He'd start again later. Gran said it was important to practice his counting.

Sparklies, that's what he was in the mood for. He went to his room and sat on the floor next to his old comic books. He'd love a new one, maybe soon. Made of paper, though, and people didn't have enough paper anymore. He reached under where his bed met the corner, brushed the dusty bits and pieces off his fingers, and pulled out the diamond bracelet Gran gave him last Easter inside a cardboard egg. No chocolate to put in the egg. War was a big nuisance.

"Here you are, boy, there's some sparklies for you. God knows I don't need them any more," she'd said, her lovely crinkly smile soon going away when her mouth turned down to its usual place.

"Ooh, are they worth lots of pounds, then?" What a most beautiful thing, the best he'd ever seen.

"No, dear, just pretty and sparkly, and that's what you like, isn't it?"

"And how does God know you don't need them?"

"God knows everything."

"Every single thing I do?" Not good.

"Just the important things, not silly little ones."

Sparklies was what he liked best of all—except chocolate. She didn't know he had an even better one, the one Roy stole from her and he stole from Roy. *Is it really stole if it was stole first?* He'd have to think about that. He'd ask God if only he knew where to find Him. Anyway, it was a most deep secret. Gran was sad after Roy took it, so Jamie taking it from Roy didn't make her any sadder because she didn't know. And where did Gran get it? She never said.

The sun was shining into the kitchen window a little today. It didn't often because of the wall right opposite, but sometimes it poked through. Jamie stood at the sink and turned on the tap, only as far as a drizzle. He held the bracelet under the drops watching as the dust turned to nothing, and then held it so all the diamonds caught the light and sent sparkles. Gran used to talk about God a lot before she got so fed up with things, and sparklies were like God shining on people. And when he held it just right, he got shined on, too. Made him feel special—in a good way, not the slow way.

Doors slammed open, first Roy's room, and then the toilet. Not shut though. Jamie disappeared back to his room before he could hear anything nasty and stashed his bracelet. The larder door crashed next. He hoped Roy would leave him alone.

"Mornin'!"

What does he want? "Good morning, Roy. What are you eating?"

"Nice sandwich I found in the larder."

"That's my lunch! Gran made it for me."

"So what, idiot, make one for yourself."

"You know I'm not allowed to use a knife."

"Well, what you going to do when Gran dies? She's old and she's going to die soon, you know. Very soon."

"Don't say that! Stop it!" Jamie put his head on his lap and covered his ears.

Roy pulled Jamie's hands behind his back, twisting his wrists.

"You're hurting me, stop . . ." Fussing only made things worse. Why didn't he ever remember that?

"Shut up, or I'll get the hairbrush again. And who got in my room and took that brooch?"

Jamie tried not to shake. Roy sometimes did terrible hurting things with the handle of that hairbrush and it made him want to do bad things even more if he knew Jamie was scared. But he wasn't going to tell. That brooch wasn't even Roy's. It was Gran's, and he'd take better care of it. Roy would just sell it off for money.

"What's a brooch? Is that the thing you stole from Gran? And I don't never go in your room. Not never. Your friends go in there sometimes, don't they? And Gran isn't going to die till I get old."

"And where do you think she got it? She nicked it from one of her ladies, take my word for it. So it's stole twice over!" Roy seemed to find that very funny. "And Gran will die, and then they'll put you out on the streets. Think how that'll be in wintertime. Brrr! Or maybe they'll put you in a home."

"Won't you look after me? You're my cousin. Gran said families help each other."

"Me look after you? You've always been a nuisance!"

"Anyhow, this is my home. You mean a different sort of home?"

"A home for idiots. Anyway, I left half the sandwich in the larder for you. Found some oranges last night, so there's one of those for you too because it's your birthday tomorrow. Say thank you." He grabbed Jamie's wrists again.

"Thank you, Roy, and I'll be fifteen, and that's big, you know. Oranges are very special. We haven't had one for ever so long. Why didn't you sell it?"

"I'm not all bad, you know."

"There might be cake tomorrow, though I don't know if Gran's got so many candles as fifteen. You'll get some, too."

"Bloody right I will! I'm off."

As soon he heard the front door slam, Jamie got into bed and curled up tight, rubbing his wrists and thinking about Gran. *Gran dead soon?* She'd always been here. How could that be true? How did someone die? He knew it meant you didn't see them anymore. He couldn't bear not seeing Gran. No one to help. No one to make him supper. No one to hug. People hated slow boys; he knew that from the things children in the street yelled at him. And because of the nasty things Roy did to him. "Good for mentals," he'd say. Although he saved him an orange. Funny, that. But really, only Gran loved him. Only Gran.

Jamie felt a big something growing inside him, a lot like that picture of a volcano Gran stuck on the kitchen wall, hot and dark in his tummy, swirling in his head and mixing everything up, something that could throw his insides up as far as the sky. He heard himself cry, a sharp noise he'd never made before, it sort of hurt his ears that mad noise.

Close your eyes, Jamie, close your eyes till Gran comes home. He hugged himself and patted his arms, made himself say, "There, there," just like Gran would. His voice still came out funny, but it helped. "There, there," he whispered. "There, there."

* * *

"Helloee! I'm home, Jamie."

He must have fallen asleep. It made him very happy to hear Gran's voice, though. He pushed his fingers through his hair and went to the kitchen.

"Hello, Gran. Ever so pleased to see you!" He gave her a big hug and didn't want to let go. His leg bumped her shopping bag. "What've you got there?

"Imagine, I managed to find some flour for your birthday cake and a little butter! What's the matter, Jamie? You look upset."

"Roy wasn't very nice today. He saved me an orange, though. But I think I forgot to eat my lunch."

Gran went to the larder. "You ate half the sandwich, though."

"No, Roy did. And he twisted my wrists. He said you're old and will die soon and I'll be sent away to a home for idiots. Are you going to die soon? Are you?"

"Oh, Jamie, Roy can be so cruel. No, don't you worry about that. Let me put the kettle on, then come and sit by me."

Gran walked a bit funny when she went into the kitchen, slowly as if something hurt. She did look old. When she came back, she fell onto the sofa with a big sigh. "My legs will be the death of me."

"See, your legs will make you die, you just said so!"

"No, no, Jamie, that's just something we say. My legs hurt because my veins get all swollen and I stand up all day cleaning houses. Now, I've never said anything before, but I want you to understand that Roy's mum was often very cruel to him when he was little. It was all her drinking, you see; and your mum was a drinker, too. Your grandfather, he was one for the drink and it wrecked his health so he died young. It's a bad thing if you overdo it. Anyhow, all those things his mum did to him made Roy angry, and angry people often do nasty things."

"Why do they drink like that if it's bad?"

"It gets a hold of you, you see. You get so you've got to have it. Don't start on the drink, Jamie, not ever."

Jamie nodded solemnly.

"So stop worrying. I'll talk to Roy. I've got something to tell him tonight, and he won't like it, so maybe tomorrow. You know how he gets." She sighed hard and frowned down at her hands.

"What's he done?"

"Oh, just storing some stuff in some of my ladies' houses, in their sheds. Stuff they don't know about. But no more questions. It's time for our tea." Her hands kept crumpling her apron up into a mess. Jamie gently cupped his hands over hers.

"Tell you what, Gran." He put on a big smile to make her feel more happy.

She smiled back. *Good, it worked.*

"You do the putting on the kettle bit and I'll take everything to the table. I can be a big help, you know."

"Thank you, Jamie, that sounds very nice. I've already put the kettle on, it's probably about to boil, but there's still plenty to do. Off we go then."

Gran got out the tea caddy. "Maybe two spoonfuls today." She made the tea, then sat at the table and watched as Jamie took the cheese from the larder, peeled off the wax paper, and set it in the china cheese dish before carrying it across the kitchen. He let the tip of his tongue pop out between his teeth because it helped steady him. He thumped it down on the table, only a little hard, right in the middle of the sun picture on the oilcloth. He'd got out of breath.

"Very nicely done, Jamie. That's the only nice piece I've got left from my family home. I'll tell you a secret." She leaned towards him with a sort of naughty look on her face. "I slipped it under my coat that last day, after the big row at tea when my dad ordered me and Ted to get out. It still had cheesy crumbs on it. Took me ages to get the stains off my blouse."

"Why did he tell you to get out? That wasn't very nice."

"He said Ted wasn't good enough for me. We were a nice family with a nice house and a garden too. He was right. But I never saw my dad again."

"That's very sad." Jamie went over to the breadbox. "Which loaf?"

"There's only Hovis, Jamie. I know you like white best, but they'd sold out by the time I got there."

"That's all right. I like brown bread too. Don't worry." He took the breadboard over to the table, then went back to get the loaf.

"Is that all, Gran?"

"Not quite. What do we usually eat with our bread?"

He must think hard. "Oh, yes, butter and jam. See, I only needed a little reminding!"

"Well, no jam, I'm afraid. Get the butter, then. You're ever so helpful, lovey. I'll see to the knives."

"Lovey to you, too. Let's have our tea!"

They'd just sat down when the front door handle smashed the wall. Gran jumped as much as Jamie, and mashed her hands together, almost as if she was washing them.

"Jamie, there's something I have to talk to Roy about, and he won't like it. You know how he gets, so maybe you'd better wait in your room."

"Oh, Gran, tea, I'm hungry!"

"Well, all right, we'll eat first, then you go to your room."

Roy slouched in without a word, fell into his chair, grabbed the breadknife, and sliced several ragged hunks off the loaf. Gran quickly cut some slices for Jamie and herself and put cheese on their plates while there was still some left. She looked from Roy to Jamie while she chewed. Roy ate like a pig as usual, and made a noise drinking his tea. Jamie knew Gran hated that, so he was extra careful with his own table manners. He might be slow, but he knew a thing or two. He tried to talk about things to keep a nice time going, but Roy rolled his eyes and didn't say a word, so he stopped trying. Gran looked as if she could hardly swallow now, so she must be very worried.

"Have you had enough, Jamie?"

"Oh, yes, thank you, Gran."

"Please go to your room for a while. Roy and me got to talk about something."

He knew she was watching him on his way up the hallway, so he turned back to look at her. It was definitely going to be one of those times.

"I love you, Gran."

"I love you, too, Jamie."

Roy made a noise like someone being sick.

* * *

They began by blaming each other, but it turned loud and ugly when Gran and Roy started all the shouting. The terrible things they yelled roiled Jamie even more than bombing did.

She said he stole things, that she'd lose her jobs if they found out. He said she was . . . an itch? And she said he had a dirty mouth. She said it had to stop, he said what's she going to do about it, and she said she'd call the coppers on him. A crash like a dish breaking. He hoped it wasn't Gran's good one from her nice home. She said he was no good, just like his mother. Then there was some quiet. A sudden funny cry like that time he'd pushed Gran over and she couldn't go to work for a few days. But at least it was quiet, which was always better.

Jamie curled forward on his bed, hands clamped over his ears in case they started again, and soothed himself with rocking—back and forth, back and forth. Gran would be cross if she saw him. "Fiddle-faddle, big boys don't rock," she always said. He held his ears tighter; he couldn't do with so much noise—big bangs, sirens, people shouting outside, Roy and Gran shouting at each other inside. *Keep rocking*, such a comfort, *softly, softly*.

Crashing, a big crashing. Would the house fall down? Shaking, people shouting, but not Roy and Gran, *rock, rock*, eyes closed, *rock, rock*. Sirens yowled, but far away.

A knock at the door, Roy shouted something. Jamie began to hum, had to stop the noise and Roy getting in. His breath had gone all raggedy; it might even stop if this went on much longer.

Say like Gran, "Fiddle-faddle, fiddle-faddle," sounded brave. Louder better, "Fiddle-faddle." More louder, "Fiddle-faddle." Can't hear them now. "*Fiddle-faddle!*"

Roy slapped down his hands.

"Stop rocking, idiot. And stop that stupid fiddle-faddling. What'll Gran say?" He had his unkind look, a hitting look. He kept making fists, uncurling them, and then fisting again. Wasn't dressed up now, except for grease in his hair. There was a big dark spot on his trousers, quite low down. Looked wet. Roy probably hadn't noticed it yet or he would have changed.

"Won't do it no more. No more. Promise. Don't tell!" Jamie sat on his hands, pulling in his chin. He risked looking up at Roy, and Roy turned away and moved to the door. He looked back in Jamie's direction over his shoulder at the postcard on the wall.

"I'm going out, got business with a bloke. Gran's not feeling well. She's had a nosebleed and her dress got blood all down the front. She's all right, just taking a nap now. Don't bother her. Leave her be. I'm going to lock the door, can't have you wandering about. You're not to go out, no matter what. Understand?" Roy got out his shiny black comb and scraped it along his side hair again. Always combing.

"Suppose the warden tells us to get down the shelter. What then? Suppose bitz comes on us?" Roy looked him in the face now. He was blinking an awful lot.

"*Bel-itz*, stupid. I'll be back soon. I think it's all over for tonight. Sit tight. No fusses. And leave Gran alone or I'll give you a good thrashing."

"Yes, Roy. I'll be good. Know what tomorrow is?"

"Yeah, for the hundredth time, it's your bloody fifteenth birthday, and don't expect nothing from me, we just had Christmas and you got an orange today, too."

Jamie suddenly felt brave. "Language, Roy, what would Gran

say?" Roy snorted too much, so rude. Couldn't he find words?

"Gran's got the stuff for cake. I'll share." Jamie smiled up at Roy.

"Bloody hell, what did I do to get a retard for a cousin?"

"Don't you like me anymore? You gave me an orange this morning." Jamie felt tears coming up, must try not to let them out. One slipped down.

"Don't start blubbering. Christ, I can't stand it! I'm going out."

2

J amie knew Roy had left when he heard the front door
hinges squeak, then the lock click when Roy turned
the key. The sirens started again, very loud. Just a bit
more rocking, just till he felt better. Just for a little bit.

Jamie thought about Gran and sat up. Supposing she had
another nosebleed while she was asleep, would all her blood leak
out? If he tiptoed, opened the door carefully, he could just make
sure she was all right. He tried it, stumbling a bit, he wasn't very
good at this, dead clumsy, Gran said he was, but he managed.
He listened outside her bedroom. He turned the doorknob very
slowly, ever so slowly, expecting it to make a noise that would
get him in trouble. He opened the door without even a squeak.

Lots of blood had gone right through her blanket and the
sight made him feel funny. There wasn't any blood coming from
her nose, though, so it must have stopped. Bad smell in here.
Farts? Probably, and time for her next bath, too. Could it be
Saturday already? She was very asleep, the blanket wasn't even
going up and down, and she wasn't snoring for once. He'd better
leave her be till she felt better, like Roy said.

He stopped moving when the air raid warden banged on
their door, but Gran didn't wake up.

"Everyone down to the shelter. Right away, please. You in there, Millie?"

Jamie couldn't go down to the shelter without Gran, and Roy would hit him if he went out on his own. Gran might shout at him if he woke her. He kept quiet so the warden would think they were all out and go away. Best that way.

Jamie tiptoed back to his room. What to do now? Fifteen was quite big. So big he could touch all his walls if he turned around with little steps. Gran had painted them last year, but not a happy color. She got the paint cheap in a sale. He'd been sick in the toilet soon after and the color was nearly the same. He didn't much like having his room the same color as sick, but he didn't say so; she would have got upset. Mustn't hurt her feelings.

So quiet all of a sudden. No noise upstairs, no shouting and nasty thumps, no crying when Mr. Blackstone hit Mrs. Blackstone before their bed started squeaking and Gran got all pink and cross. *Did Roy hit Gran?* Is that what made her nose bleed? *Better not ask.*

Everyone had gone away and left him and Gran. He wished he had some new comics. And a book. He only had one book, a little one with pictures of flowers. Gran said books weren't for boys like him. But he wanted to know about things, real outside things; he hardly ever went to see outside things. Gran had two books with writing and no pictures. They used to sing the ABCs together, him and Gran. That was fun, but he'd forgotten them now.

Jamie felt around under his bed and pulled out Biffy's box. He knocked on the lid. "Can I come in?" he whispered. He was careful and slow as he opened it and said, "Hello, Biffy, it's all right, Roy's gone out." Biffy was a green dog, nice and soft with big eyes, and they'd been together for years and years. He didn't take him out of his box a lot because Roy usually pulled Biffy's ears to make Jamie cry. Biffy could only cry inside. Well, Roy was out, so Jamie and Biffy could have a good cuddle while he waited for Gran to wake up. He just wished he could see Biffy's beautiful heart. He had to keep the stolen brooch somewhere safe where Roy would never think to look. There'd been a little split in Biffy's side, so he pushed his best sparkly deep inside so it had the fluffy stuff over it. And then he'd asked Gran if she could sew him up. He hugged himself, pleased with his tricky ways. Slow could be clever. And if he ever needed lots of money, he would just open Biffy up a little bit, without probably hurting him, and get it out.

He was hungry again, but he'd have to wait for Gran because he wasn't allowed to take food without asking. Really hungry.

Gran needed her rest, she got tired a lot. She did for ladies that lived in big houses in the West End and she always talked about how they got their money's worth. She sounded angry when she said that. Jamie didn't know why. She worked and they paid. He'd get a job in the West End one day and buy food and chocolate. *Cho-co-late.* Gran was ever so proud when he learned to say it properly. Gran said it was important to talk nicely; people treated you different. So Jamie always talked slow and tried to get all the word bits in. He was always forgetting blitz, though. Kept saying *bitz.* Saying *bler* was hard, tongue kept going in the wrong place.

Gran said Roy would get more respect if he talked nicely, but he took no notice. He should stop putting all that greasy stuff in his hair, too, looked like nothing on earth, she said. Roy didn't have a proper job and that made Gran cross.

He thought hard about what Gran said. She'd said Roy was no good. Did that mean he didn't have to listen to Roy? He was older than Jamie, not that much taller, and he wasn't slow. But Roy was no good, put grease in his hair, and didn't talk nicely. And he didn't show respect for Gran. Who was better? Jamie knew he was nicer than Roy. *Is nicer better?* What sorts of things mattered more than other sorts of things? What a muddle. He never asked Gran about things like that anymore. Maybe one day he'd know someone who liked answering questions.

Listen to me, Jamie! Get out, leave, Jamie, leave!

His head shot toward the door. "Gran? Is that you?" No reply. He tiptoed toward her bedroom again. He had to get out of the house. What made him think that just now? Roy told him to stay inside. But the voice was stuck in his head. *Leave, Jamie, leave.* Sounded a bit like Gran, only whispery. If he went out Roy would go mad again. But it was like there was someone inside his head. Jamie laid Biffy gently on his pillow so he could have a nice rest until Roy got back.

Gran kept her key in her handbag. Should he get it out and

have a look? He could watch for Roy. *Would that be such a bad thing to do?* The bag was on the kitchen table, big and old and brown and creasy. He found the big key, but her wallet wasn't there. Funny, Gran always had her wallet in her bag. She kept everything together in case she forgot something important, and it wouldn't do to get locked out. Roy locked her and Jamie out on purpose once, and Jamie had sometimes seen him take money out of her wallet. Roy said he'd beat the hell out of him if he told, but Gran knew; he'd seen her look inside it and shake her head. Her face looked so sad.

Jamie went to the front door and stood in front of it. It looked so big and heavy and hard. A new smell now, what was it? It was like when Gran burned the toast. Jamie went into the kitchen. No toast getting burned. He'd have liked some toast, even toast too much cooked. Yes, that was her lovely dish smashed on the floor. *Poor Gran.* His feet crunched on broken things.

The smell must be coming from outside. He coughed. Another smell, a smoky smell, was catching at his throat now.

Get out.

Jamie struggled into his coat and shoved his gloves into the pockets. He tiptoed to the front door and listened. He put the key in the hole—not so hard—and turned it slowly so he wouldn't make a noise. It only went one way. He'd never unlocked a door before. *Easy.*

* * *

Roy hung around the old marketplace for half an hour, but things were getting bad outside and his bag was heavy. He'd got a message that someone had a job for him, a real plum. He vaguely remembered the bloke, someone he'd gone to school with, a mate of the Reddy boys. Vicious little sods, they were. And they had it in for him, too. He'd managed to avoid them after that cock-up in the West End, and made a point of going around with a couple of toughs so the brothers knew if they gave him any trouble, they'd get trouble back. There'd be a reckoning sooner or later, though.

Hey, wait a mo! Friend of the Reddy boys? Maybe he'd been had, a setup. Better think about getting out of here, out of London. He'd left a real mess at home, but he thought he'd pretty well covered his tracks. The fire seemed to have caught hold. *Good riddance to the old hag, and Jamie, too.* The kid's mum must have been a real slag, drinking so much it made her baby come out retarded.

His own mum's drinking must have started later, because he came out smart enough. A picture of her popped into his head, uninvited and unwelcome. He'd hated that mean foxy face, the mouth always ready to stab him with curses, the scrawny hands always ready to take up anything within reach to lash him with if he didn't make his getaway fast enough. He'd got pretty good at reading the signs and disappearing before the real trouble started, especially when Dad came home drunk. Dad sometimes beat her almost senseless. Rather her than him. Out of the blue one day, a strange woman took him away and dumped him on Gran, who'd been shocked and none too happy. She'd never liked him, he could tell. His parents said he'd be brought back soon when that woman came for him. Never saw them again. Were they really dead like Gran said? He hoped so, though Dad hadn't been so bad when he was sober.

Best idea would be to get out of the city soon as he could. He'd come back when everything had calmed down and get the government handouts. There was a little insurance policy, too; he'd tucked that with his other important papers in his inside pocket. And he'd found one of the old girl's sisters, a Mrs. Myrtle Freeman. He'd watched the house for a bit. Nice place, the sort of neighborhood where someone would be ashamed to be related to someone like him, would pay to make him go away. Tomorrow. He patted the bulky pocket of papers certifying he wasn't fit for duty and wondered if the trains were still running. He started walking.

He must get himself to the Golden Lion tomorrow, too. Derek left word there he'd be back in the next few days. He'd moved out of their neighborhood years ago, but he never forgot his old friends. Not one to be snooty, Derek, and he was the bloke with all the big ideas. He'd tell him where to lay low. *Where to now?* Couldn't very well go home—it wasn't there anymore, he'd seen to that. Anderson shelter. They'd sprouted up all over. Just keep walking, got to trip over one sooner or later, or at least an underground station.

* * *

The Reddy brothers rifled through the house with sharp-eyed efficiency. They dressed like wardens on nights like these and reveled in the orders to evacuate they could give out whenever they felt there might be something worth lifting. Nobody noticed the kit bags they carried. None of the real wardens carried them, but people didn't question much when they were scared.

"Hey, Vince, we've got to meet Roy in a jiff. Be fun sorting him out, little rat!"

"Yeah, let's take turns. I've got me good heavy boots on tonight. Since it's such a special occasion!" Jed made a high-pitched shrieking noise that always grated on Vince's nerves. That was the way he laughed when he was excited and looking forward to a treat.

They left the house, kit bags only half full. They'd make another call later, but first Roy. Couldn't let it get around that some little wanker pulled a fast one on the Reddy brothers.

"It was that idiot Derek let him get away. Think he was in on it? Pisser joined up next day, very convenient." Vince felt ripe for a fight.

"Wonder how he explained why he wasn't in the army already. Well, if the twerp comes through it we'll have a little word with him, too, won't we?" said Jed. They grinned at each other in imagining the scene.

"Hey, you two, come with me. We need all hands on deck," said a big, bossy copper with broken purple veins all across his cheeks.

They exchanged glances. The kit bags were only half full. Make a dash for it? They rounded the next corner and there stood an army transport full of sullen civilians and a couple of soldiers; *too risky.*

"Here's two more. You're all needed over the bridge, St. Paul's area. All hell's let loose." The copper cleared his throat of heavy phlegm. "Whole city's on fire, they say."

They climbed in and sat glued together on a bench. They'd miss the meeting.

"That fucking Roy's got the luck of the devil," muttered Jed.

"Later, we'll get him later, have a real old ding-dong!" said Vince.

Their protests regarding their lack of firefighting experience went unheeded, so both of them pulled and tugged and sweated to a degree they found unreasonable and unsustainable. The heat was dreadful, and the filthy-smelling smoke stuck in Vince's throat and made his eyes smart. Every now and then he'd straighten up and look around for a chance to escape. A ghostly St. Paul's emerged from time to time as the smoke drifted, but there was no way to retrieve their bags and get away without being seen. Several teams of men toiled on the other sides of the square.

The fires only grew and roared and fed on themselves, however hard the men fought. After a couple of hours they didn't notice the smell. Vince didn't think he could take it much longer, although he didn't want to admit it. They'd never been through anything this bad. Incendiaries popped and flashed blindingly before the fires they started sent up wicked white flames. It was light as day. He felt and heard the grind and rumble of bombers as they swooped over again and again, following the fires and picking their targets. The whistle of the bombs as they dropped raised the hairs on the back of his neck. He wanted to run no matter what when one of the bombs went quiet a hundred feet above them. That meant they were ready to drop. They were forced to keep going, though, and had to hang onto the writhing, hissing hoses for dear life. They weren't allowed to let go.

"You fellows keep at it. You're not to leave your post for anything. I'm going round to the next street, they're down a couple of men."

Vince didn't rightly know who he was, but contempt in the man's tone was clear, and he simmered with loathing as they watched him stride off. "Bloody tin pot general," Jed muttered.

"Now's our chance, Jed. The fires're all around us now, do for us if we don't get out. See that gap over there?" Vince jerked his chin at the corner where Jed could dimly make out the entrance to an alley. "When I give the word, run for it!"

The brothers grabbed their bags and scuttled round the corner, the other men's angry shouts drowned out by hot howling winds. They found themselves in another square now, three sides of it on fire. They ran towards an alleyway that looked clear, but skidded to a stop as a streak of fire caught a church ahead of them and hop-scotched from building to building on the fourth side with cartoonish abandon. The ravenous firestorm hemmed in the brothers with horrifying speed.

Arms outstretched, they circled each other in terrified disbelief, heads swiveling this way and that, searching for any way out. They held hands like they used to as children, running this way and that to find a gap. Too deadly to broach, the flames drove them back and scorched their faces. Jed clutched his brother, whimpering and peeing like a whipped puppy. Vince, frozen and silent, gazed at him as if from a great distance; he looked so strange without brows or lashes, bloodshot eyes sunken in his sooty face. Vince supposed he must look about the same.

Bricks and girders screeched and groaned as a massive Victorian book warehouse buckled and collapsed, burying everything in its path, including the Reddy brothers.

Furious winds swirled its fallout of shredded paper like dirty snow.

* * *

Derek Lester smirked as he flopped down into a seat vacated at last by an elderly woman who wore thick wool everything and even smelled like a sour old sheep. When he told her the next stop was hers, she'd squinted at him with a pained smile of gratitude for giving her time to get herself gathered up and away. The senile old bag would have to wait for hours for another train to get her where she wanted to go, only three stations farther down the line. You had to be smart to get anywhere in this world.

He was, at first glance, a good-looking youth, not tall, but muscled and upright, smartly turned out. If someone looked closely, although no one ever did, he might notice that the fair wave of hair falling over his right eye—an eye that was slightly too close to its mate—draped more by order than accident, and that the half-open grin owed more to slyness than pleasure.

December 29, only two days to New Year's Eve and another year, 1941: maybe the year the war would end. His family had never been one to celebrate the New Year, but they'd be happy enough to see him that they wouldn't mind him bringing out the whisky bottle. He'd stashed it under a floorboard in the parlor one night after he'd pointed out to old Shipman how he wouldn't want Derek chatting about some of the more creative ways he stocked his corner shop.

Mum didn't approve of drinking, still a lot of Presbyterian Puritan in the old girl. But she'd let him have his way as she always did in the end. Her son, a hero in the making, home from the war. No need for her to know he'd spent most of it so far slaving in the barrack kitchens in Plymouth because he'd broken his right hand in a bar fight. Couldn't shoot, so couldn't fight. Perfect. Once he'd got used to working lefty, it turned out to be a useful situation, very pretty indeed since he'd got in with a bunch of Yankee sailors. They didn't get out much, not supposed to be anywhere near England, one of them told him. They told people in town they were Canadians; no one could tell, they all sounded the same to the English. Interesting what you could get out of people with a few beers. Anyway, they got everything they wanted, those Yanks—nylons, chocs, tins of food, and easy-going girls, thanks to good old Derek acting as a go-between. Good sorts, they didn't begrudge him some of the goods when he wanted to butter up a girl of his own, or have a nice little present to please the family. He'd missed Christmas, but he'd brought a little something for every last one of them.

A French doll for little Jane. Nearly new, a bloke said he'd exchanged it for food with some tatty family over there. German badges, two each for the twins, Bobby and Andy. He'd tell them he'd ripped them off the uniforms of dead soldiers. They'd love that, show all their mates. A bar of scented soap for Mum and some pipe tobacco for Dad.

And Sarah, his favorite sister. Always backed him up, got him out of scrapes, said he'd been where he should've, hadn't been where he shouldn't. Nylons for Sarah. She'd grown up pretty. He'd kill any fellow who laid his hands on her. He didn't want to think about boys doing the sorts of things to her he liked to do with some of the bints he knocked about with. A nice solid hubby for her, one who could provide the goods. Nothing but the best for Sarah.

A pair of gloves for Betty to cover up her work hands. He'd leave them with Sarah, because who knew when he'd see her next, down in Hampshire with her peasant of a husband, miles away from anywhere and working herself to death at some manor. Lucky to be married, though. Betty wasn't like Sarah, not at all. Great, big healthy girl was Betty.

All in all, he was a good son, a good brother. They'd all look up to him when they heard his tales. He looked out of the window and caught his reflection smiling back. Good looking chap, too.

It was almost dark now, only another hour or so to South Docks. The train came to a swaying halt at some little station in the middle of nowhere.

"Everyone out please, everyone out!" *Shit.*

Lots of chatter but no real information. A raid, a big one, they said. Have to wait it out, could be an all-nighter. Derek sat himself on his kit bag in a corner of the ticket office next to the men's room. He hated this sort of thing—sardine-like, all that bloody chin-up, make-the-best-of-things natter. At least all these bodies should work up some warmth. Smelly, though. Too bad some were stuck out on the platform still. Not him, though. A few people had looked at him funny because of the way he'd shouldered his way through the crowd. They could go piss themselves. What a bloody stupid waste of a day's leave.

* * *

"Hello, love, how're you feeling?" said Derek in his top-of-the-world voice. "Took me a couple of days to find you. Glad to see you're wide awake now."

Glad to see her better, but not so glad she'd be asking questions he didn't want to answer.

"Where are they all?" Sarah asked, her voice breathless and shaky, afraid of his answer.

His face grew congested with repressed tears as he shook his head. After a moment he said softly, "Don't worry, I'll take care of you." He would, too. Maybe send her to Betty when she was strong enough, although God knows what she'd do with herself down there.

"Brought you a lovely cake of French soap, darling. Make you feel like a million bucks, as the Yanks say."

Well, a bar of soap wasn't much of a consolation prize for a missing leg or a family too torn up to bury decently. Only one coffin, and he didn't know for sure if all the bits and pieces inside it even belonged to them. Direct hit on the Underground station where just about the whole neighborhood had been sheltering from the raid. Rotten luck. He watched her suffer, steeling himself to stay quiet and still.

"It hurts so much." She sounded short of breath. "It's like the doctor's still cutting at it. It was terrible. I'd just gone to the toilet when we were hit. They found me, maybe they missed some."

"No, love, they got them all out. They've gone." He dried his cheeks with a rough, embarrassed swipe.

Poor kid. He'd given the nylons to a pretty charge nurse who'd been enthusiastic and properly grateful, and promised to take extra good care of Sarah. It would have been tactless to give her the nylons. She could've worn them one at a time, but that seemed such a waste.

She breathed harder now, sometimes with a series of sharp intakes of air through her teeth as the pain stabbed, and sometimes with a long sigh as it exhausted her into surrender. Perhaps he was tiring her. A bell rang.

"Visiting hours over, love, see you tomorrow. Got to find Roy now, see about a place to kip down. House has gone too, see." She nodded slowly as if it didn't matter. "Roy's always got something up his sleeve."

"I just remembered. He was in the tunnel with us. Maybe he didn't make it, either. You'd better ask about him here."

"I will. Hope he's all right."

"Just don't let him talk you into anything again." Her vehemence surprised him, given the state she was in.

"Don't worry, I'm over all of that."

Derek found Roy in the men's surgical ward with a cast on his left leg.

"There you are!"

"Derek! How'd you find me?"

"Sarah's here. She said she saw you in the tunnel. She's lost a leg. Whole family bought it, Roy. Except her."

"Sorry, mate. Yeah, I saw them down there. Your mum wouldn't let me sit with them. Saved my life, I reckon." Roy blushed. Even he seemed to recognize how tactless that sounded. He looked down and fiddled with the buttons on his pajamas.

Derek swallowed hard. "Anything I can get you?"

"I've got to get out of London, Derek. The Reddy boys might

be after me. I went to meet a bloke about a job, got a message you see, but then, I thought to myself, it could be a setup. They're tricky, those sods."

"Tell you what, Roy. Soon as they let my Sarah out, I'll want her taken to our sister in Hampshire. I've got to get back to my unit. You remember Betty? She works in a big house there. Manor house, actually. You could maybe find a job down there. Keep you out of trouble for a bit. What do you say?"

"Sounds possible. Can you spring for the tickets? I haven't got a bean. House went up, and Jamie and Gran along with it."

"Sorry 'bout that Roy. Really sorry. Both in the same boat now. Yeah, I'll spring for the tickets. I'll leave the money with Sarah."

One more visit with Sarah tomorrow, leave her the money, and he'd get back to Aldershot. Got a girl with great big tits waiting for him down there. Didn't pay to leave them alone too long, although he'd made it clear he could get his hands on Yankee goods. She'd hang on for any of that she thought might come her way. He chewed his lower lip, rubbing his hands together in anticipation as he sauntered out into the pale sunny day.

* * *

Myrtle Freeman sailed around the table in St. Paul's, pouring tea and platitudes for the volunteers. Those not numbed by fear or exhaustion often snickered and nudged each other in quite a rude way when she went by; she was only trying to offer a little home comfort and didn't find the situation at all amusing. Raw nerves, no doubt. The length of this raid bothered her, too, but her legacy as a bastion of competence and reliability in the eyes of the dean's wife concerned her more.

The dean of St. Paul's was dear and sweet and never spared himself. A slender man with fine aristocratic features, he ought to take better care of himself. But, there you are, a man of the cloth has his calling. There had been one or two incendiary hits on the dome, but they hadn't pierced it and the dean and his helpers managed to douse them all from the buckets they'd had ready. She overheard the dean tell one of the staff that the Nazis were going for the Cathedral tonight. He'd been warned by Whitehall that very afternoon.

She wondered how Millie was getting on. She'd caught sight of her sister near a market where she'd heard they had good sausages. A long way off her beaten track, but a proper English sausage was worth the effort. They hadn't seen each other in over thirty years, and Millie had looked so old and tired and lined she hardly recognized her. She'd married beneath her and spent the rest of her life poor. On an impulse Myrtle had followed her until she turned into a house that had obviously been turned into flats. Not a very nice area, but not too bad, just low class.

A young man passed Millie on his way out and said, "'Night, Gran, going out for a bit."

Millie said, "Oh, Roy, where to this time?" The boy lifted his eyes heavenward, not bothering to answer. His greasy hair was slicked back and his clothes were terrible, flashy, a real spiv, as they called his type.

Myrtle carried on her trek, but turned to retrace her steps when she heard a door slam. It was Millie again, this time with a teenage boy in tow. Looked a little too old to be holding hands like that. A couple of children playing hopscotch in the street abandoned their game to follow them. "Idiot! Mental! Stupid! 'Tarded!" they yelled, twirling their fingers at the sides of their heads. Millie turned around and shouted at them like a common fishwife. The boy shoved his hands in his pockets and, head down and shoulders hunched, kept on walking as though he hadn't heard a thing. Maybe he was deaf as well.

So, Millie had at least two grandsons, one a spiv, the other a mental defective. Myrtle had been considering making contact, but thought better of it now. What would all her friends make of Millie and her family, especially her circle of lady volunteers at St. Paul's? No, it wouldn't do. And her own son, she had to think of him, not to mention his wife—she was very particular. No, a great pity, but there it was. Millie had brought it all on herself, after all.

A sudden dangerous crackling sent Myrtle edging out of her alcove to join the others, all gazing up at a hideous greenish glow in the dome. An incendiary had penetrated the lining and stuck there, smoldering. The dome was lined with only a thin layer of lead resting on old wooden beams; a firetrap, it would go up like tinder if the flames were allowed to gain hold.

Hardly breathing, they followed the few dark figures crawling along the beams like marauding rats. The onlookers should have gone down to the crypt, but stayed, paralyzed by the fear their beloved church was finished—St. Paul's had already burned down twice in its thousand-year history. As the glow flickered out and the dome melted back into its shadows, the onlookers exhaled and sagged, some sliding down the wall to sit on the floor, exhausted by fear and relief.

The dean lumbered down the worn spiral stairs, coughing from smoke, effort, and emotion. "It's safe," he said, tears in his eyes. He told them how some of the men had made the perilous crawl along the beams to do what they could. To everyone's relief, the incendiary fell outwards onto a balcony below of its own accord, where the waiting crew soon extinguished it. These volunteers had spent most of the day filling buckets with water and lining them up around the different balcony levels. "Heroes, every one," he said. "God bless them."

The raid went on and on. When the all clear finally sounded, Myrtle and the others stepped outside to utter devastation. The fires had burned to within twenty-five feet of St. Paul's and most of the surrounding ancient city had been reduced to a pile of rubble, hundreds of years of history decimated in a matter of hours. Myrtle took in the stone and dust, unwilling to think of what might lie underneath. No one spoke; too much to take in, *too much*. "God help us all," an old man muttered. At the sound of his voice, Myrtle straightened her shoulders, thankful to be alive. Must get on with things. She knew she should find out if Millie was all right. Her Christian duty. But then what?

* * *

Myrtle's journey home had been a nightmarish patchwork of lifts from strangers lucky enough to still have petrol and long walks. Thank goodness the gas was still on, she'd die if she didn't have a cup of tea right away, then off to bed and a lovely long sleep.

She took it easy for the next few days, dusting and polishing and tidying, trying to concentrate on her library book, wondering whether there would be anything worth buying down at the shops, but lacking the energy to go and see—Myrtle couldn't bring herself to try to make it back up to St. Paul's. She telephoned to the high street shop and had a boy deliver the basics. Not everybody on their street had a telephone and Myrtle was surprised hers still worked. It always gave her a little surge of pride when she picked it up and asked the operator for a number, even if it did cost good money. Heaven knows how that little shop afforded one. On the fiddle? Somehow they always managed to keep their shelves stocked.

After a week Myrtle pulled herself together, shrugged on her second-best winter coat, set her maroon felt hat at jaunty angle, and strolled down the avenue. She pursed her lips as she noticed an unsavory looking character hobbling towards her on crutches. He came to a halt in front of her with a clownish look of surprise on his face.

"Aunty Myrtle!"

Millie's grandson. What did he want, how did he know who she was?

"I . . . I'm afraid I don't . . ."

"I'm your sister Millie's grandson Roy. I've been watching you. Until I broke my leg in a raid, that is. Now they've let me out of hospital, I thought I'd come and pay you a visit."

Oh no, watching her? *Just walk away from this dreadful person.* Myrtle started to move around him, but he blocked her way, nimble as a goat on those crutches.

"Please let me pass. I've never seen you before in my life!"

"Well, you're seeing me now. I've got bad news. My Gran, your sister Millie, and my cousin Jamie, they're dead. Our house blown to smithereens and them along with it."

"Oh dear!" Myrtle was shocked at first, and then saddened when she realized she felt no sense of loss, no regret, no sense of missing her sister. She'd be hard put to it to dredge up happy memories of their youth, even though there must have been some before she ran off with that Ted. She suppressed a shameful feeling of relief. So this horrid person really was her nephew.

"See, I've nowhere to kip down, so I thought I'd move in with you for a bit."

"Oh, no, I couldn't possibly. I've got my son and his wife to consider, I'm . . ."

"You and your son wouldn't want my sort around, would

you? You especially wouldn't want people knowing we're related. I thought you'd turn out to be that sort." He leaned back and raised his eyebrows in a ridiculous show of surprise. "But you can't have people knowing how you turned away your dead sister's grandson. A poor chap wounded in an air raid turned out on the streets by his aunty." He bared his teeth and gums as if ready to laugh. "Tell you what, you see me right, and I'll leave you alone. Forever."

"You young scoundrel, you're blackmailing me! You ought to be ashamed of yourself with your grandmother and cousin dead. I'm not giving you a penny."

"All right then, next time you visit your precious son, I'll pay a little visit myself. And a church meeting or two might make a change." Even Roy's sneer was crooked.

"I've hardly got anything on me." She couldn't help her tremulous voice and she could tell it pleased him. He looked so smug. He'd won.

"There's only two banks around here, both still standing. One of them must be your branch. Let's go for a little walk."

He kept close to her side, sometimes catching her leg with his crutch, and marched her to the Barclays where she told him she banked. She'd had no choice but to give in to his demands. Too numb to move after this latest raid, she watched him swing his cast down the road and out of sight with one hundred pounds of her savings stowed in his inner pocket. Thank goodness Roy didn't know she'd deposited most of her savings at two other banks, just in case.

3

W hy was the sky that funny color, all yellow and red? Jamie saw a sunset like that once when they'd gone on the train to Brighton. Lovely over the water, that sun. You could see it up in the sky and down in the sea, like a mirror. Lovely. Maybe it was sunset time now. But it was nighttime, wasn't it? Not dark yet, so it couldn't be. Everything topsy-turvy today.

He walked nearly to the end of the street. He felt excited and scared all at once. He usually did as he was told, but now he was being a bad boy. He only wanted to see things other people were allowed to.

So much smoke, just like the bonfire last Guy Fawkes Night. No sun that he could see. Some of the houses all the way down at the other end had fire up high, licking them like that monster licked people in one of his comics. People got burnt and hurt when houses got fire. Was this what bitz did, made fire in houses? Gran and Roy talked about bitz a lot, but Jamie didn't quite know what it was. They did say lucky it hadn't come on their street yet, though they heard bangs from other places sometimes. Gran said Hitler was a very bad man. He could see why, now. He walked some more till a really big bang knocked him over.

Jamie sat up. His head hurt and his ears felt funny, though he could hear bangs a long way away and sounds like when he dropped a glass once, only louder. Had Roy come back and hit him? He looked back up the street. He couldn't see Roy anywhere at all. Lots of houses weren't there now, not mostly, they'd lost their windows and doors and lots of their bricks had gone, too. And there was fire in them. Where was the house with Gran's flat? He tried to walk down to it, but everything was too fired up and he couldn't see properly with his face all hot and tingly. It had probably been bitzed on and so had Gran and Biffy. He ran back down the street, crying and shouting, "Roy, Roy, come home." *Mustn't cry, big boys don't cry.* He didn't feel big, though. Even the broken houses were much taller than Jamie, and some of the fire almost touched the sky. *Look for a grownup.*

He couldn't run for long; he wasn't ever very good at running and his breath came hard and hurting. He didn't know his way to anywhere, but he had to find a policeman. That's what Gran said to do if he got in trouble. No home and no Gran, that was trouble all right. People were running and being noisy, but they didn't even look at him. He should run, too, but he was winded and didn't know where his running should take him. A big gray lorry with bells came, but no policeman that he could see. And no one he knew. And he wasn't to talk to strangers, except a policeman; that was a rule. The gray lorry's bells sounded like a fire engine. But fire engines were red, weren't they? He turned around a few times, but everywhere looked messy, where to go, what to do? He could hear his breath, felt it hot deep down inside. Was he going to get on fire? That would hurt. He cried a little, although fifteen year olds didn't ought to and he'd be fifteen tomorrow.

Jamie was hungry and thirsty, didn't get any supper. *Be a brave strong boy and keep on going. Be a soldier like we pretended at nursery school.* He put his shoulders back and walked fast, swinging his arms like a smart soldier in a uniform. He got tired after a bit and had to slow down. Tears squeezed out again. He loved his Gran. And Biffy. He couldn't bear it if they'd been blitzed. He should have stayed, just in case. This bitz business was horrible, bad as bad could be.

Black smelly water, that must be the river. Oh, would he ever get in trouble if he fell in. He must stay away from where the dirty dark water touched the ground. He could see a big bridge. If he crossed it he might find a policeman. He had to stay tight to the side because of all the lorries going over. After he got across there were more big bangs and more red fires and it was very windy, not cold wind like usual, but hot. The smoke made him cough and his mouth tasted nasty. Jamie got coughs a lot, so he had to be careful. He covered his mouth with his hand. It wasn't polite to cough without covering your mouth and besides, it helped keep the smoke out. His feet hurt and he had scrapes from when he fell down. *Must keep going. One, two, one, two.*

There was St. Paul's with its great big round thing up top. That must have been the bridge him and Gran had gone over in a bus when she took him there once. She got him a picture postcard of it and he'd kept it on his shelf where he could look at it every day. He must have got very strong now he was nearly fifteen because they'd come on a bus for a long time, and he'd just walked here all on his own. Had his postcard been blitzed too? And the stuff for his cake?

St. Paul's looked funny. It was up high, sitting on clouds. *It must have been bitzed and sent to heaven like a good person would, like Gran would be because she was good.* Churches could probably do that, and St. Paul's was a special big church. He couldn't remember the special name for churches like that. But it looked beautiful. *Heaven must be a super place.*

"Hey! What're you doing here? Don't you know there's a big raid on? You're supposed to be in a shelter, young man."

Jamie turned and saw two men in uniforms. One tall and skinny with a ginger moustache, the other ordinary, the sort Jamie might not remember next time he saw him. Strangers, but must be police, only different uniform from Constable Wilson.

"I think my house was bitzed—*be*-litzed—and I've been looking for a policeman. I think my Gran was bitzed too and Biffy and the stuff for my birthday cake." Jamie began to cry again. "Are you policemans?"

"Where d'you live, son? What's your name?" asked the ordinary one.

Jamie stood up very straight, hands by his sides. "My name is Jamie Jenkins. I live at twenty-two Hortey Street, Southwark, London, England." He said it loud and proud. Gran had practiced that with him over and over, and today he'd got it right first off. And got in the aitch. *Remember be-litz.*

"Blimey, you're a long way from home. You come along with us. We're going to take you to the station. It'll be safer than out here."

"Slow, don't you think?" the tall one sort of whispered to the other. Hard to whisper low with all the noises going on.

"Ssh, you'll hurt his feelings," said the other one.

"You won't hurt my feelings," Jamie said. "It wouldn't be kind to call me stupid, but slow is all right. I just take longer to learn things than other people. But I know things. Lots of things." The men looked surprised.

They hurried along some side streets and came to the fire station. Inside they passed lots of funny big boxes and some gray lorries and one red one.

"What're those for?" asked Jamie.

"Get a move on, Simon, busy night." The ordinary one seemed crotchety. Maybe being easy to forget did that to people.

"A few minutes to cheer him up won't be missed." Jamie liked this tall one best.

"Those are pumps, they carry water to fires and get pulled by taxis," said tall Mr. Simon, pointing at the big boxes. "And those are fire engines. They all used to be red like that one, but they're supposed to be gray now. We ran out of paint. Soon as we get some more, we'll paint the red one." He looked down at Jamie, his eyebrows up like he had a question. Funny those eyebrows weren't ginger like his moustache.

"I like red best," Jamie said.

"Yes, but red is too easy to see from the air."

Jamie didn't know why that would be a bad thing, it sounded like quite a good thing. Red was a happy color. He must ask lots of questions so he didn't have to think about being sad. Gran told him to keep his mind busy if things went wrong. "Especially yours," she said.

They came to a room with some ladies with telephones and big bits of paper with pictures up on the wall.

"What're they doing?" Jamie asked.

"That's a watch room where people telephone to tell us where there are fires. Those are maps on the wall and they stick pins with little flags in them so we can see quickly where the fires are and send the pumps and engines to put them out."

"There are lots of fires. Why are the pumps and things still in here?"

"Can't crowd them together too much. And we have to keep some back in case fires start up in other places. Probably hard for you to understand. Enough questions for now, I think!" Tall Mr. Simon sounded a bit crotchety himself now.

They went down lots and lots of stairs to a huge room with no windows. There was a sort of kitchen at one end where a pretty lady was making a huge pot of tea.

"That's the ticket, Joyce!" said the ordinary man. "I could just do with a cuppa. Look who we found outside. This is Jamie. Reckon he's been bombed out. Got a sandwich for him, have you? I reckon he could do with a feed." He whispered something in her ear.

"Poor little chap," Joyce said. "You just come and sit down here by me, Jamie, and I'll find you a bite to eat. Do you like tea, dear?"

"Yes, please," said Jamie. "Can I have milk and sugar in it?"

"Milk of course, love. No sugar to spare with this rationing, I'm afraid."

"Here, Joyce, I've got a twist of sugar in my pocket. He can have it." The ordinary man was quite kind after all.

"Thank the nice man, Jamie."

"Thank you, how very kind." He'd heard Gran say that.

"Well, such lovely manners. Who looks after you at home?" She combed Jamie's hair off his face with her fingers.

"My Gran. Roy, he's my cousin, lives there too. Roy and me have different mums and dads. Roy's died in a train crash. Mine just had to go away somewhere they couldn't take me."

"I see, dear. And where is Roy now?"

"Roy, he went out and Gran was taking a nap. I was outside looking for Roy and I think our house got bitzed."

"Do you mean *blitzed*, dear?"

"Keep forgetting. Be-*litz*. You know, when houses get bangs and fall down and get fire in them." *Careful, talk right or people won't treat you right.*

"Bombs, dear. When there's lots of them, we call it blitz. "

The lady called Joyce poured Jamie a big cup—milk must have been in the cup already—and stirred in the sugar for him. It felt very comfy on his scratchy throat.

"Did you see the bomb fall?"

"No. Something hit me and I fell down. I couldn't see and my head hurt."

"That would be blast, from the bomb exploding. It can do that. You were lucky, it must have been a long way away from you." She clicked her tongue a few times, scaring Jamie a bit because when Gran did that it was to tell him he was doing something wrong. But she smiled, so it must be all right. *Pretty smile.* Didn't Gran say *blast* was a naughty word, though?

"Maybe Gran's just got a hurt head and can't see properly. I should go back and look. But I'm so tired, I can't walk anymore."

"He seems to have walked all the way from Southwark," tall Simon said as he sucked up his tea, making the sorts of noises polite people shouldn't.

"Good gracious," Joyce said. "You must be a strong boy. But don't you worry. These wardens will telephone through and ask people to check up on your house and your Gran. You leave it all to them."

"Wardens? Aren't they policemans?" asked Jamie, breath coming hard again. "I was told to find a policeman if I was in trouble. Gran and Roy will be really cross with me if I didn't do it right."

"They are sort of policemen, Jamie, you did quite the right thing."

"Good. It's not nice when people are cross. Can they ask about Biffy, too?"

4

"Wake up, Jamie, there's someone to see you."

Jamie looked around and sat up so fast his head got all swimmy. "Where am I?"

"You remember, dear, you're in the fire station, you got bombed out," Joyce said, stroking his hair. "I'm going to get you some breakfast, but first this lady wants to talk to you."

Joyce pulled a chair up to his bed and a lady with beige clothes and face and hair sat right on the edge of it, all that beige pulled tight by hands that clutched the big blue handbag on her lap. She glanced at Jamie's face before moving her eyes down to his chest.

"Did they find my Gran?" The lady's shoulders went up, almost to her ears and she made fists. She looked unhappy, almost as if she'd been made to swallow a spoonful of medicine. *Though no one would ever make a grownup take medicine, of course.*

"Jamie, I'm afraid I have very sad news for you, dear. Your house has gone, and so has your grandmother. I'm so very sorry. Was anyone else living there?"

It might be a mistake. Gran had always been there and said she'd never leave him. Roy might know where she was.

"Only my cousin, Roy, but he locked us in and went out, don't know where. Maybe he got back by now." No tears came. The lady had an odd smile, a worried smile, like it hurt her to stretch her lips.

"Locked you in? Why ever would he do that during an air raid?"

Roy did all sorts of funny things. No telling why, but he was quite smart, so he had to have his reasons. "Said he had to go out and couldn't have me wandering. Gran was taking a nap. He's going to be really cross now. Because I wandered. He'll hit me."

She turned the smile off and frowned instead. She looked at his face now and seemed more normal. She kept scratching at a rough spot on her neck. It didn't look very nice; she should leave it alone.

"No one's going to hit you, Jamie. We're going to put you on a train with some other children and you're going to stay on a farm in the country. That'll be nice, won't it?"

"Can't I go to the seaside? I went there once. It was lovely." *Will Gran know where to find me? Just in case there had been a mistake. Should I ask?* Grownups get angry when people say they've made a mistake.

"I'm afraid not, Jamie. But the farm will have animals and lots of fields to play in. And it's actually not far from the sea. You'll have to help Mr. and Mrs. Lake, but not much. Of course, you must behave nicely and do as they say." *Scratching again.* Maybe being unhappy made her itchy.

"What're fields?"

"Why, Jamie, haven't you ever seen one?"

"Perhaps I seen one and didn't know. I don't go out much."

"Well, it's a great big piece of land that is only grass, or some sort of crop like wheat or barley, and it doesn't have any houses on it."

"No, I never seen a field. What's a crop and them other things you said?"

"Oh, Jamie, you'll see it all when you get there. It's such a change from London, and no bombs, either."

No bangs and bitz. Nice. "No be-litz? And no Roy?"

"Lots of peace and quiet. How old is Roy?"

"He's nineteen, and Gran says he's no good, just like his

mum." Jamie felt his cheeks go hot. He shouldn't say things like that about his cousin. *What if someone told?* He wanted to rock. Mustn't rock. *Sit on hands.* That would help. *But no Gran? Couldn't be right.* His tummy felt heavy.

"Then Roy must take care of himself. Why isn't he in the army? All healthy young men should be in the army." She looked fierce now.

"Don't know. I think he mostly takes stuff from empty houses."

"No, Jamie, there'll be no Roy in the country. It'll be an adventure."

"Is it tomorrow now? If it is, it's my birthday. I'm fifteen." Fifteen sounded grownup.

"Well, you stayed overnight here, so, yes, I suppose you can say it's tomorrow. Many happy returns of the day, Jamie. Fifteen. My word, you are getting grown up." The funny not-really-a-smile was back.

"Thank you. Gran was going to make me a cake, she got all the stuff, but I suppose it was be-litzed."

"Yes, Jamie, it was. I'll see what I can do."

She didn't say goodbye, just stood up, turned around, and walked out. She was a funny one. She said sad things but didn't seem very sad, and she smiled that hurting smile in between. She was unhappy, but that was different from sad. Wasn't it? Some people probably found it hard to say sad things and just pretended not to mind. Jamie was beginning to feel sad, but he'd save it till later.

Peace and quiet and adventures sounded nice. He couldn't have Gran and Biffy and birthday cake, but at least he didn't have to have Roy. Sad and glad, that's how things always seemed to turn out.

Joyce came in with a cup of tea and some biscuits.

"You'll never guess what, Jamie."

"What?"

"One of those men who found you yesterday just brought in your green dog. He went all the way to the station near your house and got it for you. His day off, too. It's really messy, so I've got to wash him off and trim some of his fur that got singed, but he'll be almost good as new."

Jamie looked up at Joyce's smiley face and burst into tears.

"Oh, Jamie, I thought you'd be pleased." Now he'd made her sad.

"I'm ever so happy for Biffy, but ever so sad for Gran."

"Oh, Jamie, give me a big hug now, you'll feel better when you're down in the country."

Joyce felt nice. She was soft and smelled sweet. Gran hadn't hugged him much since he got big. He buried his face in the big roses on her dress. All ladies should dress in pink roses and smell sweet. He must take a bath at least two times a week in case one of them wanted to hug him again one day. He ought to be ready, just in case. And a very special lady might like Biffy's sparkling heart. He'd leave the heart where it was for now. Maybe for years and years. The hug was beginning to make him feel funny, so he sat up. He had to go to the toilet.

* * *

The train was noisy, but in a nice way, as if it was talking. He felt very excited because he hardly ever went outside, never mind to an adventure. You learn things at an adventure. Lots of children were on the train, but he sat next to Mrs. Meyer, one of the ladies who was taking them all to the country, and she wouldn't let the others tease him. Children always teased him, that's why Gran never let him know any. Mrs. Meyer acted nice and said he was a polite boy. He told her Gran was fussy about polite, he always had to mind his manners. She told him they were going to a town near the New Forest.

"Has a new forest got littler trees than an old one?"

She laughed and said, "The new one has very big trees and it's actually very old, but they called it that a long, long time ago, and the name stuck."

"I saw St. Paul's up in heaven, you know. It was sitting on top of the clouds."

"It wasn't really, Jamie, I saw the picture in the paper. You saw it sitting inside smoke that looked like clouds because lots of the buildings around it were on fire. St. Paul's was spared. It was a miracle."

"Oh. You mean like a Jesus miracle?"

"Something like that. Lots of the first bombs weren't big bang ones. They were incendiaries, meant to set things on fire so the next lot of pilots could see where to drop the big bang bombs."

Would he ever understand all the things grownups knew about? "That's a big word, *insendies*. I want to learn it."

He practiced "incendiaries" with her until he got it right. And he simply must remember to get blitz right. The lady said why not look out of the window, there was lots to see, but things kept going past before he could see what they were. There were so many green things. Little hills, lots of grass. Fields, he declared, and Mrs. Meyer said he was quite right, they were. Jamie decided he liked green grass and trees. And animals. Like little dots until the train slowed a bit and the lady could point and tell him sheep or cow. Pretty things, they were. The train stopped at stations sometimes, but not very often. The train sometimes went through without stopping. *The people on the platform must be quite cross about that.*

There were some places that had houses, and you could see right into the back gardens because they were close to the special road the train ran along. There were lines with wet clothes hanging on them, and some of the children giggled once because the train slowed down right opposite a line with some very big pairs of knickers on it. Jamie had been to a house with Gran that had a back garden once when he was quite little. She was doing cleaning for the people who lived there. They had some children, he could hear them laughing inside. He'd walked round and round in the garden for a very long time. No one came out to play with him. Probably weren't allowed.

The train came to a stop with a big screaming sound. "Here we are!" the lady said.

They climbed off and walked down a long, long street to what they called the church hall. They all had to sit in chairs and be quiet as church mice. Did God make church mice behave better than other mice? The little girl sitting next to him stared at him all the time. He could feel it even when he wasn't looking her way. She had no manners at all, so when no one was looking he pulled the corners of his mouth into his best monster face and when her face started to crumple sat on his hands and stared at the wall opposite. When she was taken away, still crying, he noticed something drop from her neck and roll under the chair. He could have called out, but rude girls shouldn't have pretty things. He dropped one of his gloves and crouched down to pick it up. A little sparkly thing on a chain. He slipped it into his glove, a good safe place.

Most of the children were taken away by different grownups, and some of them cried. They were probably scared and missed their grans, and Jamie knew how they felt. Wasn't anybody coming for him? At last, one of the ladies brought over a man and woman. The woman looked nice and smiley, but the big man with black hair was frowning. Something about the lady's mouth, she tried too hard to smile, blinked too much while she did it. People often tried to hide under their smiles, and it never worked, not really. She was a nice lady, even so. She was scared of the frowning man, kept blinking and looking at him, hands held tight together just under her belt. His hands were tight but separate, as if he wanted to hit someone.

"Don't waste time, Elsie, there's the cows to be milked." Loud, hard voice.

The lady looked tired, like Gran often did by suppertime.

"Well, you're a nice looking young lad. You must be Jamie."

"Yes, miss."

"You can call us Mr. and Mrs. Lake. We live on a farm, and you're going to stay with us for a bit and help us with some of the jobs we have to do."

"Yes, Mrs., um . . . "

"Lake."

"Sorry, miss. Mrs. Lake." *Got to keep my wits about me . . .* Roy said he didn't have any wits. More unkind stuff, and not so very true. *Not very.*

"Well, he's simple all right, but at least he doesn't look a fright like the last one," the man said. He sounded very grumpy. "Small for his age."

"Shh, Tom, be nice." He didn't look the sort who would find nice easy.

"Oh, come on, Elsie, let's get back."

Jamie picked up his case and followed them out of the hall, waving goodbye to Mrs. Meyer. He ran back to her suddenly. Mr. Lake shouted after him to stop his nonsense, but he kept on going.

"Sorry, I forgot to say thank you. Thank you."

"I loved having you sit next to me, Jamie," she said. "But now you'd better get back to the Lakes, they seem to be in a hurry. Good luck." Mrs. Meyer looked as if she might cry.

The car was very bumpy and made Jamie feel a bit sick because he was sitting in the back and kept falling around. He tried looking out of the window and just thinking about what he could see. Fields, mostly, so it was a good thing he knew what they were.

He gasped when they stopped in front of a huge house. The bricks looked different from the house where Gran's flat was.

"Is this all yours?" he asked. "Do other people live here, too?"

"Yes, it's all ours," said Mr. Lake. "We've got a son away in the army and our daughter, Pamela, helps her mother around the house when she's not at school. They take care of the chickens and ducks, too. You'll be helping me with all the other jobs. There's a lot of work, so you'd better get used to it." He sounded angry. He looked strong and had big red hands that still held the wheel tight as could be, even though the car had stopped moving. "I don't want to hear any whining, and no complaining to those women who come round checking up, either. Far as I'm concerned, you're here to work."

"Yes, Mr. Lake. I always wanted to get a job so I could earn money and buy food for Gran so she won't have to work so hard."

"Well, you won't be earning any money here, and your gran's dead, remember? You just be grateful for a bed and your meals." Mr. Lake turned and glared at Jamie, who tried to keep the tears down. Another person saying Gran was dead. Horrid word, *dead*. Mrs. Lake stared out of the window, thinking of something far away. She was much smaller than Mr. Lake, and she'd closed up her face so it didn't tell anything. Her hair would be quite pretty if she looked after it. It looked like string, what with the color and needing a brush through it.

Jamie felt better when he got out in the fresh air, even though it was cold. Their feet crunched on the icy path up to the big wood door. Mrs. Lake took him up a lot of stairs to a white room with a funny ceiling that went this way and that way. It had a bed, a chest-of-drawers, and a chair. Roy and Gran had a chest-of-drawers, but not Jamie, he only had a shelf. This was nice. He could put things away and close up the drawer. His things would be private.

"It's not much," she said, "but it'll have to do, I'm afraid."

"It's very nice, thank you, Mrs. Lake," Jamie said. He smiled at her and she smiled back. She was kind, but he didn't know about Mr. Lake yet. She left him to unpack. He took off his wooly gloves and looked at the necklace. Tiny diamonds, but they'd light him up in the sun. The only other things he had were a patchy Biffy with his hidden sparkly heart, some socks and underpants, a shirt, and a pair of trousers. He put his new treasure inside a sock. There was a little parcel he hadn't seen before. Maybe from Miss Joyce. He opened it carefully. Chocolate, his favorite. He wished he could eat chocolate every day. He loved saying that word with all its bits. He put it in the back of the drawer for later. Was that Mr. Lake's voice? He went to the top of the stairs and listened hard. His ears didn't seem the same since the big bang.

"Jamie, get down here for supper. We go to bed early in this house. Wash your hands in the bathroom first."

Mr. Lake said something called grace before they ate. There was a lot of stuff on the table, and Pamela was there, too. She had nearly white curly hair, different white from Gran, and there was more of it. Her big round eyes stared at him all the time. She'd be pretty if she didn't wear such a mean face. She never said hello. He didn't know what to do when she kept looking at him like that. Made him feel fidgety. Gran said staring was rude. He kept quiet and ate the bread and dripping Mr. Lake put on his plate and drank his water. He wanted tea like them, but he didn't say so. There was jam, but they didn't give him any of that either. There was cake, too. Mrs. Lake put a small slice on his plate and he remembered to say thank you before eating it. Her face was sweet when she smiled at him, but it looked sad most of the time.

"Don't you go spoiling the boy, Elsie, he'll eat us out of house and home." It wasn't very nice, not wanting Jamie to have cake.

"It was just a little, Tom. He's a growing boy, and he'll need to build up his strength." *At least Mrs. Lake has good manners.*

"That's all very well. Food costs good money, and sugar's too scarce to waste on the likes of him."

When Jamie finished he was sent up to bed. It took him a long time to get to sleep. Gran was probably in heaven and he hoped she was happy there. He wished he had a picture of her. He must think about her every night so he wouldn't forget. He pretended she was kissing him goodnight, smiling so her eyes squeezed up and got buried in wrinkles round the sides.

He dreamed of crackly fire, big bangs, and lines of doors that locked themselves loudly, one after the other. Then he was walking and walking and walking, all alone in the world, and no one came. He felt he'd only been asleep a minute or two before Mr. Lake shook him awake.

"Rise and shine. Get your clothes on and come down to the kitchen. You can have a glass of milk and some bread and butter before we get started. I've got some gumboots about your size, so come down in your socks. No need to wash now, you can do that before dinner. Get a move on!"

5

Elsie watched him trail Tom out to the farmyard. Jamie was a nice-looking lad, rather short, but quite normal-looking. She liked the brown wavy hair that needed a trim, and his girlish sensitive face. Still slight, maybe he'd fill out in a few years. With his big brown eyes and long eyelashes he might have grown up to be a heartbreaker—if he weren't retarded. *What a shame, such a waste.*

That poor boy was shivering already; he needed a jacket. Elsie would have to find an old raggedy one so Tom wouldn't get angry. While they were having breakfast, Tom said he'd show him how to feed the pigs first while his man started on the milking, and after that Jamie was to clean out the sty. Jamie said his cousin Roy had one of those in his eye once. "So did pigs get them too?" Tom rolled his eyes and poor Jamie looked confused. Watching him eat bread with a smear of butter while they ate bacon and eggs was painful, but the boy didn't complain, had seemed to fold into himself. Used to being second best.

Elsie worried about Jamie. Tom did cruel things to those boys. They seemed to arouse in him a primitive need to lash out, to brutalize when they came near. He kept asking for slow boys because they were free and no adult listened to them. Tom had a wild animal's instinct to destroy the weak. Only the land girls ever met with his approval. When the government came up with the idea of recruiting young women they referred to as "land girls" to work on the farms in place of the laborers who'd gone off to war, Elsie thought it was the answer to their prayers. Another was coming next week. The last one had left after a month without explanation; they never stayed long. In a better mood than usual when they arrived, Tom was in a worse one then ever when they left, using Elsie like a rutting stag at night and alternately ignoring and berating her during the day.

Elsie was surprised they'd sent Jamie after the fuss they'd made about the last boy, although she knew they were running short of families to take the evacuees. Tom said normal boys were lazy and told too many tales to get out of work, and who would believe cretins, after all? The last boy, Jack, ran away. The local constable called out a search party right away and the poor Jack's body had been found frozen stiff in Old Ring Copse. He was too thin, they'd said, and later that evening a detective inspector arrived at their farmhouse.

"Mrs. Lake," said Inspector Morris, fixing her with eyes that blamed and judged. "We're trying to put together Jack's last day here before he left. What time did he go to work?"

"Well, we got up at about five, like always. We had breakfast, and then he and Tom went out to milk the cows."

"What did Jack eat?"

"Oh, I don't know. Same as usual, I expect, bread and butter and a glass of milk."

"How about later?"

"Well, we had our midday meal, and he would have had some meat and potatoes, cabbage, too, I think. I don't remember if we had a pudding that day. Then they went out again. There's always work to do on a farm."

"I know, I was born and brought up on one. What was he wearing?"

"You can't expect me to remember that! A pullover, I suppose, a jacket probably."

"When we found him he only had a shirt on. Will we find more clothes in his room, warm clothes?"

"I suppose so. I can't be expected to know what he did with them. He wasn't quite right, you know. He could have left them anywhere."

"We know he was mentally retarded, Mrs. Lake, and we also know he wasn't as bad off as all that. He stayed with one of our constables for a few days before being sent over to you. I don't suppose you knew that. What else did he have to eat that day?"

"There would have been supper and then bed. Bread and dripping most likely, perhaps an apple."

"The pathologist said there was no food in his stomach, Mrs. Lake. How do you account for that?"

"How should I know? Perhaps he had a stomach upset, that would account for it." She hadn't meant to starve the boy, but Tom said he had to be punished. Nearly every day Tom said that.

"He had lost a lot of weight. He was weighed before he left London. I don't suppose you knew that, either. He was nine stone then. He was quite a bit lighter when we found him. About seven-and-a-half stone. Twenty-one pounds in six weeks?"

"I don't think they get a lot of exercise, usually. They don't go out much because their families are ashamed of them. Hard work takes off the puppy fat very quickly, you know."

"Why didn't you report him missing? He was only a child, or don't you think they're worth the trouble?" He had almost snarled.

"He was seventeen, Inspector. I leave these things to my husband." Her words sounded feeble, her voice shaky.

"You can't have it both ways. Too retarded to keep his jacket on in a freeze, but too mature to bother reporting missing. Come, come, Mrs. Lake."

"I don't know what to say. I'm sure my husband had his reasons."

"Yes, well, we're not completely satisfied, Mrs. Lake. I'm going to look through his things now."

He thinks we killed him. We did. Tom did.

He looked through the chest of drawers and found some of their son Gerald's old warm underwear. Socks and a pullover, too. Tom must have put them there earlier. The police didn't take any action, except to caution them that they must report runaways immediately. Other fish to fry. She'd heard they'd broken up a big black market ring a couple of weeks later.

Elsie felt ill thinking about Jack again. She'd had to lie, but Tom was a brute. He made the boys get close to animals they'd never seen before; their bulk and wild eyes would terrify any city-bred child. He shouted, hit them, he didn't let them have enough to eat, and he wouldn't let her make sure they were warmly dressed. They disgusted Tom, and so did Elsie these days. Well, he disgusted her for that matter. He'd made her compliant in his gross inhumanity. But she was powerless in the face of hard facts; she had her own children to protect, Pamela and Gerald, and he held the purse strings. And she was afraid of Tom.

Even if Tom hit her for it, she'd have to warn him to be careful this time. They'd better not lose a second one. When Pamela was grown and gone, Elsie would leave, too. Tom was no better than a murderer, but Pamela couldn't see it. She was hard, like her father, and their only warm feelings were reserved for each other. Gerald was more like his mother, much to Tom's disappointment. "Namby-pamby," he called him. Nothing namby-pamby about the army though, and he'd volunteered, not waited to be called up, like some.

Elsie's parents lived not too far away. They were getting on and could do with some help. She could go to them and maybe get some kind of job in Lymington. They had such a pretty house with lovely views of the sea. She'd like a steady, quiet life in the company of decent people. She'd done well in school, well enough for university, but her parents had been uneasy with the idea. Not many around there go to university, especially girls. They'd pressed her to go to a secretarial school, get a nice job, and find a husband after a few uneventful years. She'd done all that, always accompanied by a niggling unrest she could never quite dispel, and Tom had seemed like a great escape from the monotony of small-town life.

Tom had been handsome and charming in those days, and she'd fallen for him almost right away. He'd worked with his father then, a controlling and abusive man. Just like Tom was now, although there was no hint of it then. Nothing he did was ever good enough for his father, but Tom just swallowed his feelings and carried on. Elsie had admired Tom's fortitude. In the last days of his life, Tom's father made Tom promise never to give up the farm and throw away his life's work, no matter what. "Don't disappoint me, Tom," he'd croaked, clutching his son's arm with an emaciated claw. This last manipulative coup haunted Tom still. And Elsie.

There were hard years after the old man died, and Tom began to change. He was miserable and felt trapped, and his temper became ever more explosive. She'd tried to be understanding.

"Why don't we sell the farm?" she'd asked Tom one evening. "We could buy a little business, a pub perhaps."

"You stupid cow," he'd shouted. "Don't you know my father damned near killed himself to keep this going? I can't just walk away from it. I can't disappoint him like that."

"Tom, he's dead. He can't be disappointed anymore, and you know no one could ever please him in life; he was that kind of man. It's not your fault. We have our lives to live. I want you to be happier, for us to be happy like we used to be."

"Oh, so now you're not happy? The fairy tale's over? Gilt's off the gingerbread?" He slapped her face and stalked upstairs.

That was the start of it, as if she'd betrayed him somehow. She'd tried to explain how she loved him still, just wanted him to be happy, but he wouldn't listen. She'd not been keen on sex after that slap, the first of several. Anger and resentment squelched those feelings a little more with each clash, and eventually killed them entirely. That had made things much worse, of course, and his resulting mistreatment alienated her further. All her loving feelings for him had seeped away. It left an emptiness that was almost painful. War was good for farms, and she'd hoped he might be more at peace now they were on a firm financial footing, but rage still ate him raw.

It's not as if she wanted much out of life. Her parents wouldn't approve of her leaving Pamela, though they'd have strong views on that. And Pamela certainly wouldn't leave her father. She was stuck, at least until the girl left school.

* * *

Elsie opened the oven a crack to check the Yorkshire pudding. Rising nicely, nearly done. On Sundays they had a better cut of meat than usual, although Sunday wasn't any different from the rest of the week on a farm. They weren't churchy, even though Tom carried on his father's practice of saying grace before meals.

Pamela was home to help in the kitchen, not that she ever did much. She came downstairs to lay the table for lunch, their main meal of the day. She was giggling and opened the back door, poking her head out. Elsie could hear Jamie wailing over Tom's curses.

"What's going on, Pamela?" she asked, running to the door.

"It's the idiot, Dad's hosing him down, and he doesn't seem to like cold water. I watched it all out of my bedroom window. He fell into the pig muck. That sow can be pretty aggressive, and I suppose Jamie's afraid of her. They always sense it, don't they?"

"That's awful, it's freezing outside." Elsie wiped her hands on her apron. "He'll catch his death of cold."

"Well, he can't expect us to put up with that stink indoors, can he? He'll have to learn, just like everyone else. And who'd want him to use our bath in that state?"

"You know, Pamela, you've become very callous. Can't you find any sympathy in your heart for that boy?"

"Should've been drowned at birth, that's my opinion."

"Oh, Pamela, listen to yourself."

Elsie had few illusions about her daughter, but Pamela's heartless words still shocked and saddened her. Pamela didn't need her; she followed her father's example and learned nothing of consequence from her mother. Elsie had tried to instill some sense of humanity in her children, but she'd failed with this one. Gerald, thank heavens, was a credit to her. Pray, God, he'd stay safe in this dreadful war.

Tom dragged Jamie in by the scruff of his neck. He was sobbing and shivering, ashen from fear and cold-pain.

"Tom, he's got to get out of those wet things," Elsie whispered. "He's going to get ill."

"Get him some of Gerald's old things. Nothing too good, mind. I know what a soft touch you are. Let him towel off and get changed. Bit of work after lunch should get him to rights again."

"Don't you think a warm bath—"

"I'm not paying to heat up water for a stupid boy who's afraid of a pig! Get on with it. I'm hungry and I want my lunch on the table in ten minutes."

Elsie climbed the stairs, heavy with distress. She found some old clothes, which were at least warmer than Jamie's poor things.

Pamela had finished laying the table and was poking at the potatoes, still smirking over Jamie's plight. Elsie ignored her, got out the roast, and brought the cabbage to a boil. The gravy was simmering, left over from the day before. She drained the potatoes and began to mash them with fierce, stabbing movements.

"My, aren't we in a pet," Pamela said.

Elsie spun around and the girl recoiled from her furious face.

"You insolent little brat, how dare you speak to me like that!" Pamela began to laugh. As Elsie started forward as if to slap her, Pamela danced away. Elsie closed her eyes for a moment to get herself under control. Reacting like that helped nothing. She should ignore her daughter's unpleasantness from now on to keep some semblance of peace.

Lunch was spent in near silence after grace. Elsie thought she'd go mad from Tom's nerve-jabbing plate scraping and wet chewing, interspersed with Jamie's bouts of shivering that he tried hard to suppress. Pamela alternated pouting with contemptuous glares at her mother and Jamie; she rewarded Tom with an occasional sweet smile.

Tom scraped his chair back. "Time to get back to work. Come on, Jamie, look lively."

Elsie had to speak up. "Tom, I really don't think he's up to it."

Tom leaned his fists on the table and brought his face level with hers. "Oh, you don't think so? Why don't we all just take a nice little holiday?"

He stamped out with Jamie trailing behind him, his narrow shoulders slumped like an old man's.

He was going to get ill, might run away, and the trouble would start all over again.

"Come on, Pamela, let's clear up." A little holiday would be nice. Alone.

"I'm tired. I want to take a nap."

"After the work's finished, Pamela. I'm not the maid around here."

"Might as well be." Pamela stood in front of a little mirror next to the door, running her fingers through her waves and pinching them forward or back as she monitored the effect. Her mouth pursed into what she probably thought was a film star pout, but she only succeeded in looking like an unpleasant and petulant chit.

"What's got into you, Pamela? You used to be a sweet child. You're only sixteen, how did you change so much?"

Pamela swung around. Hands on hips she leaned toward her mother like a harridan berating her neighbor over the fence. "Oh, you're so boring. I hate my life. Daddy at least treats me with some respect. If you want respect, you have to earn it, you know."

Earn it? By mistreating helpless children? "What have I done to lose your respect, while your father enjoys your full approval?" Elsie's breath came fast and shallow. Her head pounded in step with her heart.

"You don't love him anymore, I can see that. He works so hard, and when he gets fed up with the stupid things you do, you just go all wobbly, like that idiot out there."

"How dare you speak to me like that, Pamela, how dare you! Get out of my sight!" Elsie turned away and leaned on the sink, clutching the rim as if it might fly away.

The front door slammed. Still shaking, she began the washing up. Tom had stolen their daughter, somehow. She couldn't take much more of this. Looking out of the window, she caught sight of Pamela, looking rather foolish as she minced with grim purpose across the yard. Gone to complain to her father, she supposed. More rows.

Supper was another episode of silent tension. Jamie looked exhausted and soon asked if he could go to bed. He thanked her for the meal, and she dredged up a smile and wished him goodnight. Tom said nothing, didn't look at him. Pamela went up soon after, saying she had homework to do, although she was a poor student and almost never studied. She'd leave school at the end of the summer term, as there was no point in going any further.

"What do you think Pamela will do when she leaves school?" Elsie asked Tom.

"I don't know. What does she want to do?" Tom replied.

"She hasn't said. Hasn't she said anything to you?" He'd know if anyone would. Didn't he realize Pamela hardly spoke to her mother anymore? Did he notice anything?

"No, she hasn't mentioned anything. There's plenty of work around here, anyway."

"It would do her good to get a job and get out in the world." And away from home.

"No need for that. Leave her alone, do you hear? You're always on at that girl," and Tom finally looked at her, scowling with fierce challenge.

It was true what Tom said. There would be plenty to do on the farm because Elsie would be gone by that time.

* * *

Jamie and Elsie retreated into themselves a little more each day, going about their daily tasks without speaking unless they had to. Jamie's eyes didn't meet Elsie's anymore, and he looked as pale and listless as she felt. *Poor boy.* She smiled and stroked his hair when no one was looking. She left little treats in his top drawer when she could. There wasn't much more she could do for him. At least he knew she liked him. That had to count for something. Pamela had hardly spoken to Elsie during the two weeks since their fight, and of course she never spoke to Jamie.

She'd love to leave this house. Even if she and Tom were still happy together, she'd want to leave. It had never been her home; she'd not been allowed to move a picture or bring in any small item to her liking. His parents' hefty furniture swamped the rooms and she sometimes felt the pieces watching her in solemn disapproval. First Tom's father, and then Tom, wouldn't hear of changing anything. Even the chintz curtains managed to exude morbid gloom from their faded panels.

The next Monday, Elsie stood washing up the breakfast things when she spotted a bicycle coming up the road to the farm. The land girl. She wiped her hands and walked across the yard to the gate. The girl got off her bike, panting a little.

"Hello, you must be Mrs. Lake. I'm Valerie Rand. How do you do?" A friendly, open face.

"Yes, I'm Mrs. Lake. Come in for a cup of tea, you must be cold after that long ride. My husband's in the cow fields, I think." She seemed cheerful; might be nice to have around.

"Thank you, it is a little chilly. Do you have any other help?"

"Well, we've got two young men who come in the mornings

and a young retarded boy, Jamie. He hasn't learned the ropes yet, it takes them a while, you know."

"Yes, but once they've learned, they've learned, or so I'm told."

Elsie didn't answer, but busied herself with the kettle. "Beaker all right for you?"

"Oh yes, rather. I like my tea; dainty little cups empty much too quickly."

They chatted about matters that make up the warp and weft of village life. A sensible girl and pleasant looking. She was on the stocky side, but fresh-faced with curly, gingery-fair hair. She looked strong, which would be useful, but gave the impression she wouldn't put up with any nonsense, which Tom might find inconvenient. More turmoil, at least for Elsie.

"Well, thanks for the tea, I'd better go and find your husband now and get to work." She grinned at Elsie and strode off, not seeming to notice the cutting January wind.

That land girl program was something Pamela would benefit from. Most of the farmers had lost laborers to the war effort, so the girls helped fill in for them. Tom would never let her do it, though. And Pamela would fight it tooth and nail.

* * *

It was Elsie's washing day, so she lit the water heater and went upstairs to collect the dirty clothes. She checked in Jamie's room to see where he'd put his clothes, but didn't see any. She opened his chest-of-drawers and found pants and socks neatly folded in the bottom drawer. He only had one change of clothes, and nothing warm at all, apart from the clothes he'd put on after the pig muck incident. It took so long for things to dry, they'd not been washed since. She'd add some warm things little by little, things Gerald wouldn't miss, although Tom would probably notice. She found the chocolate in the back of the top drawer that he'd brought with him; he'd taken tiny nibbles of it, trying to make it last.

When she got downstairs with the basket, she was surprised to find Valerie sitting at the kitchen table. Elsie looked flushed and indignant. *Oh, Tom, not already, couldn't you have waited?*

"Mrs. Lake, tell me about Jamie."

"Well, I told you, didn't I? He's retarded, and Mr. Lake is trying to teach him the work."

"Trying to teach him? Trying to beat it into him, more likely," Valerie said. "I was watching him work, he hadn't noticed me yet. They were rounding up the cows, but Jamie seemed scared and ran away from them when they got near him. Your husband went berserk, boxed his ears and threw him down in a pile of cow manure. Now he's crying his eyes out and your husband is shaking him like a madman. I can't work for a man like that! I'm leaving, so be sure to tell him what I said. I'm afraid I'll have to tell my supervisor why I'm not coming back."

Elsie said nothing as Valerie turned her back, went out to her bicycle, and peddled off down the road.

Tom came around the corner into the yard dragging Jamie by his ear.

"No, please, no cold water, no water," Jamie screamed until Tom slapped him and told him to shut up.

Elsie went upstairs and put dry clothes and a towel on Jamie's bed, another blanket, too. She came back down to the kitchen to the same scene as before, only with Jamie looking downright ill this time.

"Jamie, go upstairs, I've put dry clothes and a towel on your bed."

"Who was that on the bicycle? That wasn't the land girl, was it? She was supposed to be here after breakfast."

"She was here, Tom. She went out to find you. She saw what happened in the field with Jamie and said she didn't want to work for a man like you."

Elsie held her breath as Tom balled his fist, but he said nothing and went out again, shutting the door with a click that managed to be both quiet and resonant. He'd take it out on both of them later. She boiled some milk and put a little precious sugar in it and went up to Jamie. He was slumped on his bed, rocking back and forth and still sobbing. Elsie sat next to him and drew him to her.

"Jamie, I want you to drink this warm milk and get into bed. Try to sleep a bit, you'll feel better. I'll call you when lunch is ready. You're a good boy, Jamie."

"Mr. Lake doesn't think I'm a good boy."

"Yes, but I know better. Into bed now."

Jamie's sobs quieted as he sipped the warm milk while she held the cup. He smiled weakly and closed his eyes. Elsie stroked his hair, lifeless now, like his beautiful eyes.

"I'll be back soon," she whispered. She tucked him in, giving him a little wave as she left. One hand rose and fell in reply.

Jamie didn't answer when she called him for lunch. She went up and found him asleep. She felt his burning forehead and went down to the bathroom for aspirin. She coaxed him awake long enough to get two tablets down him, then tucked him in again. Tom was taking off his boots when she got back to the kitchen.

"Where's that damned boy?"

"He's asleep, Tom. He has a high temperature. He'd better stay inside today."

"How do you know Little Lord Fauntleroy isn't playing games?"

"I felt his forehead while he was still asleep, it was burning hot. I gave him a couple of aspirin. I'll have to call in Dr. Gibson if he gets worse."

"Don't you dare get that doctor in. These people can't mind their own business. We don't want any more talk. Doctors cost money, too, or had you forgotten that?"

When Tom became aggressive he held himself as if he carried a football under each arm, rather like a gorilla she had seen in the zoo once menacing one of his females. Now he looked at her with a hatred shocking in its intensity. She put his plate in front of him and they ate in silence. No grace this time. He shoveled his food down as if stoking a boiler and left right after.

She'd get out, and she would make sure Jamie did, too.

Elsie moved through the day with compulsive precision. She finished the washing, hung it on the clothes horses in the old pantry, checked on Jamie, administered more aspirin and warm milk, cooked and cleaned, fed the chickens and ducks—the endless enslavement of a farmwife. Tom came in, ate in silence, and went out in silence. He went to bed early and fell asleep at once. She lay awake for hours, finally falling into a dead sleep, only awakening with a jolt when Tom clattered down the stairs in his boots.

"Get that boy up, Elsie," he yelled back up.

"I'll go and check on him."

Jamie was much worse, much hotter to the touch. He opened his eyes, but didn't seem to know her and he'd developed a deep racking cough that heaved his chest like an earthquake. She went downstairs. She had to get help.

"He's much worse, Tom, he needs the doctor."

"I told you, woman, no doctor. Don't you dare! Understand?"

"Yes, Tom." *Must get him help.*

"Damned useless little runt."

As soon as Tom left she telephoned Dr. Gibson. He was with a patient in the surgery, but his wife promised to give him the message.

Elsie sat at the kitchen table, terrified for Jamie, for herself. She'd have to leave now. She paced a bit, sat a bit to ease the knots in her stomach, went up to check on Jamie—who couldn't stop coughing and couldn't talk—paced a bit, sat a bit, and jumped when Dr. Gibson put his head around the door.

"Good morning, Mrs. Lake, lad not feeling well?"

"I think he's really ill, Doctor. Could you come up?"

Dr. Gibson couldn't take Jamie's temperature with all the coughing, but listened to his chest and shook his head.

"Double pneumonia, I'm afraid. I'll have to take him to hospital. How long has he been ill?"

Elsie took a deep breath. "He's been poorly for a couple of days. Then he fell in some cold water and took a turn for the worse."

Dr. Gibson stood over her. "Fell into cold water? The pond?"

"Not exactly." She looked him in the eyes. "Actually, he fell in a manure pile. Tom cleaned him off with the hose." He looked at her over his glasses, closing his bottom lip over the top one. There, she'd said it; she wasn't going to cover for him anymore.

"Can you help me get him downstairs? Or do you want to get your husband?"

"Oh, God, no!" said Elsie. "He'll kill me for this. He told me not to call you."

"Mrs. Lake, this boy is seriously ill; he could die. How could Mr. Lake not want him taken care of?"

Elsie sat on the bed, sniffling now, and told him the whole story—the other boys' treatment, and now Jamie's. Dr. Gibson was appalled and concerned for her and Pamela.

"Has he ever hit you, Mrs. Lake? Forgive me, but I feel I must ask."

"Yes, but just a slap, really." She saw him shake his head and sigh. Even a slap would be unthinkable to a man like Dr. Gibson.

"What about Pamela?" he asked.

"Oh, he adores Pamela, she'll be fine. But these boys? He hates them. And me, too."

"Would you like to come into town with me, Mrs. Lake?"

"No, I'd better wait and tell him. Then I'll probably go to my parents. They're in Lymington, you know. I'll call a taxi when I'm ready to leave." *If he lets me leave. But I'm not the sort of woman who just runs away like a scared rabbit. But that's just what you are, Elsie Lake, nothing but a scared rabbit.*

"Well, better get this boy in, let's get the blanket around him. Perhaps he can support his own weight a little."

They struggled down the stairs with their burden and got Jamie into the back of the car. He was quiet now, not coughing so much.

"Sure you won't come with me?"

"I'll be all right, please don't worry yourself." He would worry, of course.

"You realize I have to tell the authorities about this?"

"Yes, I suppose you do."

Elsie spent the rest of the day in a sweaty state of tension, trying to build up her courage for the inevitable showdown. Tom came in for lunch and didn't ask about Jamie, so she kept quiet. Pamela didn't talk to her at tea and didn't look at her, either.

At supper Tom said, "Where is he?" Elsie told him. He put his knife and fork down very carefully. Pamela watched them, her expression alternating between anxiety and anticipation.

"You went against my instructions. You went against me."

"He was very ill, Tom. The doctor said he might die."

"And good riddance."

"Don't you think there would have been trouble if he died and we did nothing? Like before?"

"Are you saying that was my fault?"

"Yes, Tom. It was your fault. It's all your fault. You are cruel and abusive to those boys, and to me, too, for that matter. And I'm going to tell the authorities not to send you any more of them. Tomorrow, I'm going to stay with my parents. Pamela can manage the house for a while. You can get a woman in to clean and cook." She couldn't look at Tom or Pamela, couldn't lift her gaze from her plate.

Tom jumped up, crashing his chair to the ground. Too numb to move, Elsie watched him, outside herself somehow, resigned to the crushing blow he wanted to deliver. But he turned and left without a word.

Elsie looked around the kitchen. She'd cooked her last meal in this cold, hard room. No more wiping down the dark-green tiles, no more scrubbing Tom's scuff marks off the floor, and no more heating water for scouring pots and pans. She would leave this lot piled in the sink. Kitchens ought to be cheerful, the heart of the house. She'd like a pretty kitchen. Perhaps some day, in another place, another life. She jumped when Pamela's voice pierced her thoughts.

"How could you do that to Dad? Look how you've gone and upset him! And all for the sake of that horrid boy." *Horrid girl.*

"Pamela, he would have died if I hadn't got him to hospital. He may still die."

"I hope he does. And what about me? You're going to leave your own daughter?"

"You don't need me, Pamela, you don't even like me. And, you know, you're not a very nice person to be around." There, she'd said it.

"I knew it, you hate me! I hate *you!*"

"Go to your room, Pamela."

Elsie had just turned on the radio in the half-dark living room when Tom came in. The BBC always aired Big Ben chiming nine o'clock before the news started, and the last clang still reverberated. Even in the gloom she could see his eyes were red and wild as if he'd been drinking.

"So, you're going to tell people."

"Yes, they have to be told." She didn't mention she'd told the doctor everything already, and he seemed to have forgotten the land girl.

"Do you know what I've been doing, Elsie?"

"No, Tom. What?"

"I've been out in Old Ring Copse digging a great big hole. For you."

So this was it. Elsie closed her eyes and sought an image

of Gerald's face. She would think of nothing but her dear boy. Please, God, take care of Gerald. Jamie was safe now; she'd done one thing right. This was it. She'd tried.

Get a backbone, Elsie; you found it once today. Think of Gerald.

Tom went out to the kitchen and Elsie went to the hall telephone. She'd called the taxi service after lunch, but they were out of petrol. Said they'd come if they could get their hands on any. She'd call Dr. Gibson. What was Tom doing in the kitchen?

"Operator, would you connect me with Dr. Gibson, please. It's urgent."

A hand clamped down on her shoulder. "Hang up."

6

G ood morning, Reggie. How are you?"

"Morning, Audrey. Busy, busy. The patients never stop coming," said Reggie Coleman.

"I don't know how you do it, Reggie. Still short-handed?"

"Oh, yes. Don't see that improving in the near future. Could do with a few more nurses, and volunteers, too. What about that daughter of yours? Still loafing about?"

"Rosie only took a few months off after finishing school, you know. She asked me to tell you she'd come in tomorrow morning and help with the patients. She's a little nervous about how she'll manage seeing anything grisly. And, I must say, she's a little afraid of you, too. Says you remind her of her headmistress. That woman could turn anyone's insides to jelly, even mine."

"Well, I may be a hospital matron, and I know I'm pretty strict with the girls—have to be—but I'm fair. I'm no ogre."

"I know, Reggie. You haven't changed. When we were in the sixth form, most of the juniors were afraid of you. Did you realize that? All that 'get on with it' attitude can be intimidating. Especially to people who are more inclined to let things slide. It even took me a while to see that big heart!"

"Oh, put a sock in it, Audrey, you sound like a penny dreadful. Go and visit the patients. There's one in particular I want you to see today. Jamie's a mildly mentally retarded boy. Most people would just call him slow. Brighter than some I've seen. Getting over pneumonia. Grandmother and house gone in the blitz." Reggie told Audrey the story. "He's a nice boy, mannerly . . . Well, I must get on."

"Oh, is he the one they wrote about in the paper?" Reggie nodded and grunted. "Poor boy. Yes, I'll certainly visit him."

* * *

The farmer's cruelty depressed Audrey. The newspaper article had told of other mistreated evacuees. Pure evil. Most of the children had been sent back home a few months into the "phony war" as they called it, when nothing much was happening, and a lot of them had been caught in the blitz—many had died. Now they were being sent back to the countryside in droves and there weren't enough people organized yet to oversee their welfare. Sitting ducks for monsters like that farmer Tom.

Audrey greeted the sour staff nurse and asked for Jamie Jenkins. She followed the starchy back down the row of white-clad beds to the end, where a scrawny boy sat up with the sheet pulled up under his chin. His haggard face looked hunted.

"This is Lady Audrey McInnis. She's going to visit you for a little while, so mind your manners," Nurse Dawley said through barely opened teeth before sweeping off to find someone else to bully.

Jamie goggled at Audrey. He looked scared stiff, poor child.

"Good morning, Jamie," she said with a smile.

"Good morning, miss. What must I call you?" He'd started to rock back and forth a little. That wretched nurse frightened him.

"You can call me Lady Audrey, Jamie," she said, disquieted. Was he going to have some sort of a fit?

"I've never heard of anyone called Lady before."

She couldn't help smiling. "It's not a name, Jamie, it's a title. Like mister, or miss."

"Oh."

God, hope he doesn't think I'm laughing at him. Perhaps these people were sensitive. It was so hard to know the right things to say to a boy like this.

"How are you feeling?"

"I've still got a cough. I get tired a lot. But I'm all right."

Brave boy. "I'm glad to hear it, Jamie. You've had a difficult time. Matron told me the farmer where you lived wasn't very kind to you."

"No, he wasn't. He cleaned the animal stuff off me with cold water out of doors. It made me ill. He hit me a lot. He hit Mrs. Lake, too. I saw. Round the face."

He panted heavily now, and rocked faster. *Try to calm him down, mustn't have a scene.*

"Oh, Jamie, I am very sorry. There are bad people in this world, but most of us are quite nice, you know." Audrey found herself breathing harder, too.

"My Gran warned me about bad people. About not talking to them because they get you in trouble. But the only bad person I knew before was Roy. I don't know many people, so it's hard to tell."

That sounded coherent. "Who is Roy?"

"My cousin. My Gran said he's no good. He lives with us. He went out the night we were *bl-itzed.* Never came back. He locked us in. And I always say *blitz* properly now."

Jamie began to cough. Audrey looked around and caught Nurse Dawley's venomous look from her desk at the end of the ward. Never mind, she wouldn't dare reprimand her. Should she pat the boy's back, maybe put her hand on his shoulder? *What if he hates being touched?* She herself didn't like strangers touching her, after all. *Time to go.*

"Enough talking for you today, Jamie. You learned to say a lot of things properly, good for you. I'm going to ask my daughter, Rosamund, to visit you tomorrow. What can she bring you? Anything you like. If she can, that is."

"I love chocolate. And comics." The rocking had slowed.

"I think we can manage comics. I'm not sure about the chocolate, but I'll see what I can do. Goodbye, Jamie. I'll be back, I promise."

"Thank you very much, Lady, er . . ."

"Audrey."

One of his hands ventured out of the sheet and gave a little wave. She smiled and waved back. He wasn't so bad.

Audrey made her way back up the row, visiting each patient. She asked after their progress, their families, their pets, and let them know someone took an interest in them. There was only one soldier this week, hospitalized after yet another operation to put a shattered leg to rights. He appeared down in the dumps and clearly in a great deal of pain.

"Good morning, Corporal."

"Morning, Lady Audrey."

"Does your leg still hurt a lot?"

"Yeah, it's a b . . . er . . . well, it's bad."

"I'm so sorry. You're a very brave man, like all our soldiers."

He smiled half-heartedly, as if tired of playing the part. "I'd just feel better if Sylvia came to sit with me sometimes. She came the first night and said she wouldn't be coming much. Has to work so hard on the farm she just falls into bed after supper. But she's my wife, she ought to make the effort." *Oh, God, another precarious encounter.*

"You sound angry, Corporal. I'm sure Sylvia's doing the best she can. I'll have a word. Perhaps I can arrange a lift for her."

"Thank you, Lady Audrey. You're very kind." He looked happier now.

The young man's misery saddened her. She knew Sylvia, who used to work in the village bakery until becoming a land girl on a farm outside New Milton. Audrey had gone to a friend's house for tea the week before, and on the way back she'd spotted Sylvia nuzzling Eric, a young laborer from their own estate, as they went into a pub. Eric had been deferred because of poor eyesight, but the army was getting less fussy as the casualties mounted. Farming was the only thing standing between him and the trenches. *So, he thought it was acceptable to take up with an injured soldier's wife, did he?* She'd deal with it. Well, Geoffrey would.

* * *

Audrey picked at her food, unable to shake off her low mood. Geoffrey kept on reading one of his interminable papers, lips pushed out like they always did when he was vexed. He was busy and preoccupied most of the time these days. He had frequent meetings with their region's chief constable, strangers from London would suddenly appear as weekend guests and spend most of the time in closed meetings in the study, after which Geoffrey often disappeared for a few days. She had learned to keep out of the way and never ask questions. But she felt lonely and cut off, especially from Geoffrey. They lived near the coast, so she had to assume they were making plans in case of invasion. *God forbid.*

He finally noticed her mood. "What's the matter, Audrey? I've never seen you look so down."

"The hospital was very depressing today, darling. Did you read about that local farmer who mistreated the young retarded boy? I visited him today. He's very sweet, talks well, and has lovely manners. He's had a rotten time of it, and I can't get over how people can be so cruel. And then there was this young soldier. He's had another leg operation and he's in a lot of pain. His wife hasn't been visiting him, says she's tired at the end of the day. I know her. Do you remember Sylvia? She used to work in the bakery."

He looked at her over his glasses, smiling. "Not really, dear. I don't go in there often."

God, I never used to prattle like this. "No, silly of me, of course you don't. I saw her go into a pub with our young Eric last week, and they looked much too friendly. I think you should have a word with him."

"Disgraceful! I most certainly will," Geoffrey said, slamming down his papers. "He'll put a stop to it at once if he knows which side his bread's buttered. If I sack him, he'll be conscripted, and don't think I won't do it!"

Geoffrey went back to his reading. She missed him now he was busy with all those secret meetings—war stuff, of course. Poor man. All sorrow and disappointments pushed down so he could keep going without faltering. Their lost little girl, having to keep the family estate going instead of following the scholarly career he'd craved, and now the call of who knew what onerous responsibilities. And he never spoke of his service in the Great War. None of them did. To this day she'd see those few who were left of that generation—Geoffrey, her brothers, cousins, friends—lose track of themselves from time to time, gazing into some grim scene, or perhaps trying to catch a glimpse of a long-gone companion.

Audrey nursed her own sorrow, still mourned her little girl. Geoffrey's steady presence and attention bolstered her in way that kept her on an even keel. Although pleasant and affectionate when around, he was hardly ever there when she wanted him now. She couldn't tell him what it was she wanted him there for, because it would sound so feeble. She just wanted him near.

She'd risk another interruption. She cleared her throat.

"Geoffrey." He looked up enquiringly, didn't seem annoyed. "That young boy, Jamie. I don't know what's to become of him. I suppose he'll go off to some institution. But I was thinking, darling, let's have him here for a few weeks while he gets his strength back. He needs some kindness."

"Well, I don't know. What's he like? I mean can he take care of himself? You know what I mean. He's not given to doing anything, well, odd, is he?" She was amused in spite of herself. He looked as if he'd sucked a salty lemon.

"Oh, I don't think so. He speaks nicely and seems very civilized. Why don't we give him a chance?"

"Very well, my dear. I'll leave it to you."

Of course he would. "I'll speak to Reggie, I'm sure she can fix it with whomever is in charge."

"No doubt. Reggie can make anyone do anything!"

"True enough," Audrey said. "I'm sending Rosie to visit him tomorrow. She's going to start volunteering at the hospital, you know."

"Do her good. She needs some purpose in her life. Too much moping around after that young blighter pulled the wool over her eyes." Geoffrey's ears began to acquire the pink tinge that could only grow fiercer whenever the subject of Rosie's former beau came up.

"Yes, but not for long. And at least she broke if off with him before things went too far. She has a good head on her shoulders."

"She does." He took off his glasses and drew some deep and, she hoped, calming breaths as he massaged his temples. "Audrey, I'm afraid I've got to go out again tonight. Don't wait up."

"Oh, Geoffrey, you'll wear yourself out."

"Don't worry, I'm all right. I must confess I'll be glad when it's all over—assuming we come out on top, of course. And I'll be glad when I can spend more time with you."

"Me too, darling. Drive carefully."

He got up and she followed him out to the hall. His usually ramrod-straight back sometimes sagged lately. He didn't look himself, not like the dear Geoffrey she wanted back—always impeccable and straight-laced, and always so comfortable to be around. She still fancied him, and he still seemed to find her desirable, too. Down to earth for their set, too, and brainy according to his old school friends. Running the estate left no room for intellectual pursuits, though. Maybe she'd misread him. Maybe his war activities provided more than a wearying duty and he enjoyed the challenge.

He shrugged on his overcoat and turned as if he wanted to tell her something. Instead, he pressed his lips together and went out through the door she held open. He forgot to kiss her goodbye.

* * *

Rosie took a deep breath as she stood at the door to the men's ward. She glanced over the rows of beds and was relieved to see there didn't seem to be anything grisly on view. She hadn't the faintest idea what to say to these people, and especially to the retarded boy. Her mother had assured her that he was easy to talk to, but then she always made light of things. She looked around some more. Everything white, different shades of white. Clean, sanitary, bright white. A touch of color would have added a little cheer for the patients, but matrons and nurses probably didn't think in those terms. Hygiene and order, that's what they liked. Depressing.

She jumped when Aunt Reggie's voice boomed, "Get on with it, Rosamund, it'll be doctor's rounds soon. Start at the end with Jamie, on the right there. Nurse Dawley will be back soon."

"Yes, of course. Sorry."

Rosie squared her shoulders and strode down the ward as if she were quite in command of herself. She looked at the boy, and he looked back at her.

"Who are you?" he asked, leaning back hard into his pillow as if she might hit him. She must have looked grim. She smiled as wide as she could and sat down by the bed.

"I'm Rosamund. My mother came to see you yesterday. Lady Audrey. You must be Jamie. May I sit with you?"

"Yes. Your mother is a very nice lady." *Still wary.*

"Oh, before I forget, she sent something for you," said Rosie as she put a paper bag in front of him.

"Oh, will it be chocolate, will it? And will it be a comic?" He reached out for it, all caution forgotten.

"Why don't you open it and see." *He's not so bad.*

The gaunt face glowed with sudden animation. His cheeks grew pink and his eyes glittered as he opened the bag carefully and got out his presents.

"Two comics. And a big chocolate. Thanks ever so!"

"Don't mention it, Jamie. I'm glad you like it."

He clasped his hands like a maiden aunt in church. "Oh, but I must mention it. Gran says we must always say thank you," he said with comical prissiness.

"I know," Rosie said. "That's just something we say when we mean that we are pleased you like something. Do you want me to break off a bit of chocolate for you?"

"Yes, please. Nurse Dawley better not see. She's always cross."

"She's not back yet. I'll break off a bit and hide the rest in your drawer."

Rosie watched, fascinated, as Jamie sucked on the chocolate square, eyes closed as if he were in paradise. His eyes opened when he made his final swallow.

"I've still got a cough, but I think chocolate is good for it."

"I think chocolate is good for everything, don't you?"

"Yes. What's your name? I forgot."

"Call me Rosie. Everyone else does."

"Rosie. That's easier than what you said before."

She opened his drawer and felt around for a space. It was full of something furry.

"What's this in your drawer?" She held up a green soft toy that had seen better days.

"That's Biffy. Nurse won't let me have him in bed. I like to cuddle him, but she said he's not *genic*, whatever that is. He's my best friend. He's been in a fire, that's why he's all messy."

"He's very handsome. He has a kind face."

"You've got a kind face. You're pretty. Do you wear pink roses?"

"Thank you, Jamie. What do you mean, pink roses?"

"There was this lady before, and she had a frock with pink roses. It was pretty. Like you. And your name. I think all pretty ladies should wear pink roses." He spoke in a confidential whisper as if imparting state secrets.

He started to cough, it seemed his long speech had been too much for him. His chest rose and fell like the bellows in the study at home. What should she do, call that horrid nurse? Pat him on the back? Would he mind being touched? She felt awkward, helpless.

"Are you all right?" *He's just a boy.*

Jamie laid his head back on his pillow and panted.

"Is Nurse Dawley back?"

"No, why, do you want me to get her?"

"No. I need more chocolate. For my cough."

Rosie grinned as she rummaged in the drawer and broke off another piece. She popped it into Jamie's mouth and he sighed as he sucked. *Just a boy.* How silly she'd been. He was quite normal, really, nothing weird about him, only a little slow. She heard footsteps behind her. "Jamie," she whispered. She put her finger to her lips to warn him. He stopped sucking and closed his eyes again, concentrating on the richness melting in his mouth.

"Now then, Miss Rosamund, Jamie still tires easily. Time to visit some of our other patients, I think."

Rosie, in an effort to distract vinegar-lips from noticing Jamie's chewing, asked her how he was coming along as she got up to leave.

"As well as can be expected," she replied with a snort that expressed a broad sentiment of disgust.

Rosie turned and waved at Jamie, who waved back, eyes open now his chocolate was safely swallowed. He looked giddy and happy. She didn't think he was used to being happy, and hoped it wouldn't wear off too soon.

Rosie returned the next day with some toffees she'd managed to find, not easy with rationing so stringent these days. She knew where the sweets were hidden in the pantry and had crept in there at night after Cook had cleaned the kitchen and gone to her room. Jamie insisted that she have one too, and they chewed like camels as they tried to pretend they were talking.

"Jamie, did you know that you're going to stay with us for a bit when you leave here?"

"Am I? You and your mum are ever so kind. What was she called?"

"Lady Audrey."

"Yes."

"We live on an estate."

"What's that?"

"It's a big house with a lot of land. Some of it is a farm."

"Oh no, not a farm, I can't do farms, I can't," cried Jamie, his voice rising in panic as he clutched at the sheets with frantic jerky hands.

"Ssh, Jamie, we know what happened to you on that farm. You don't have to work, or even go to that part. We have some horses, but we grow wheat, mostly. No cows or pigs. We've got a nice dog; you'll like him. Don't be afraid. I'll take care of you."

Jamie, his sheet pulled to his chin, was coughing quietly and breathing hard.

"Promise?"

"Promise. We just want you to have a rest and enjoy yourself. My parents are kind people. Not like those others."

"How will I enjoy myself?"

"What do you want to do?"

"I want to learn to read. I learned the ABC's in kindergarten, and Gran said them with me sometimes, but she never had time to teach me how to make them into words. Said reading wasn't for the likes of me, anyhow. Perhaps she didn't know how. Do you?"

"Of course. I think I still have some of my old books. I'll look for them. I don't know if I'm much good as a teacher, I haven't tried. We'll do our best."

Jamie laid back, his face flushed and excited.

"I'm going to read a book. Like proper boys do."

7

Jamie had been a little scared of Laddie at first, but now they were best friends. After Rosie and Biffy, of course. He didn't even mind when Laddie chased him around on the grass. Laddie liked Jamie to chase him, too. He loved watching the dog's big ears flopping around as he went, all untidy and yellow. And he'd got another friend, Mr. Evans, the gardener. He was quite old, but very kind, and he explained things. This morning they'd plant seeds together inside the glass house. The seeds would be vegetables when they grew up. Then this afternoon he'd practice reading with Rosie again.

Jamie had done well this week and had nearly finished the first book. The story wasn't very interesting. It had pictures on one side and the words on the other side. But being able to sound them out was exciting. Some you just had to remember the shape because they were too hard to spell out. But he could read. Yes, he could say that.

He'd never been with so many people. Every day. He kept learning things. People were nice to him. He felt cheery, and more clever.

"Mornin' young lad," said Mr. Evans, his big old hands supporting the small of his back.

"Good morning, Mr. Evans."

"Now then, come and see here."

Jamie followed, almost trotting to keep up with his long steps. Mr. Evans had some earth in two long pots. He had something like a letter with a picture in the other hand.

"See, now, we make a little ditch like this. I'll do this one, you do t'other."

Jamie was very careful, so careful he forgot to breathe, until such a huge gasp happened out it quite surprised him. Mr. Evans opened the picture letter.

"Put some o' these seeds in your hand like this. Take a tiny pinch, not too many now, and sprinkle them along. Tha's the way! Only a few, don' want to crowd them."

Jamie had a little trouble with this. He had clumsy hands, but if he tried very hard, he'd get it. He pinched his fingers together till it hurt, and just opened them a tiny bit to let the seeds go. Along to the end he went. His tongue hurt a bit where he pushed it against his teeth to stop him dropping the seeds too early. But that was fine; he was getting it right.

"There you go, good fellow! Now, gently does it, spread the earth back over top. They're just babies, don' hurt 'em! That's good, Jamie. Now a little water to make them grow, don't drown 'em, though."

"What're they going to be?"

"Tomatoes, Jamie, gorgeous red, tasty tomatoes. Better than any you buy in shops."

"Will I taste some?"

"Oh yes, even if you're not here when they're ripe, I'll see to it you get some."

"Thank you, Mr. Evans. I wish I could stay here. I don't want to go away. I like it here." They said he'd just stay with them for a few weeks until he felt well again. But he secretly hoped it would be forever. *Nothing is ever forever.*

"I know, yer a good boy. But the authorities have their own ideas, you know."

"My idea is best. Stay here forever."

Mr. Evans smiled at him. "I reckon you'll be coming round a good deal."

* * *

Jamie and Rosamund were almost finished with their book when Sir Geoffrey came into the room. He seemed to have a frog in his throat and was oddly noisy, clearing it several times and frowning too hard.

"Afternoon, Jamie."

"Good afternoon, sir."

"Jamie, the authorities have been on the phone. They have a place for you at the Blexton Institute."

"What's that?"

"Well, it's like a home for people who have, er . . . special problems."

"They're slow?"

"Well, some of them I suppose. And they don't have families who can take care of them."

"Can't I stay here? I like it here."

"No, Jamie, I'm afraid not. You see, we don't have much say in it. We're not your official guardians. They say you have to go. Tomorrow. We've enjoyed having you here. I'll send a car for you once a week for a visit. We mustn't lose touch."

Sir Geoffrey took a deep breath, frowned even harder, and managed to both clamp his teeth and push out his lips. "Took us by surprise, I must say." He spun around and left.

So this was it, the end of the dream, the wishing. Jamie looked up at the painting of Sir Geoffrey's father. He looked like someone who was used to telling people what to do. He wore a uniform and his wide shoulders stuck straight out sideways and his chin jutted up and out as if to say, "Listen to me, this is how we're going to do it." He looked more stern than Sir Geoffrey; he might have fixed things. But maybe not as kind, maybe wouldn't have had Jamie here in the first place. Wouldn't have put up with that busy spider spinning a silky string between Sir Martin's biggest medal and the light just above.

Jamie dropped his eyes to his lap. He must make the best of whatever came. Even at the farm there had been a little piece of chocolate sometimes and a nice smile from Mrs. Lake. *Why is Rosie crying?* He sat up and put his arm around her shoulder. Then he was crying, too, couldn't help it.

"Don't cry, Jamie, I'll come and visit you, promise. And we'll carry on with your reading. You'll be all right."

"Then why're you crying?"

"I'll miss you, Jamie. And it's so sudden. They didn't give us a chance to get used to the idea."

"Can I leave Biffy here with you? I have to make sure he'll be safe in that place before I take him there."

"Of course, Jamie. I'll take good care of him."

"I'll miss you, too, Rosie. And it's not just reading. I want to learn to write." He'd tell her about the book he had to write some other time.

"All in good time, Jamie, all in good time."

Gran always said that when she meant probably never. And perhaps the people at that place thought reading and writing wasn't for the likes of him. Even Gran thought something like that. Well, Jamie was a real reader now, and there was nothing they could do to take that away from him. Nothing at all. He'd do it every night in his head if he had to.

* * *

Lady Audrey and Rosie waved goodbye as the car drove him away. Both looked very sad, but they couldn't be as sad as Jamie. Rosie promised to come soon to help with his reading, and Lady Audrey promised to send a car on Saturday. She told him she'd take him to the seaside when the weather got warmer. Something else nice to think about in bed, something to drive the shadows away.

He pulled his arm away from the woman's hand. Too tight, made him feel he'd done wrong. He looked out of the window, but could only see her staring at the back of his head. Everything was thin on her face—eyes, lips, nose—and even her hair was thin. Dressed all in black and brown, she looked quite ugly. That was unkind, thinking those things. But it was unkind of her to take him away from the Manor, and without even a little smile.

The house was the most huge he'd ever seen, even more big than Rosie's. The woman acted nasty, holding his arm too hard again so it hurt. She'd left the car going, so she wasn't going to stay. *Good.*

The hall wasn't so big like at the Manor, and it had lots of doors round it. A lady in white sat at a desk. She got up and said good morning to the other lady.

"This is Jamie Jenkins. I'll be going now." She didn't even say goodbye.

"Jamie, I'm Mrs. Clancy. We'll go to the sunroom in your wing now, and you can meet some of the others."

"Yes, miss."

They went down halls, upstairs, downstairs, until they came into a big ugly room full of boys. A dark-green room. Not pretty green like grass, but dirty looking, like old cooked cabbage. Lots of windows up high. There was a smeary one farther down where you could look through. That had bars on it. No sun coming in that Jamie could see. Not cheery, this room. A sad room full of sad boys. And now he was one of them.

"Here we are, Jamie. This is one of the attendants, Bernhardt Visser. There's always someone in charge here to keep an eye on things." Bernhardt didn't say anything, just nodded. He was big and definitely not the smiley sort. "This is where you come during the day, and you'll share a room with George and Philip at night. This is George. He's a spastic."

George sat in a chair with wheels. His body looked all twisty and his mouth made awful shapes. He seemed to say hello, Jamie wasn't sure, although he tried hard to say something. He would remember the name George because Gran had a friend called George.

"This is Philip. He doesn't talk, I'm afraid."

Philip stood in a corner, staring at something, Jamie couldn't see what. He had a very white face with big lips and spit ran down his chin. He smelled a bit, as if he didn't wash much. *Doesn't he know any better?* A big boy jumped in front of Jamie, backing him up to the wall.

"I'm Alan. I kill people, so you'd better do whatever I tell you." He grabbed Jamie by the hair and pulled him into his mad red face. The man in charge grabbed Alan's shoulders before Jamie could scream and pushed him into a chair

"Behave yourself, Alan, or you'll be in the jacket again. Want another shock treatment? How did you like it last time?" Alan stared at his shoes. The big man talked funny.

Jamie was so scared he couldn't stop shaking. He couldn't

talk. Didn't look at the bad boy.

"I'm sorry about that, Jamie," said Mrs. Clancy, patting the back of her hair, afraid she looked untidy, perhaps, although all those little curls were so tight it didn't look as if even the blitz could shift them. "We'll keep Alan in check, I promise. He doesn't really kill people, you know, he's just a bit rough sometimes. I'm going to leave you here for a while so you can make yourself at home."

Home? What kind of a home is this? Nothing cheery, no brightly colored cushions, no pictures on the wall. The Manor was full of pictures, although some of them were of people who didn't look very cheerful or pretty. Even Gran would tear a page out of a magazine and pin it to the wall if she thought it had a happy look. Jamie used to have lots of pictures on the walls of his room, until Roy pulled them down and tore them up.

Jamie looked around. Some boys were big and some were small. Some stared at him, some looked at nothing. None of them talked to each other, although a few seemed to be talking to themselves. The sun probably never shined in here because the darkness kept it out. *Why am I in a place like this? They're not like me. They probably can't read or talk nicely.* His tummy felt heavy and his breath came hard. He was sad, but not sad like when he lost Gran. Sad like if he went to sleep he might not bother waking up.

George had got his chair up next to him. He could make the wheels move with his hands. He grunted, and then his eyes and head jerked to a corner where there was one empty chair. Jamie went over and sat down, holding his knees to keep his hands still. George wheeled up next to him and grunted again. Something had gone wrong with George a long time ago, like it had with Jamie. Only things were more wrong with George. Jamie turned and put his face close to George's. He looked over the scrunchy face and into the jumpy eyes. George struggled and pushed to tell him something, but he had a bad body, all over bad, so he couldn't walk or talk properly. Maybe he was smart on the inside and nobody knew.

"Are you smart, George?" Jamie asked.

George made a face, perhaps a smile, and pushed out a noise that could have been "Yes."

8

Roy shoved his hands in his pockets as he shuffled from foot to foot in the freezing February wind. At least the trains were still running; he'd checked that early on. He peered down the street looking for the bloody ambulance, half an hour late already. *Always emergencies with these fucking Huns bombing the world to hell and back.* He heard it coming before he saw it round the corner. Silly little bell sound, didn't sound like something to take any notice of.

"Roy Beck for Sarah Lester," he told the driver, who nodded and opened the back doors. Sarah, already in a wheel chair, had a blanket over her lap that lay embarrassingly lopsided.

"Good morning, Roy. This is very good of you." Such a tight smile, tight words. Snooty little cow. She might have forgotten how she'd snubbed him down in the underground tunnel, but he hadn't. Ought to be grateful, really. She'd saved his life. Her family had been killed where they sat. She only survived because she went to the lav.

He thanked the driver, who wasn't much friendlier, and whirled the chair around and into the station. He heard her gasp.

"Could you move more slowly? I'm still in a lot of pain."

"Sorry, love. Know what you mean, I've only just got off crutches myself."

"Yes, Derek said you broke your leg. I'm sorry about that."

"And I'm sorry you lost yours." She bowed her head and sighed. Oh, this was going to be a merry journey.

One of the porters helped him get the chair onto the train and find them two window seats opposite each other. He helped Roy lift her off the chair and into her seat before folding it and taking it away. He hoped to God she wouldn't need to go to the toilet. Sarah pulled a book out of her satchel.

"Do you mind if I read? It takes my mind off things."

"'Course not." Good, God knows what they could have talked about.

The carriage started filling up, and for Roy's bad luck a couple of wrinklies came to sit next to them. The old man, skinny as a string, sat next to Sarah, edging himself as far away from her empty left side as he could. Did he think it was catching? His fat wife sank into the seat next to Roy, squeezing him against the cold metal wall.

"Shit," he muttered. Sarah's head shot up.

"I beg your pardon?" said the old man.

"Nothing," Roy said, sullenly.

"I should hope not!" Silly old git, he was knee high to a grasshopper. Did he think he could take Roy on? He caught Sarah's glare and looked out of the window.

After a long, boring wait, the train pulled away. Their carriage was close to the front, so they caught the full blast of the locomotive's deafening labors. His view of London was a cruel scene of random destruction, most streets looking like a mouthful of rotting teeth—too many gaps, some houses broken and stained, and others still whole against all odds. He laid his head back. May as well have a kip.

He woke with a start as the wrinklies hauled themselves out of their seats and he fell sideways when he lost his mainstay. The train was slowing. Stubbly fields and a few cows were all he could see now. He'd never been to the countryside before. He wasn't going to like it, he could tell right off. Sarah was looking at him, sort of smiling.

"What?"

"It was funny when she got up and you fell about like a beetle in a jam jar."

"Very amusing." Her smile switched off and she returned to her book.

The old man had left his paper on the seat. Better than nothing. He skipped the war news on the front page. *Same old shit.* The papers were pretty thin these days. Not much sporting stuff anymore. Not much sport going on, of course. He opened the center page. His stomach flipped as he stared, transfixed, at the photo. He glanced Sarah's way. Mustn't give anything away. Jamie's sloppy grin took up nearly half a page. *How the hell had he made it?* He read faster than he ever had before, which wasn't fast enough.

The headline was huge: *Evacuees Mistreated!* They told a few stories about children being badly treated, then got on to Jamie, who had most of the space. He had been found wandering the streets, grandmother died in the house, evacuated to Hampshire, abused by a farmer, got pneumonia. *That bloody little sod! Still alive. Shit, shit, shit!* The next line gave him pause. Taken in by Sir Geoffrey and Lady McInnis of Brockenhurst Downs. Well, the little runt had really fallen on his feet. No mention of Roy, though, so that was a good thing. Maybe he hadn't mentioned being locked in. Or about the fight. He folded the newspaper and sat on it.

"Sarah, where does Betty work?"

"In Brockenhurst Downs, near New Milton. Why?"

"Just wondering. Big house, is it?"

"Yes, she works for Lady Audrey McInnis. Funny to think of Betty in a place like that."

"Love to get a look at the place. I'll be looking for a job, don't forget."

"I'm sure they're short of men at the moment. Only thing is they'll want references. Do you really have any?"

"Of course I do!" *Bitch.*

Roy lapsed into deep thought and deep scheming for the rest of the journey.

"Roy! Roy! New Milton's next. You'll need to get a porter."

The porter got the chair and told him to wait until everyone else was out of the carriage. He supposed that worked best, but he just couldn't wait. He had to stop Jamie before he let something drop and people started asking questions. Had to stop him.

He pushed Sarah into the waiting room. No one was there.

"Didn't you say we'd be met?"

"Yes, I don't know by whom, though."

Roy went to the ticket office.

"Has anyone been in asking for a Miss Lester? Someone was supposed to meet us, and she's in a wheelchair."

"Oh, yes, sir. Lady Audrey has sent her car. There it is outside."

Roy looked at the big shiny Bentley in gleeful appreciation. No wonder the clerk had called him sir. No one had ever called him sir before.

"Come on, Sarah, we're going in style!"

He couldn't resist whirling the chair around again with a flourish.

"Roy! That hurt."

"Sorry, love."

The driver got out of the car when he saw them emerge and walked around to meet them as if he were in a funeral procession.

"Would this be Miss Sarah?"

"Yes, it would."

The man made his grand way to the boot and opened it.

"Would you please assist the young lady into the car? I will then fold the chair and put it in the boot."

No offer to help. Well, it would be pretty awkward with two of them, actually. He'd better put his best foot forward, not get on anyone's bad side. He got Sarah in, but not without some *ahs* and *ouches*. How could it hurt so much when it wasn't there anymore? Maybe the stitches. She was a complainer, all right. The driver got into his seat at his own pace. Roy had never seen the King, but he probably walked that way. *Putting on airs, silly old goat.* And it wasn't as if he owned the bloody car.

They drove for a good half hour through narrow roads with hedges and open fields instead of the blocks of flats Roy was used to. Of course, he'd been up West lots of times, but they had great big houses there, nothing like these little old ones dotted around.

He finally saw a really big one.

"Whose house is that?" he asked.

"That is the estate of Sir Geoffrey McInnis." No "sir" coming out of this old sod.

"Your sister's house is not far now, Miss Lester."

They turned down a lane, bumping over ruts that made Sarah turn pale. The cottage looked tiny and the walls didn't seem entirely straight. Betty must have been waiting for them as she rushed out of the door and to Sarah's side of the car. Revolting the way she blubbered and kissed Sarah's face over and over until the driver was ready with the wheelchair. She hadn't said a word of welcome to him yet.

"This is so very kind of you, Stanton." Betty was still teary.

"It was a pleasure, miss. I do wish the young lady all the very best."

Betty lifted Sarah out of the car herself, beefy piece that she was.

"Come on, love, we'll get you warmed up and in bed in no time."

Stanton turned to Roy. "You are to stay in the servant's quarters up at the Manor until you have made other arrangements. Come with me."

Getting better and better. Be careful Jamie doesn't give me away. Must stay out of sight until the right moment.

"Goodbye, Betty, nice seeing you again. Bye, Sarah."

"Thank you, Roy. Bye!" Like a cats' chorus. He watched them go into the cottage and slam the door. Not really that noisy, but felt like a slam in his face.

"You can sit in the front seat now, if you please." Why? Well, he wasn't going to argue.

The car pulled around to the side of the Manor.

"Are all these places for cars?" he asked.

"No, they were all built as stables. Two have been converted for the cars." They drove into one. "I will take you to the kitchen door, and you will be shown to your room."

"Yeah, thanks. I was reading in the paper about a young boy, name of Jamie. Is this the place he's staying?"

"Not any longer, sir. He was removed to the Blexton Institute just a few days ago. We were all sad to see him go."

Damn. He'd got away again.

"Sad? Why?"

"Oh, he's a lovely young gentleman, and had quite a green thumb in the garden. Evans will certainly miss him."

"Who?"

"Evans is the head gardener."

Stanton rapped on the kitchen door and a plump girl in a uniform opened it. She looked Roy up and down and smirked. Definitely liked what she saw. He'd explore that later.

"This is the person who accompanied Betty's sister from London."

"Roy Beck, pleased to meet you," he said.

He stepped into another world, a world where the kitchen was nearly bigger than Gran's whole flat, where he had to climb hundreds of stairs to get to a bedroom that was better than any he'd ever had. And he hadn't even seen the posh parts yet.

He wanted this world, would find a way to worm his way in. But first, he had to take care of Jamie.

* * *

The institute looked huge and magnificent from a distance, but close up it looked less impressive. The stonework was grimy and slivers of carving had fallen off all over. He stopped outside the door and heaved a sigh. He must remember his proper talk like Gran used to try to make him do. A nervy knot tightened in his stomach at the very thought of Gran and the expression on her face as she died. That face never left him alone. He'd thought he was rid of her, but she still hung around, hounding him night after night.

The cheek pads he'd put in an hour before took some getting used to. At least they'd remind him to make his mouth move differently. No one knew him down here except Jamie, and he was easy to fool. He'd never recognize him, especially after the dye job.

The woman at the front desk looked him up and down and sniffed. "Can I help you?"

"I telephoned yesterday. I have an appointment with Mrs. Clancy at two o'clock."

"Wait here, please. I will let her know you are here." She trudged away down a long dark corridor.

No respect. He'd show them all one day. He went over to a chair under a small window and sat, hands clasped between his knees.

Two sets of footsteps, one slow and heavy, the other brisk and noisy. Roy stood.

"I'm Mrs. Clancy. Graham—what was your surname?"

"Pleased to meet you, Mrs. Clancy. Graham Green."

"Well, Graham, I think the best thing would be to show you around first, then we'll go to my office for a chat."

"Yes, fine, thank you."

"We'll start with the boys. Most of them are not too bad."

The room was dreary and depressing and smelled of piss. He caught sight of Jamie sitting in a corner next to a twisted little creature in a wheel chair. He turned his head away in time to see a boy with thick lips peeing into the next corner. A man had been yelling in a thick accent at a large gangly teenager with small brutal eyes, almost nose to nose, until he noticed this last occurrence. He strode over to a cupboard and pulled out some towels and threw them at the teen. "Alan, you clean that up."

"Why should I? Philip did it, make him clean it."

"Philip can't do anything. You'll do it because I said so. You want trouble?"

The boy grabbed the towels, pushed Philip aside, and started to mop up, muttering obscenities under his breath.

Mrs. Clancy watched all this with her hands curling and uncurling by her side. She sighed.

"That was two of our difficult ones. Philip is profoundly retarded and Alan is really very difficult. Not very bright, but more disturbed than retarded. And the man on duty today is one of our other attendants, Bernhardt Visser. He is a Dutch refugee. Bernhardt! Come and say hello to Graham. He might be joining us."

"We could do with the help." The man said gruffly, extending a hand. Roy smiled in his friendliest fashion and tried to match the Dutchman's grip.

They worked their way around. The women's room was unsettling, a restless wandering and chattering that almost became a scream. The worst day room was the adult males. Total chaos, a cacophony of rage and stink. Two very large men watched over this room. Graham couldn't wait to get out of there. Mrs. Clancy looked at him and smiled.

"Don't worry, it takes a special breed to work with the adults. Our open spot is with the boys. I don't think we'll worry about the girls just now. Let's go back to my office."

Once they were seated on each side of Mrs. Clancy's desk and the tea was poured and the biscuits set out, she sat back and looked at him with a little frown.

"What brings you here, Graham?"

"I wanted to get out of London, and I'm not able to fight, unfortunately. I brought my papers." He passed them across the desk. She glanced over them and handed them back.

"They seem to be in order. But are you fit enough to work with these boys?"

"Oh, yes, indeed. I just can't march for miles, and I can't shoot. One of my eyes isn't right."

"Oh, I would never have guessed. They both look quite normal."

"Thank you. Yes, I'm lucky that way. Not being too unsightly, I mean, not that I can't fight." He found himself stammering and blushing. *Damn!*

"Have you ever had anything to do with the mentally ill? We don't require qualifications because the job is fairly straightforward and you can learn as you go. But it helps if you have had some exposure."

"Yeah . . . er, yes. My brother was retarded. I looked after him a lot."

"Oh, very good. Where is he now?"

"He's dead, and Mum, too. Last big raid. My employer in the city gone the same night. Whole building flattened. It's been terrible. I need a change."

"I'm so sorry, Graham. What was your last job?"

"I was a clerk in an export office. Had to do all kinds of things, you know, pitch in. Even help move the goods sometimes. No references, I'm afraid."

"Well, I think you might be the right type of person. Let's see how it goes for a while. Two pounds a week, how does that sound? And you'll get your meals and a room and one day off a week."

"Very good. Thank you, Mrs. Clancy. When do you want me?"

"As soon as you can."

"I can start anytime."

"Tomorrow morning at eight?"

That was that. Slave wages, but a foot in. It shouldn't take long to do what needed doing.

9

Mrs. Clancy told him yesterday he'd been here two whole weeks. And Rosie hadn't come. Not one time. Jamie rolled over and shut his eyes again. He didn't want to get up. Didn't want to go to that horrid big room with all those nasty boys. He'd woken up in the night and tried rocking, but it didn't make him feel better anymore. He said *fiddle-faddle* over and over in his head; he couldn't say it out loud in case people thought him mad. Didn't help.

The first night he'd slept all right. Must have been very tired. He didn't sleep well any more though. The room was much too big, even for all three of them, not that Jamie wanted any more boys to share. He'd got used to Philip and George, though, glad of the company. If only the room had a bit of cheer, some color. It hadn't got any colors in it. The walls weren't even a proper white. The blankets were a funny mix of brown and green, so they didn't help. *No pictures. Why not?* They allowed him one book on the stand next to his bed, but everything else had to be put away. Rosie had given him a little wooden dog that looked like Laddie, and they even made him keep that in a drawer. He would take it out now and then and kiss its snout. He'd rather kiss Laddie's warm soft yellow one. Thank goodness he'd left Biffy with Rosie.

He heard the new man, Graham, come in and lift George out of bed to put him in the chair so he could take him to the toilet. Graham told Philip to get a move on and Jamie heard his feet scuff along the floor. Philip never picked up his feet properly like he ought to.

"Jamie, why aren't you out of bed?" Graham was going to be cross. He was often cross.

"I'm ill today. I think I'm going to be sick."

"I'll see to the others and come back." He sounded quite annoyed.

There was something funny about Graham. He talked quite posh, but it wasn't right. Sometimes he said the words different like he forgot how he said them before. He had really yellow hair, like one of Gran's lady friends. And his mustache grew ever so big, like the haystacks at Rosie's. You couldn't see most of his face.

Yesterday Bernhardt told Graham he needed a touch-up, didn't he know he had a black parting? Graham got really angry and told Bernhardt to shut up. His face turned red and he left the room. Bernhardt laughed, another funny thing. He'd never seen Bernhardt even smile before. Jamie asked Bernhardt what were touch-ups and partings, but he'd just looked at him with squeezed up eyes and told him to mind his own business. Bernhardt had bluish eyes, but not pretty like the sky. Like puddle ice.

Jamie felt breath on his face and opened his eyes just a very little.

"Roy, it's you!" he said as he shot up. Graham looked shocked and his mouth hung open like a goldfish. He'd forgot he had a goldfish once. Ages ago.

But no, it wasn't quite Roy. He peered into Graham's face. He looked a bit like Roy, though. Even his voice, though he tried to talk posh.

"If you didn't have a mustache and if you had greased-up black hair you'd be like Roy."

"Well, I'm not. And don't you go spreading stories. Tell me about this Roy." Graham looked very stern.

Jamie told him about his cousin and Gran, and the whole story of the day their house got bombed. Even the blood on the blanket.

"I'm sort of sorry not to have Roy anymore, even though he was never nice to me."

"Come on, Jamie, get up, you're going to miss breakfast. And I wouldn't talk about that. People will think you're making up stories. Who've you told about all this?"

"But it's true! And I didn't tell anybody. Who is there to tell?"

"Oh, I believe you. But people are funny, you know. Can't trust them."

Roy got up to go, stubbing his toe on the foot of the bed. "Fucking hell!" So much for posh.

"You are Roy. You are, you are! You're in pretend dress up! I'm so happy. I didn't want to have nobody. Why're you pretending like that?" Funny how excited he was, considering Roy left him and Gran to die. *Most likely a mistake. Must be. Can't have meant to do that.*

"Ssh, shut up, idiot. Look, Jamie, I got people after me. The rozzers know I knocked over this house in Kensington, they got my prints. The people that helped me didn't get all the stuff they thought they should. The Reddy brothers, they're all after my bones. You wouldn't want something bad to happen to poor old Roy, would you? I'm like your brother. You do love me a bit, don't you, like I love you? So help me by keeping your mouth shut."

"All right, Roy. I don't want anything bad to happen to you. I'll keep it a secret. I'm quite good at secrets. But you have to be nice to me now."

"You see that you do keep mum. Yeah, I'll be nice."

Roy's eyes looked mean, even if his mouth said nice. His shoulders went up a bit and his eyebrows met together in the middle, like Gran's when she worried about money. He'd have to be very, very careful. Now he knew Graham was Roy, he might use the wrong name. He'd made a mistake, sitting up like that and doing all that telling. Oh, bother, he couldn't pretend to be ill anymore, he'd have to go down to breakfast.

Neville came to breakfast. He was the other man in charge, except he acted scared of the boys, especially Alan. He never looked right at them. Maybe he was too short to be in charge. He couldn't make Alan behave. He was shorter than Alan and didn't look strong.

Meals were scary. Some of the boys threw food, and some

of them spat it out. Some of them had to be fed with a spoon, like babies. Jamie usually kept his eyes on his plate and ate as quickly as he could. But there was a chair next to George today, and no one was feeding him.

"Can I help George?" he asked Neville.

"I suppose so. Don't take too long. Eat your own breakfast first."

So hard to get the food into George's mouth. And then hard for George to swallow. He kept on going. George had a big cloth tied around his neck, so spilling food didn't matter very much. Jamie was sorry he'd started it, then ashamed for being sorry. He should do this every day. He thought he did it quite well, clumsy of course, but gentle.

"Watch how much you waste. Don't you know there's a war on?"

Jamie turned to see Bernhardt scowling at him.

"I only meant to help. I know there's a war on. My house got *bl*-itzed."

"Where do you come from, Bernhardt?" asked Neville. He wanted Bernhardt to forget about being cross with Jamie. Nice of him.

"Holland. I got out on one of the last boats after the Germans invaded."

"Big boats?"

"No, mine was a small one, no shelter and very bad weather. We landed at night and I fell into the water. Freezing." The man shivered as if he were cold again.

"Frightening for you."

"I am never frightened."

Bernhardt turned his back on Neville and cuffed Alan for hitting the boy next to him. Neville blushed and chewed his lip.

"I'll finish with George," he told Jamie.

Relieved, Jamie watched Neville spoon food into George's mouth, which kept moving around, hard not to miss. He got more in than Jamie had, but not very gently, not very kindly.

* * *

Same like always in the sunroom. George sat next to Jamie's chair in the corner. No one else ever sat there. The boys knew it was their special place, even if most of them didn't seem to understand much of anything. Alan sat across the room and stared at his feet, only looking up sometimes to scowl at Jamie. Some boys painted at a table. All they had to paint on was old newspaper. Why didn't they have proper white paper? Perhaps more of the boys should have something nice to do. It might take them out of their sad selves.

If they painted pictures, why couldn't they use them to make the walls pretty? The room was very big, but so sad. The green of the walls was too hard to describe. He didn't have the words, except rotten old cabbage and that didn't sound quite right. And there were lots of patches that pictures could cover up. It was a shame that the beautiful big window had hard black bars all across it. It spoiled the view. The view was lovely, the sort of looking out you needed when you were sad. You could see people coming and going, doing the things he supposed regular people did all day.

Jamie opened his book. Kind of Rosie to let him bring it, but not kind of her to stay away so long. *Did she forget me already? Think about something else.* He'd read aloud to George and show him the pictures.

"Peter and Jane have a dog. His name is Spot. Do you see, George? That's Peter, that's Jane, and that's Spot. Do you know your alphabet?"

George's head moved all over, but mostly up and down. That was nodding.

"Can you make words?"

George sort of shook his head.

"Next time Rosie comes to see me, you can sit with us. She'll teach us both."

It seemed to Jamie that some other boys were listening, so he talked louder and read on until the end of the book. He felt proud.

"Do you want to see the pictures?" he asked some of the nearest boys.

"Nah!" Alan yelled before they could answer. He rushed to the painting table, picked up a dirty water jar, ran across to Jamie and tipped it over his book.

"You and your book, you poncy little bugger. Fuck you!"

Bernhardt wrapped his arm around Alan's neck so he choked and threw him on the floor. Alan screamed so loudly it jarred Jamie's ears, and he couldn't make out most of the words, except some bad ones he'd heard Roy use. It was plain Alan's arm hurt a lot. His face got white and twisted, rather like George's. *Could George have hurts no one knew about?*

He looked down and realized his present from Rosie was all spoiled. He felt his anger shake loose, setting itself free so he couldn't catch it anymore, getting sharper as it rose, joining with fear and sorrow until it went off like a firework.

"I hate you, hate you, hate you! You're bad. I'm glad you're hurt. I wish you were dead, I do. You should be dead! I never want to see you again. I don't want to be here. I hate it, hate it, hate it! I hate everybody here!" Jamie cried as he screamed at Alan until he felt too empty for any more tears, too sad for tears, his voice worn down. All of him worn down. Silence hung over him now, so heavy he could hardly hear or see. With a great effort, he wiped his face on his sleeve.

Neville took a cloth from the paint table and wiped off the book for him.

"See, Jamie, it really isn't so bad. You can still read the words, and the pictures still look quite nice." *True, not so very bad.* He thanked Neville, who looked sad himself.

"Take some deep breaths now, Jamie, close your eyes for a bit."

"What's going on?" Mrs. Clancy asked. Jamie jumped. He hadn't seen her come in. She must have heard the noise.

"Alan went after Jamie again. He fell down. He does not learn, that one," Bernhardt said.

"My arm hurts, he broke it on purpose."

"I'll take him to sick bay," said Mrs. Clancy.

Jamie didn't feel sorry. Alan hurt people, so Bernhardt had hurt him and made him cry. *Serves him right.* After Mrs. Clancy left, Bernhardt came over to Jamie and stared at him for a few minutes. Now Jamie understood how Laddie felt when he watched him do his business. He felt embarrassed, too, and kept turning his head from side to side, trying to find a good place to look. The room stayed quiet and still, such a big hush. Bernhardt bent down until his face almost touched Jamie's.

"People might come and ask questions. Alan fell over when I pulled him away from you. Didn't he?"

Bernhardt was afraid of getting into trouble. He didn't know grownups would be afraid of getting into trouble. He'd think it through later after lights out.

"Yes, that is what happened, and it wasn't your fault. Alan is bad. You were helping me. He's hurt me before."

"That's right. You just keep saying that. Do you understand?"

"Yes."

* * *

Another week. Mrs. Clancy was good about letting him know how long he'd been here. Every Monday he asked and she told. Nothing ever happened. Alan had been in hospital for three days because he had a broken arm. He had a hard white thing on it now, a cast they called it. He always sat as far away from Bernhardt as he could and only asked Graham or Neville for permission to go to the toilet. Today was Bernhardt's day off and that scared Jamie. Alan stared at him all morning. He didn't know if the make-believe Graham would help him; Cousin Roy certainly wouldn't. Neville couldn't. Philip stood with his face to the wall close to George and Jamie. That was a new thing, staying close. He was used to them now after sleeping in the same room. He probably felt safer staying close.

"Jamie, there's a parcel for you," called Maureen, the bouncy lady who worked for Mrs. Clancy.

"For me? What is it?" Jamie had never had a parcel, but he knew they could be full of wonderful things.

"We won't know till you open it, will we?"

"Is it from Rosie?"

"It doesn't say on the outside. Perhaps there's a card inside."

Jamie tore it open. A box of chocolates. A good day. He didn't see any card or paper. Maureen looked, too. It must be from Rosie. He grinned and hugged the box to his chest. A very good day. He closed his eyes and rocked a bit, very gently so people wouldn't notice. Something about the silence made him sit up and pay attention.

Alan, on the move like a sneaky cat, walked slowly to the painting table. Roy used to creep the same way to get behind

Jamie and smack the back of his head when Gran wasn't looking. Everybody had stopped what they were doing and gazed at their own colorful squiggles as if held tight by their patterns. He went to the nearest wall, and made his way round to Jamie's corner. Jamie couldn't quite catch his breath. Alan stood behind Philip now. He lashed out with his cast and knocked Philip to the ground, making the boy cry out, the first sound Jamie had ever heard him make. Alan cried out too and clutched his bad arm. Then Philip's eyes fell closed and he looked asleep. Graham rushed over and pushed Alan aside. Alan darted back and snatched Jamie's chocolates before running away and right out of the room.

Many of the boys started hooting and crying, and one clenched his fists and screamed nonstop. The littlest one wet himself before lying down in the corner and curling up with his face to the wall.

Jamie still couldn't find proper breaths, so he closed his eyes and rocked. It helped this time, helped him breathe properly. He heard Mrs. Clancy's footsteps. Her shoes made tapping steps, not like the men's. He opened his eyes.

"Leave him on the floor, just straighten him out and try to keep his head still. Neville, did you call 999?" Mrs. Clancy looked worried. She turned to Jamie. "Where did Alan go?"

"Don't know. Stole my chocolates and ran away."

"Graham, stay here with Philip. Neville, you come with me. We've got to find Alan. He'll have to be sedated again. Time for another course of shock treatments, I shouldn't wonder. But we'll ring the doctor from my office telephone first."

Neville hunched his shoulders and his mouth turned down. Scared of Alan. Roy—Graham—looked seriously angry at what Alan did.

Lunch was quiet. Everyone seemed happier without Alan. Boys behaved better. Alan's badness seemed to touch them all in some way. One bad boy at the table meant lots of bad boys at the table. Like catching a cold. They should keep Alan in a place all on his own.

* * *

Jamie rocked on his heels as he looked out of the window. Green leaves had started to open on the trees now, and he could hear birds singing if he listened hard. Pity about those bars. He loved being able to move around without worrying about Alan. Neville looked more cheerful, too.

"Jamie! It's me, Rosie."

He spun around, couldn't believe it. It was her. He ran across the room.

"Rosie, I thought you forgot me! I'm so happy." He jumped up and down he was so happy. He knew the whole room was staring; he liked that they saw he had a pretty girl visitor.

"Jamie, Mrs. Clancy said we could use a small room next to her office. We can practice reading and have a nice chat. She's had a word with this gentleman, so he knows it's all right." She took his hand and they left the room.

After they settled down on a small couch, Jamie took a deep breath.

"I missed you so much, Rosie. How's Laddie? Does he miss me? Why didn't you come? You promised."

"I missed you too. Laddie's fine and of course he misses you. Mummy didn't send the car because it broke down and the garage didn't get the part until yesterday. Daddy doesn't want me coming here. He's afraid I won't be safe. Anyhow, he's been away in London and took his car with him. I'm quite safe here, aren't I?"

"There's one boy, Alan, he's very rough. He hurt one of my friends this morning. I don't know if they found Alan, he ran off. I expect my friend's in hospital. I think it's good in here. In this room."

"I'm sure Mrs. Clancy will let us use it again. Are you happy here?"

"No, I hate it. They have all sorts here. Some of them can't talk. And Alan hurts me. And it's boring. And he threw dirty water on my book to spoil it. I was reading it to everyone. He's jealous. I had the chocolates you sent and he stole them away."

"Oh, poor Jamie. But I didn't send you any chocolates. You must have another girl! Here, I've got another book for you."

They practiced reading with the new book and Jamie was happier than he'd been for ages. When it was time to say goodbye he'd try to be strong. He was nearly a man, after all.

"Excuse me, Jamie, I'll be back in a minute."

"Where're you going?"

"To the lavatory. And you're not supposed to ask."

"Sorry." Another thing different about this Manor. They said lavatory instead of toilet.

Jamie heard a voice coming from Mrs. Clancy's office. It sounded like Bernhardt, only he was talking funny, using words Jamie didn't know. No words he ever knew. How could he hear anything with the door and windows closed? He looked up and saw a couple of little open windows high in the wall between the rooms. Then some words he knew. Bernhardt said "in Old Ring Copse." He knew that place. Hinges squeaked and a door clicked shut. Could Bernhardt be Mr. Lake's friend? Better be careful. He jumped when Rosie came back.

"Sorry, did I startle you?"

"That's all right." The voice had gone away.

"Jamie, tomorrow afternoon, Mummy and I are coming to take you home for tea and a game with Laddie. I saved it for last so you won't be sad when I leave."

"Goodie, I can't hardly wait!"

They walked slowly back to the sunroom, as slowly as Jamie could make it. Just outside the door Rosie kissed his cheek. He'd never wash that little patch where the kiss belonged.

"See you tomorrow. Bye."

"Bye-bye, Rosie, bye-bye."

* * *

Jamie could just see George in the moonlight. He wasn't asleep yet.

"George, you know what? I felt like I knew Graham once upon a time. But I never did know a Graham before. And then one morning, my eyes were a bit closed and I thought it was my cousin Roy. But I thought it couldn't be. But it was. He hit his toe and said a bad word, a Roy word, so I knew then. He says he's in disguise because people are after him. I promised not to tell, but I can tell you because you can't talk."

George grunted.

"And that Bernhardt. I heard him on the telephone in Mrs. Clancy's office. He was talking funny words. And I heard him say a place on the farm where I used to work. I hope he's not Mr.

Lake's friend. Mr. Lake is a very nasty man and he hates me." He jumped. "What was that?"

A long, squeaky noise, sounded as if it were just outside their door, and then a strange bump. Jamie got out of bed. George grunted, moving his mouth and hands, didn't want Jamie to go.

"All right, George, I won't do anything silly. I expect the door's locked, anyway."

Jamie turned the knob. Not locked. Exciting things sometimes happened when you went out of doors when you weren't supposed to. Exciting things weren't always good things, though. But exciting did feel nice for a while. He turned to George and put a finger to his lips. He peeked around the door. He almost made a surprise noise when he saw new stairs coming down from a secret door in the ceiling and then Bernhardt climbing up them holding a box under his arm before disappearing through that high door. George gave a little grunt and Jamie knew what he meant. *Mustn't get caught.* He closed the door quietly and got back into bed. He told George what he'd seen.

"Shhhh, shhhh," George managed to get out.

George was right. He should mind his own business. Keep his mouth shut, about absolutely everything.

10

T he sun wasn't out yet, but at least the rain stayed away. Manor day today, a wonderful day. He'd play with Laddie, help Mr. Evans, and have a nice walk with Rosie. And a big tea. There'd be scones with cream and jam. *Perhaps a cake.* Even thinking about his stolen chocolates couldn't make him sad today.

Jamie got out of bed and went into the bathroom. He needed extra time, so he must get in there before the others. He'd got to have a special wash this morning. He started on his teeth, always liked to get that done first. A scream startled him, made him stop brushing for a moment. Most probably one of the boys being bad. He heard their door open.

"Jamie, where are you?"

"In the bathroom."

He put his head around the door and saw Neville lifting George out of bed.

"Can I have some extra time? I'm going out to tea. I've got to be really, really clean."

"Take as much time as you like. Just get out of there for a few minutes so I can put George on the toilet. Then you're all to stay in your rooms."

"Why?"

"Never you mind."

Jamie sat on the edge of his bed. The scream. Someone hurt. *Would they let me go out to Rosie's? Must let me go.* He felt disappointment rising up his throat and swallowed it down. Nothing bad happened yet, so wait before being sorry. Silly to be sad for nothing. But still.

"Fiddle-faddle!"

"What?" Neville's voice got high when he was upset, like now.

"Nothing. Did Alan come back and hurt someone?" Jamie hoped he'd never see that awful boy again.

"No, he didn't hurt anyone. Now, no more questions."

Neville wheeled George back into the room and left. Jamie heard him lock the door, just like Roy did that time the bombs came down. At least Jamie could get on with his wash.

It was hard, washing all of a big boy with nothing but a little warm water in a basin. He started with his face and rinsed, all except the kissed patch. Then rubbed his underarms hard and rinsed. He got one foot up and in, and that was hard because he wasn't very good at balancing. Then he dried it and got the other foot up. The water was very soapy now. He wondered where the dirt went. Inside the soap? But then the soap got on him again when he washed the next bit. Perhaps the dirt just got more spread out. He soaped his willy and his bottom. That sometimes made him feel funny, so he closed his eyes and thought of boiled cabbage, and that kept everything in order.

Roy came in the bathroom once when his willy had got big from the washing, and he laughed and laughed. Said he didn't know Jamie had it in him. When Jamie asked what he didn't know he had in him, he laughed even more. Sometimes Jamie woke up with it that way, but he knew he mustn't touch. Gran had caught him playing with it once. He only did it because it felt nice and tingly, but she said it was wicked and dirty and he must never touch unless he had to for toilet or washing. So he didn't. Nearly never.

He hated the idea of people watching him wash. Boys here didn't understand much about being clean. It was very important. Especially to girls, because they hated smelly boys, he'd heard Gran tell Roy a long time ago. Lately, even Roy spent ages in the bathroom before he took a girl out to the flicks. Alan didn't wash much. There were a lot of things about Alan he hated. Gran said he mustn't hate people, but she didn't know Alan. *Alan is wicked and God should punish him.* Gran said wicked people went to Hell after they died to be punished. Why didn't God punish them before they died? Then they could learn to do better. He should ask. But ask who?

George seemed sleepy and Jamie was too excited to read. They waited for a long time before Neville came back and said they could go downstairs.

Breakfast passed very quietly. Unusually, all three attendants stood around the room, silent except for a word here and there to tell the boys what to do and not to do. When they went to the common room, Jamie made sure he was last. He stopped by Bernhardt, who always stood by the huge brown door, holding the key in the same hand that held the list tight to his chest.

"What's happened?"

"You'll be told when Mrs. Clancy permits. Go and read your book."

In his excitement, Jamie had left his book in his room. What would he do all morning? He went and stood at the window. If he stood on his toes he could just see the road. There was a long van, a white one. Two men carried a long board and something lay on it under a white sheet, something that broke, most likely. The van moved off and he watched it appear and disappear between the big old trees as it went on its way.

He'd try his hand at the paints.

* * *

After lunch, Mrs. Clancy came over to Jamie with a man.

"Jamie, this is Detective Inspector Falway. He needs to ask you about your chocolates."

"Why, did you find them?" That would be a very good thing, especially if no one had nibbled on them.

"Not exactly," the man said.

"What's your name? Forgot. Sorry. Didn't mean to." *Pay attention, or people would think he was stupid and then he'd never get out of this place.*

"Falway. You can call me D.I. Falway."

"All right." *Must answer nicely, must be allowed to go out.*

"Tell me about your present. The one you got yesterday."

"Maureen gave it to me. It was all wrapped up. Came in the post, you see. It was chocolates. A box of Cadbury's. My favorites."

"Who do you think sent them?"

"Dunno. Don't know, I mean. There wasn't a card. And Maureen said there wasn't anyone's name on the outside."

"Who knows you like chocolates?"

Why all these chocolate questions? "I don't know a lot of people. Rosie knows. But I asked her, and she said it wasn't her that sent them."

"Rosie?"

"That would be Miss Rosamund McInnis, Sir Geoffrey McInnis's daughter," said Mrs. Clancy. "The family takes an interest in the boy. Here she is now. He's to go to them for the afternoon."

"Hello, Rosie," said Jamie. "I'm ready. This is D.I. Way."

"Detective Inspector Falway. You're Miss McInnis?" he asked.

"Yes, is there a problem?"

"We're just trying to clear up a mystery. Jamie received some chocolates in the post yesterday. Did you send them?"

"No. If I had chocolates for him, I would have brought them in myself," Rosie said in a bossy voice Jamie hadn't heard before.

"Said it wasn't her!" Jamie wanted to go. *All these questions, time to leave.*

"Inspector, why do you ask?" said Rosie.

"Just an ongoing investigation, Miss McInnis. Nothing to worry about."

"I see. Will there be anything else?"

"No, miss, that's all for the time being. Have a nice afternoon," he said.

Rosie nodded her head at him and turned her back. Funny she hadn't asked more questions. She knew she was better than him, Jamie could tell by the way she acted. Rosie was a person who knew her place. And she knew other people's places. Gran always said people should know their place in the world and stick to it. She'd explained best she could about posh and poor, but it meant more than some people having more money than other people. It also seemed to mean who was better and who wasn't, but in funny sorts of ways. Of course Rosie was better than Jamie and had more money, too, but she never acted like it around him. She didn't have a job, so he supposed she used Sir Geoffrey's money, like Roy used Gran's if she had any to spare. Even if she didn't. Did that make Rosie poor? He'd tried talking to her about class, but could see talking about it made her uncomfortable, so he'd better leave it alone for the time being.

People act their place more than they talk about it, and they need watching. What they say doesn't tell you what's really in their head. If only people would answer his questions properly.

* * *

Lady Audrey drove the car and let Jamie sit in the front seat next to her. She smelled nice like Rosie did, only different. She gave him a big smile. She was very pretty, in an older sort of way, much prettier than proper old, of course. She was what Gran used to call a carrot-head. They'd had one living next door. Gran said that carrot-heads are nearly always bad-tempered, but Lady Audrey wasn't. Not a bit.

"It's lovely to see you again," she said. She sounded as if she meant it, her voice going up at the end as if she was having a treat.

"Today is a very good day," said Jamie.

Rosie told her mother about D. I. Falway's visit. She said she hadn't asked questions, didn't want him to think she was too interested. Lady Audrey said it might have been something to do with the black market. Odd someone would mail the box to Jamie, who said he'd never seen a black market.

"Can we go see it?" Jamie asked.

Lady Audrey replied the black market wasn't a place. "I'll explain later." Her mouth corners twitched like people's do when they want to laugh. He wished people would explain when he'd said something they thought was funny, because that usually meant he got it wrong, and he'd like it better if he could get it right.

* * *

Laddie gave Jamie such a big welcome he could hardly get out of the car. His yellow body wriggled and jumped, until he suddenly dashed off. Why would Laddie run away from him? The dog appeared again, this time with a tennis ball in his mouth. He dropped it at Jamie's feet. Not running away, just getting his toy.

"You two play with Laddie for a bit. I'll let you know when tea's ready," said Lady Audrey. Cook could just as well let them know. Jamie had spent a fair amount of time in the kitchen, and he'd never seen Lady Audrey do the bread and butter or put a cake in the oven.

They threw the ball until even the dog was tired. Jamie loved Laddie and wanted him to be happy, but he hated it when the ball got slimy. And his breath wasn't too nice these days because it smelled fishy. Rosie didn't seem to mind the slime, simply wiped her hand down her skirt. He could see the streaks. *Would her mum be cross and make her change for tea?*

"Where's Mr. Evans?" asked Jamie.

"In the greenhouse, I shouldn't wonder," said Rosie.

They found the old man watering his seedlings.

"Well, if it isn't young Jamie! Wan' t' do some waterin'?"

"Oh yes. Please."

"Here's a can for yer. Fill it up at yon tap." The old man gestured with his chin.

"I'll help you with that, Jamie. It gets heavy when there's water in it," said Rosie.

"Oh, I'm very strong. But if you want." People liked it when you needed their help. Even though he didn't.

He did need her help after all, but didn't say so. *How could splishy-splashy water be so heavy?* There were rows and rows of little plants to be seen to, and Jamie's arms felt very achy. After the watering was finished, Rosie rubbed the tops of her arms. Good, she wasn't any stronger than him. Evans showed Jamie how he thinned the seedlings.

"Got to have room to grow. Got to be plenty of food and water for the ones we keep. Pinch 'em just so. You do a couple, now."

Evans watched and guided; make nimble fingers and gentle fingers, don't take too many, give them breathing room.

"It's sad," said Jamie after he'd worked through a couple of trays.

"How so, lad?"

"The ones we pinch. They never get a chance. They might've grown up strong."

Evans straightened up and squinted at Jamie. "Tha's the way of the world."

"I think I hear Mummy calling," said Rosie. "It's time to go in for tea. There's a cake today in your honor."

"In my what?"

"Just for you, because we're happy you're here."

Jamie looked around the breakfast room as he ate. He looked at all the pictures to stitch them down in his memory, smiled as he looked out over the garden, and hardly said a word. This was his place in the world—white tablecloths and serviettes, cake, pictures, gardens, and lovely people and Laddie. Rosie. When he was too full to eat even another crumb, he closed his eyes and sighed. He felt his smile sliding away as the goodbye time closed in. Had to leave soon.

Rosie kissed the other cheek. That way he could keep his face cleaner. Just make sure she kissed the other side each time. Her soft lips didn't feel real, more like something out of a dream.

That night, Jamie stared up at the ceiling and thought over his day at the Manor. A special day. He let his mind travel around the breakfast room and stop at each picture. He liked the one with the sheep best. A boy and a dog just like Laddie sat under a tree near the sheep. That boy looked a bit like Jamie. He had a cheerful face and carried a sort of pipe in his hands, a pipe that made music, Rosie said. Jamie could see how making music would be a happy thing to do. And also being with sheep and a Laddie dog, those were happy things, too.

Graham, being Roy now, finished putting George to bed and sat down by Jamie.

"Jamie, did you tell anyone else what you told me?"

"What did I tell you?"

"You know, about your Gran and the blanket and our row." Roy sounded all wound up, his voice sharp and thin.

"Oh, that. No, I'm tired of that. It's a long time ago. There's no one to tell except Rosie. I don't tell Rosie bad things in case she cries. Except when Alan hurt me and stole my chocolates. I did tell her about that . . . Why?"

"Well, it's something you should keep to yourself. People

might not believe you. They might think you're not quite right."

"They know I'm not quite right. I'm slow. That's why I'm here." Roy could be slow himself sometimes.

"No, I mean, a bit mad, crazy. It's a crazy story."

"You think I'm crazy? Don't go telling people I'm crazy!" Then they'd never let him go. Roy could do that; he was mean enough to do that. The fear crept up on him, the fear that was never far behind, just waiting behind him for the next bad thing.

"'Course not. Only I know you, and other people might think different. So, be a good chap. Just between us. Anything else you want to tell me?"

"Well there is the door in the ceiling."

"What door?"

"Outside this room. A door in the ceiling with stairs coming out of it. I saw Bernhardt carry a box up there. Then I went back to bed. He'd've got me in trouble if he seen me watching. But I heard a noise, see, that's what made me go and look."

"You didn't see him come down?"

"No, like I said, I went back to bed." He had to tell Roy things so many times, maybe he truly was slow in his own way.

"Jamie, that's another thing to keep quiet about. You'd get in big trouble if anyone heard about it. Bernhardt was probably going up there to fix a leak. The box probably had his tools in it. You know, a toolbox. Don't say a word, not to no one. Promise?"

"Promise." If it was that important, maybe he should tell someone. The right sort of someone. *Wait and see.*

"G'night." *Not so wound up now.*

"Goodnight, Graham."

Roy was smiling, looked as if he just got a big present. Funny things going on in this place. The Manor didn't have goings on, much better that way. Smoother.

George twisted towards Jamie and grunted as though something hurt him.

"Don't worry, George, I'll be ever so careful."

* * *

Roy lowered himself to the ground, leaned against the big oak in the back pasture, and popped out his cheek pads. He had plenty of fags, thanks to no one but his own clever self. He loved every bit of smoking. The smell as he struck the match, the first taste of the smoke, the first little dizzy hit. He closed his eyes and took the first drag.

"Well, you can't win 'em all."

That chump Alan stole the chocs, but he couldn't have foreseen that. He'd have to get the little retard before he spilled the beans, though, couldn't trust him not to let it all out. He'd figure a way. And they couldn't prove nothing from his story about Gran, anyhow. The old bag must've been burnt to a cinder. Silly old cow asked for it. He hadn't ever asked her for that much. More's the pity Jamie wasn't toasted along with her like he'd planned. No need for people to start asking questions, though.

Lucky he'd seen Jamie's name in the paper. Nearly missed it. Only took a few cups of tea and a gossip in the Manor kitchen to find out where they'd put him. Made him sick the way they went on about Jamie. He'd rung up the place and asked if there were any job openings. He could have worked on the grounds or inside. Inside was easier and he could keep an eye on the little angel.

Roy dragged his fingers through his hair. *Strewth!* He hated this sticking-out hair; give him a good jar of goop any time. Kept it in place. Made him look like he should, a man with the goods. Style.

He'd work alone from now on. Shouldn't have gone in with the Reddy boys. Them wanting more than their share, they'd buggered off and left some toughs watching. Good thing he'd legged it. Hadn't even had time to wipe his prints off the place or even off the stuff. He'd had to throw the open bag behind him to make them stop to shove all the stuff back in. He never would've outrun them otherwise. What a wicked waste. He'd read in the paper they were wanted, and him, too. Someone must've fingered old Roy. *Fucking bastards.* Well, he'd just have to lie low. Rather be in the nick than behind the shed with the Reddy boys. He read the paper every day now. Best to keep up with things.

He could trust Derek. He should leave word for him at the Golden Lion to find out how things stood with the Reddys. Maybe Derek could find out where they were and turn them in. They couldn't kick Roy's head in from choky. Well, he was safe tucked away down here for the time being. Needed to get back to real life sometime, though. These Blexton boys were animals.

Now, Bernhardt up in the attic, wasn't that a turn up for the books. *What the bloody hell is he up to?* Of course, he was a foreigner. Spy maybe. He'd get the rope if he were a spy. He'd have to watch him. Must be worth a bit, what he'd got hidden away.

He'd read there'd been some local jobs pulled lately. He'd better keep his nose clean, didn't want any questions. Best hang around people a lot, so they wouldn't think it might be him creeping off to pinch stuff. Perhaps that was Bernhardt's game. Well, he'd watch and wait. Watch and wait.

And that Jamie. They must know the poison was meant for him. They'd be on the lookout. Have to wait, just a bit longer. He'd talk to the lad every night, make sure he held up. He'd find his chance to shut the little bugger up sooner or later. And that pathetic bag of bones George couldn't talk. Jamie was as good as on his own.

Roy stubbed out his fag on a buttercup and watched it shrivel up around the hole in its face. He hated buttercups. Gran used to hold one under his chin and ask if he liked butter. Full of sloppy talk, she used to be. Gran told Roy about her parents, how she'd gone to proper schools, talked nicely, went to church. She was always on about how talking nicely got you places. *Where'd it get her, though?*

Roy wanted to know Gran's parents' names, told her she should let them know how hard up she was. Gran wouldn't say a word, wouldn't let on; even so, Roy found their names through the records office, and then her sister's name. It made Gran start talking when he told her he'd done that.

Gran's parents had thrown her out when she got knocked up by a brickie. Said they were dead now, but admitted she had a sister. Roy left out how he'd tracked down dear old Myrtle, visited her just before he came down here. Myrtle had been snotty, then a little frightened when Roy came up really close and looked down on her tight, bright-brown curls. Myrtle had given Roy a hundred pounds and said she didn't think they should meet again, it couldn't work out, they had nothing in common. Well, he had his little nest egg now, but he might want more. He'd have to see how things went. Interesting Myrtle never asked about Gran until Roy told her she was dead. Myrtle didn't seem all that upset.

Gran had her pride, she said that all the time. Being poor's nothing to be proud of, not at all. Roy wasn't going to put up with it. He'd get rich and go knock on Myrtle's smug front door again and show her he was a big man of the world. He'd have his black oiled hair back, too, and some good togs.

He'd get it all, but first things first.

11

S ir Geoffrey sat in his study, feeling grumpier than he should as he waited for Sir Ronald Marsh to make his appearance. Ten minutes late, making a point. Too impressed with himself since his knighthood. Actually expected Geoffrey to go to him, silly sod. Well, to be fair, not that unreasonable since the fellow was up to his ears in high crimes these days; nevertheless, unwritten rules and all that. Nothing Sir Ronald would have caught on to!

The fact was Geoffrey couldn't warm up to the chief constable, simple as that. Those small mirthless laughs that punctuated his conversation—little puffs of air shot through his nose with the faintest of *heh, hehs*—raised his hackles within minutes. And the vowels that elongated as time went by in a hopeless attempt to move up a couple of rungs in the social ladder made him cringe. The fellow was clever, no doubt about it, so why couldn't he be content with his professional accomplishments instead of putting on airs that made him look like a chump? Look at the way he barged through the world with his chest thrown out as if to bulldoze any obstacles that might stand in his way. And that silly little moustache!

He heard the car pull up and stayed where he was. He normally greeted guests himself but felt a little formality was in order.

"Sir Ronald Marsh, sir." Stanton's intonation was sonorous, rather as if he were announcing the Grim Reaper.

"Morning, Ronnie, nice to see you again, as always," Geoffrey said, rising.

"Yes, heh, morning, Geoffrey, keeping well, I trust, heh, heh!" *Fellow's huge, seems bigger than ever. Better put him in the big chair. Hope he doesn't get that revolting hair oil all over it. Too bad Audrey won't have antimacassars.* "Let's sit by the fire. Still a bit on the chilly side. Sherry?"

"No, no. On duty you know. Needs must." *Pompous ass.*

"That's all, thank you, Stanton. What news, Ronnie?"

"We've got to beef up coastal defense, got to prepare for the worst."

"God, is it that bad? The papers don't give one that sense." *My pals in Intelligence do, though. You're not the only one with secrets.*

"Londoners could tell you. They're being blown to pieces, and they can't take much more."

The men sat morosely, staring into their laps. Geoffrey yearned for peace, to be left alone. The more all these cares and worries pressed on his mind, the more he felt the precious memories of his little Fiona receding. Her chuckles and antics had started to fade like the sepia print he kept hidden. My God, twenty years or more and he still couldn't look at it; felt the sight of it would cut into his gut like a guillotine. Even his lovely Rosie hadn't been able to ease it, couldn't take her place.

"God help us all if Jerry goosesteps his way across England, Geoffrey." *And he may well do that.* Fear fogged his mind and he had to fight it down.

"Quite. How're your wardens doing? I've seen a bit of carelessness. We've got to be more careful. The Home Office is thinking of banning everyone from the beaches. They're going to put more concrete pillboxes up, too."

"That seems harsh, Ronnie. People need their little pleasures, and surely an afternoon at the beach isn't asking too much. Perhaps we could designate one or two beaches that the wardens could patrol. Just a few hours in the afternoons."

Sir Ronald puffed out his cheeks as if weighing the matter.

"Well, it's a thought. The National Guard has to patrol the beaches anyway. So limited hours might be manageable. I'll check with Whitehall. Can't be seen making waves, though." *You won't do a damned thing, never one to stick your neck out.*

"Closing the beaches and making waves." Geoffrey laughed and Ronnie looked offended. "A pun, Ronnie."

"Yes, quite unintentional, heh, heh. By the way, keep your ear to the ground, old chap. We think there's a spy ring operating locally. We know who one of them is, but we don't want to spook him. We need the others."

"How do you know?" *Showing off again?*

"We get some radio chatter, but he's clever, never on for long enough to let us in on anything, and we don't know where he hides it. He's being watched, but he hasn't led us anywhere so far. Given us the slip once or twice." Ronnie had relaxed now; mind clearly stationed where it felt comfortable.

"Foreign or local?"

"The one we're watching is foreign. Dutch. Intelligence tells us he's a member of the Dutch Nazi Party, a traitor to his own country, too. His confederates might be local."

Geoffrey wondered what made a man turn traitor. Anger, disappointment, feeling you yourself had been betrayed? He'd known angry men, men who couldn't make their way in life and blamed everyone else for their failures. He'd seen that kind of bitterness. Of course, some people will do anything for money, not that they get that much by all accounts, not enough to make it worth risking the rope. But their sort can't think of anything but their own grievances.

"You're sure about this Dutch chap?"

"Alerted by a double agent. He tells a good story—refugee from the Nazis and all that—but the Intelligence boys checked on him and found out who he was. Immigration's got no record of entry, either. We've got a lot of strong contacts in Holland. MI5's got a good record of rounding up these characters, or at least finding out who they are and watching them until it suits them to close in. Got to give them credit. They've put a man in where he works. Doesn't seem to come up with anything, though."

"I say, Ronnie, do you know anything about an incident at the Blexton Institute yesterday? It had Audrey a bit worried.

Something about a black market box of chocolates the police thought Rosie might have taken to a young boy she visits there. All very odd."

Ronnie looked shifty. "Yes, well, I was going to bring that up. Just between you and me, you understand." He'd turned pompous again.

"Of course, mum's the word."

"Someone sent the boy a box of chocolates. We know it was addressed to him because one of the girls who works there took the parcel up to him. There was another boy in the common room who'd been aggressive and troublesome on a number of occasions. He snatched the chocolates and ran away. They looked high and low, but couldn't find him. The cleaning woman found him next day in the supplies cupboard. Dead. Lying on top of an empty box of Cadbury's. Black market stuff, of course. A box of Cadbury's is rarer than hen's teeth, worse luck."

"Good God! What killed him?" *Distasteful.*

"Arsenic. There was a little of it spilled into the box. He'd eaten the lot. The garden shed had been broken into and the rat poison was missing its lid."

"Christ, Ronnie, my daughter's often over there. Is it safe?"

"I think she's safe enough. But is he? We have to ask, who would want to poison young Jamie Jenkins? The inmates couldn't come up with something like that."

"There can't be any question of money. He's a nice boy. Simple, but polite. Doesn't deserve that."

"You know his grandmother died in the big one in December. Our people checked with the local wardens after that farmer who had been abusing the boy was arrested. He told them a strange story about that boy and the grandmother being locked into the house by a cousin, Roy Beck. That blighter's known to the local coppers up there, wanted for housebreaking in the West End, in fact."

So the cousin was a bad lot. Perhaps Jamie had seen something he shouldn't. Knew about the housebreaking. Plenty of that going on. There had been an article about it in *The Times* quite recently. People left their city houses to escape the bombing and moved to the countryside. Might just as well issue an invitation to the Roy Becks of this world. He'd read there were plenty of fences around, and plenty of buyers, too, by all accounts.

"Where is this Roy? He might think Jamie knows something."

"We don't know where the fellow is. He dropped out of sight."

"Did you trace the parcel?"

"Package was mailed in Christchurch. Post office there gets pretty busy, and the woman who runs it is usually on her own and run ragged. Doesn't remember a thing. Anyway, what D.I. Falway wanted me to ask you, is could you put the boy up here for a while? Just until we know more, you understand."

"I'll speak to Audrey now."

"Don't tell her anything but the chocolates story."

He knew Audrey would jump on it, but he felt it only fair to let her in on the situation, to go and tell her himself rather than get Stanton to send her in.

Audrey was writing letters in her sitting room when he found her, face dreamy. He knew that look, that mood, the one he loved so well, that would disappear in a minute. He kissed her hair and inhaled her perfume as she looked at him in the mirror, her eyes wary now. By the time he finished his story her eyes glittered with indignation. She reached the study first.

"Morning, Ronnie. Nice to see you." She spoke in the carrying voice she used to address the Women's Institute. Geoffrey loathed and loved the authority in that voice. "Dreadful story. I insist the boy be brought here immediately. He's a lovely chap, and we never wanted him in that place. The authorities insisted, didn't give us a choice."

"That's very generous, Audrey. I'll make the arrangements. Today not too soon?"

"We'll expect him in time for tea."

"Don't mention this to anyone else, if you don't mind. Just tell Rosie some story about needing to protect him from one of the other boys. We want to keep this under wraps, give ourselves a chance to investigate the institute staff on the quiet."

"Anything else we need to go over?" Geoffrey said.

"Just one thing. A woman's gone missing. We understand she had a romantic interest in one of your laborers. One for the boys, we're told. Her husband was badly wounded and she plays the field a bit."

"Yes, we know about her, Sylvia something," said Audrey.

"I've seen her at the baker's shop where she used to work, and I met her husband when I visited the cottage hospital a few weeks ago. That's where I met Jamie, by the way. Anyway, he told me she's always too busy to visit, but on my way home from a friend's house, I'd noticed her going into a pub with a young man, one of our laborers. Geoffrey spoke to him. He'd lose his military deferment if he got sacked."

"We've got that Mrs. Lake missing, too, you know, the one whose husband mistreated a retarded boy."

"That was Jamie, did you know that?" asked Geoffrey. *Don't these people talk to each other?*

"No, damn it. They should have briefed me. He comes up a lot, doesn't he?"

"Well, he couldn't have had anything to do with it!" said Audrey. That voice again.

"No, of course not, Audrey." Amusing how that tone of voice put Ronnie on the defensive. "Anyway, Lake says she told him she was leaving, and she was gone when he got up in the morning. She's not at her parents, which is where she told him she'd be, but she told no one where she was going. We suspect the husband may have killed her, but there's no proof. She called Dr. Gibson out to attend to the boy—Jamie—and told him she was afraid of her husband. We've talked to him, naturally. We know the taxi service wasn't running. No petrol."

"Do you think there's a connection? A rampage of some sort?" asked Audrey.

"We've handed out fliers on both of these women, but their descriptions are so much like each other and fifty thousand other British woman, I don't hold out much hope. Messy business. Well, must be off. I seem to find myself on some sort of treadmill these days."

He sounded hopeless for a minute, a tone far from his usual bluster. Geoffrey felt a little ashamed of his earlier behavior.

"Thanks for your help, Ronnie. Don't you have time for lunch? We'd be delighted to have you."

"No, thanks all the same, Geoffrey, most kind. Got to get back to the office."

Audrey and Geoffrey rose to show him out. Ronnie was quite a decent fellow, really.

* * *

"Where to, Sir Ronald?" asked his driver.

"Home for lunch. Ask Sally to give you something in the kitchen. I'll go back to the office at one."

"Very good, Sir Ronald."

He hadn't mentioned his new directive to Geoffrey. It showed how worried Whitehall was. Not encouraging. Each chief constable must form a spy ring of six individuals, each unknown to the others. They were to report to him directly and act as informants—saboteurs even, in the event of a German invasion. He'd got five already. All walks of life.

Would Geoffrey be too obvious? He'd have to think it through. He needed people who had good reason to be out and about a lot, and Geoffrey had good reason, what with running the estate and so on. He'd got a postman, and the proprietor of the most popular pub in town, even a dustman. Eyes and ears. But if Jerry landed, Geoffrey's property would be the first to be singled out. The buggers were like that, only the best for their officers. What they'd done in France was banish the estate owners to a corner of the house, or worse, and taken over everything else. Though that meant there might be a lot of information worth overhearing. And Geoffrey told him once that he spoke German, had spent his summers on the farm of a family friend near Erwitte. And Audrey spoke finishing-school French, no doubt.

Is Geoffrey reliable? All that silly business playing the aristocrat and trying to put him in his place. *Good heart though, with the boy. Not many take one of those on.* And Audrey. *Magnificent woman.* That red hair and slender waist always stirred him more than was comfortable.

He'd need help with food storage, too. Each area needed a secret food storage facility. Not going to be easy. Geoffrey might be able to help, probably the best person, actually.

Sir Ronald's stomach growled. His wife wanted to put them both on a diet. He didn't consider himself fat, just well built. She was rather more solid than he'd like, though. Not like Audrey. *Fine figure of a woman, that.* He sighed.

He'd give Geoffrey a ring later and make sure he came to the office this time, official business and all that.

12

Sarah's eyes fluttered and closed, finally. She looked frail under the blankets, sadly incomplete with only one long mound where there should be two. Never plump, she needed feeding up. Betty thought she'd ask Lady Audrey, generous soul that she was, for some extra bacon and stew meat rations, just until Sarah got some flesh back on her bones. They'd been ever so good to them up at the Manor when the news came through. They'd paid for her to get the train up to London. Derek and her had seen to the funeral and visited Sarah in hospital. They'd had to leave her there until she was well enough to travel. Derek, always on his way to somewhere else, asked Roy to bring her down and he'd come to see her in a few weeks. Of course Betty agreed to take her sister in and hadn't bothered to ask Frank. What could he say? "Family is family," Betty told him, even though she knew he hadn't got any and couldn't grasp the idea. Poor girl, however would she get on in life now?

The clock downstairs chimed nine. Another hour till the pub closed, although the landlord sometimes let a few regulars stay on. Would Frank be sloppy drunk or nasty drunk tonight? Sarah had spotted the bruises on Betty's legs when the wind blew her skirt up yesterday in their little back garden. Sarah hadn't believed the "I tripped" story, but finally let her be.

Betty hoped Frank would be quiet tonight—it wouldn't take much to wake Sarah. She'd only been here a week, and Frank had already got drunk down the pub twice. He wasn't too pleased about Sarah being in the house. Afraid the girl would tattle about him, although who could she tattle to? Just about everybody blown up, both the little ones, even the neighbors on both sides. Derek wouldn't be any help. He was in the army now and had quite an important assignment from what she understood. Roy had stayed long enough to drink with Frank in the pub one night and gone straight to the station after closing. Frank kept talking about how Roy "knew his way around." Betty remembered Roy being quite a wild boy. She hoped he hadn't grown into a bad lot. Derek seemed to attract bad lots.

Frank kept saying how Sarah looked down on him. She could seem a little stuck-up sometimes. Their family wasn't ever anything special, nothing to brag about, but none of them laborers or maids. Until Betty married Frank. She'd been that happy when she met Frank at their local one evening and he'd asked her out. She'd always been popular, especially after the boys had put a few beers away. Fat plain girls had to be jolly and easy to get along with, you had to face reality. But she never got asked out much, not for a proper outing to the flicks and a bite to eat, only for doorway groping and wet kisses. They hardly ever tried to do much with that hardness they pressed into her, only once or twice.

Mum and Dad hadn't been that impressed with Frank—none of them had—but they'd put a good face on for their little wedding. She hadn't expected to have to work so hard, but she didn't mind. She loved sex, and he said he loved her big body, loved to bury his face between her breasts as he squeezed her bottom, and loved feeling his sinewy thin legs between her plump thighs.

Frank wanted a baby, he even more than Betty. That's where it had all started to go wrong. Two years, no baby, and he'd turned on her. It started with the drinking and hitting, and after that he called her names, even sober. One night, just before Sarah came, she'd refused him because she had her period. He'd gone berserk and lashed out and lashed out until she found herself curled up in a corner, holding her head and crying. When she'd calmed down and raised her head, he was slumped in a kitchen chair snoring like an old dog, drool looping from his slack lower lip.

Peculiar, him reacting that way to not having a baby. Was it somehow tied up with proving himself a man? Frank was about her height, shorter than most of the other laborers, but they'd learned not to tease him about it, learned the hard way, she'd heard. Or was it being brought up in a Dr. Bernardo's home? Frank said it hadn't been a happy place, but wouldn't say more. He needed his very own family that was probably it.

Betty still loved Frank, God knows why. But the morning after that beating, she sat across the kitchen table from him and looked him straight in his red squinty eyes.

"You hit me like that again and I'll leave you. I mean it."

"Leave me?" His face arranged itself into a cruel mask. "And go where? No family that I can see. Unless you think a one-legged chit of a girl and a brother at the front are going to be any use. And who do you think's going to take up with a fat cow like you? You've got a face like a pudding and you can't make babies. And this cottage is tied to my job, not yours."

There wasn't much Betty could say to that. Frank about got it right, beastly spiteful though it was. Still he hadn't hit her for a while. She had to go to the doctor again soon. She'd see what he had to say this time. She was due to get her period in another week or so. She hoped to God that didn't start another row. Not in front of Sarah. She didn't want to be shamed in front of her sister. And Betty wanted Sarah to feel safe and comfortable in her home.

Betty never thought about the others, especially the little ones. She couldn't bear it. She pushed them all down and away. Time to get into bed and try to sleep, or at least pretend to be asleep. She wasn't in the mood for his drunken fumbling tonight. Never was, these days.

The doctor had said last time that it wasn't necessarily the woman who had something wrong, sometimes the men didn't have enough of something or other. Betty had asked him about that again. She hadn't mentioned it to Frank. He'd go mad.

Supposing it was Frank's fault? He couldn't blame her then. But he would, of course, he'd make her life a living hell. What if Betty found someone else to have a romp with? Tested it out. Shocking idea, she didn't know what made it pop into her head. But the thought excited her, made her shiver. How on earth could she manage something like that in a small place like this? How could she get away? And anyway, who would want her? There were plenty of willing lonely girls around, after all, lots of them pretty. Interesting thought, though.

Miss Rosamund said she would visit Sarah tomorrow. She'd mention that to Frank. He would want Sarah and Betty to be at their best. It might make him simmer down.

13

Rosie watched Jamie trying to eat his boiled egg. Or, rather, trying to decapitate it with the edge of his spoon. Absorbed in the task, his forehead raised and creased under his wavy fair hair as he worked at it. He wasn't getting anywhere. The egg wobbled and cracked, but it wouldn't be sliced.

"Jamie, I like to do my eggs this way," she said. "Look." She put the egg in the eggcup and, with the bowl of the spoon, cracked it gently all over the top. She pulled off the little pieces of shell and put them on the side of her plate.

"See, now it's easy to chop off its head," she said as she spooned off the top. "See how I've cut my toast into soldiers? Dip them in like this," and she brought the eggy toast up to her mouth where it dripped on her chin.

"Oops," Jamie said, laughing.

"Well, I usually manage better than that. Here, you crack the egg and I'll cut your soldiers."

They ate alone as Rosie's mother was in bed nursing a headache and her father had a fencing problem to attend to in the upper pastures. Rosie was looking forward to Jamie's first day back with them. Life had been very lonely since she'd broken up with Robin. Damned war, what a bother, what a thumping big bore.

They planned to practice reading together after breakfast, and then they'd take Laddie out for a long walk. Jamie said he wanted to help Evans every day, so he could do that in the afternoon while Rosie caught up with her letters.

The breakfast room was Rosie's favorite place in the house, especially on a beautiful spring day like this. The windows, huge and partly mullioned, had cushioned seats beneath them where she loved to curl up with a book. Sun streamed in and reflected off the lemony walls and leached the light out of the satinwood dining table, always faintly scented with lavender polish. Outside, hundreds of tall daffodils nodded in the border that lined the path down to the lake. Rosie's eyes focused abruptly as she saw a figure dart out from behind the boathouse and into the bushes that led from the lake to the woods.

"What's the matter, Rosie?" asked Jamie, his eyes following hers.

"I thought I spotted someone out there. By the lake." She looked for a few minutes more, but saw no one. "Maybe a deer, or maybe even Laddie, I haven't seen him since I got up."

"Maybe your mum went out for a walk."

"Mummy's in bed. When she's got one of her migraines— that's a bad headache—she usually has to stay there all day." *And if Mummy got some fresh air and exercise, maybe she'd have fewer of those wretched headaches.* It got more and more difficult to be sympathetic as the years went by. People lost loved ones and picked themselves up and got on with it. *Twenty years, for God's sake!*

"Aren't you going to see her? When Gran had headaches, I used to put a flannel in cold water and put it on her head. She said it made her feel better."

"No, that's all right, Jamie. Mummy likes to be left alone when she's ill, doesn't want anyone near her." Mummy never needed her daughter for comfort when she was going through one of her sad times. Never needed her for anything.

"Oh. I like someone looking after me when I get ill."

"Everybody's different, Jamie, you know that."

"Yes, I'm learning about that. I didn't see people much when I was with Gran. But she talked to me lots. She told me about people. I've finished my toast soldiers. I'll just use the spoon now. I like eggs your way."

"Good. You nearly ready? Tell you what; let's go for our walk before we read. Do you mind? I fancy a look at the lake today. We might find some wildflowers."

"Yes, I'll pick some flowers for your mum. They always make people feel better."

"Better wipe your mouth, it's all yellow."

Betty sidled in. "Can I clear away, miss?" Rosie nodded. Betty Lester—she couldn't remember her married name—had rather a sly manner and was not to be trusted in Rosie's opinion. Rosie hated the way Betty always carried her head low and spied on the world from under her eyebrows. Her eyes wandered all over the place, even though her head stayed straight. She didn't miss much. Mummy had just shrugged her shoulders when Rosie told her how she felt. The girl was fat and as plain as a pikestaff, too. She'd heard rumors about her husband beating her, but never saw any signs of it. Lucky to be married at all with a face like that.

They went out of the French doors and walked down the path to the lake, always farther than it looked. Most things were green now and the huge rhododendrons were in early bud, even though they wouldn't flower until the end of May. They'd be magnificent; they always were. Queens of any Hampshire garden.

"Jamie, we'll have a picnic in the New Forest in a few weeks. Mummy takes us every year for a ride down the Ornamental Drive. It's got all these huge great bushes with great big flowers. They're called rhododendrons. People come from miles around to see them. Wouldn't you like that?"

"Yes, I would like that." A big smile lit up his face. So handsome, so sweet, so nearly perfect.

"Rosie, can George come one day? He's my best friend in that place. He's there all alone now. That makes me sad. I expect George is sad."

"Of course. But how can we get him here?"

"His chair can be made small. If there's someone here that's strong, he can carry him into the car. I saw them do it once when his cousin came. But his cousin can't come anymore because he moved away. George didn't cry when he told him because he's a big boy. But he wanted to, I could tell."

"That's so sad. Here we are. Jamie, you mustn't ever come here on your own. If you can't swim, it's dangerous. Promise?"

"Promise. What's this little house?"

"It's the boat house. It's only a little lake, but we have a couple of small rowing boats so we can get to the island in the middle. We sometimes take picnics over there when it's hot."

"Can I go? Please?" She realized Jamie couldn't quite believe all the new treats he was hearing about.

"You'll have to learn to swim. Think you could try?"

"Hmm. I'll have to think about that."

Rosie opened the door to the boathouse. No cobwebs slung across, *thank heavens*. She hated their sticky, ghostly touch. The grimy windows didn't let in much light and the place smelled of mold and damp wood. The boats, upside down at the end, were dusty and the ropes and oars hanging on the walls were swathed in cobwebs. Strange the door had been clear. As her eyes adjusted, she noticed a pile of boxes next to the cupboard. She didn't think they'd been there last year. And they looked quite clean. She'd have to ask Daddy. They were all taped up, so she didn't like to open them. Jamie had a sudden attack of sneezing.

"Come on, let's go outside, it's too dusty in here," she said, taking him by the hand. When they got into the sunshine, Jamie's eyes ran as he sneezed some more.

Rosie looked around; she felt nervous. Silly on a lovely day like this. Still, there had been someone, she was quite sure.

"Let's walk all the way around the lake, Jamie."

"Is it a very long way?"

"Not that far.

Jamie ran ahead, doing a little skip and jump, his arms flailing as he worked to keep his balance. His face, half joyful, half tentative, seemed torn between experience and hope. He'd started to fill out, begun to grow into his gangly legs. A pang very close to love struck Rosie at that moment. She'd never known brothers or sisters. The sister who'd come before her, and soon left again, only a wraith, a perfection never to be stained by the absolutes of language, a being whose quintessence remained beyond reach.

Years ago, after overhearing Cook tell a new maid that there had once been a sister, she'd asked about her at dinner. Her mother went up to bed with a migraine, and her father's fine, uncluttered face hardened and then closed. He offered nothing. Nothing for a bewildered little girl to hold onto. She'd understood then that she had uttered the unspeakable. And how she had longed for a brother, a rough-and-tumble brother who could be her best friend. Now she had a gentle boy for a brother, and one who needed her. Better, perhaps.

She'd looked inside a box in her father's closet one day when they were out. Right at the bottom, under some other old papers, she'd found a birth certificate and a death certificate. Fiona Catherine McInnis, born February 22, 1919. Fiona Catherine McInnis, died August 28, 1920. Cause of death, influenza. No pictures. She'd have liked pictures, to see this child who'd abducted her parents' hearts. She hadn't felt sad, just angry they couldn't forget Fiona and instead be content with Rosie. It did no good to dwell on things.

"Jamie," she called. "Have you seen Laddie this morning?"

"No, I haven't. I miss him. Where did he go?"

"I don't know. It's odd he wasn't with us at breakfast."

They whipped around as they heard barking and frantic yipping. A roaring figure cut out of the woods, closely pursued by a snarling dog on a mission.

"Bernhardt!"

"You know him, Jamie?"

"Yes, he's from where I was before. Laddie, leave him alone!"

Rosie whistled and the dog braked and dropped, fixing Bernhardt with intense beady eyes. The man, red-cheeked and thin-lipped, prudently stood still. He didn't look at Jamie.

"What are you doing here? This is private property!"

"Then I apologize, miss." He performed a stiff little bow. "I was just taking a long walk. It is my day off today. I did not know I had crossed into a private place." He stared into the dog's eyes, an unwise thing to do to a dog that's already agitated.

"I'll hold the dog and you can go back the way you came," said Rosie. She called Laddie to her side and grabbed his collar.

Bernhardt nodded, turned on his heel and strode off as if he had urgent business elsewhere.

"He's foreign. Do you know where he's from, Jamie?"

"I heard him say at breakfast once. Holly?"

"That can't be . . . oh, Holland, perhaps."

"Think so. He didn't say hello or goodbye to me. That was rude."

He was the man she'd seen earlier, she was sure of it. He hadn't just been walking. He'd been skulking.

"Jamie, I have to go and talk to Daddy. Why don't you find Evans."

"What about reading?"

"We'll do it later, promise."

* * *

"Daddy, I need to talk to you."

"I'm on my way out. Got some fences down in the upper pasture."

"It's important."

"All right, Rosie, what is it?" He looked down at her. So tall and fit, he must have been very handsome once.

Off-hand at first, he became intent as she went on.

"Dutch, you think. That rings a bell. Rosie, I'll take care of this. Don't wander too far around the grounds, please. And don't mention it to anyone. Off you go now, I have to telephone through to Sir Ronald."

Her father's grim demeanor unsettled her. He turned his back and lifted the receiver. She'd forgotten about the boxes in the boathouse.

Rosie found Jamie in the old greenhouse. She loved the old glass-and-iron structure, built in the traditional conservatory style—the sort of place where Cinderella's coach might have been conjured out of a pumpkin.

Jamie was busy transplanting seedlings. "Annuals, Rosie. They only go on for a year, then they die and you have to keep the seeds and start all over again next spring."

His voice had changed a little since she first met him, even though that hadn't been long ago. He didn't have the breathy tone of a child any more. It could be that new confidence had infused his personality, or perhaps he was just beginning to grow up. He'd turned fifteen, after all. She watched him for a while and smiled at his puckered face, mouth drawn back in an agony of concentration, with just the very tip of his tongue showing between his teeth. *Fifteen years old sometimes, five at others.*

She was surprised to see her father dip his head to enter. He almost never visited the place.

"Evans, I'd like a word, please."

"Yassir."

She watched the two of them, annoyingly out of earshot, as they discussed something; something serious, judging by the way her father's brow furrowed and Evans's lower jaw jutted out as he shook his head in the swaying manner of an old bull. Evans shuffled back, his thoughts far away. He sat on an old stool with a sigh.

"Well, I'm to have some help with the garden. Sir Geoffrey reckons he owes me a spot of help at my time of life."

"Oh, Evans, do you mind terribly?"

"Oh no, miss. It'll be a rare treat having a young'un to do the heavy work. You're about done with that, Jamie, time to get some elevenses. Why don't you two run off now, I got something to see to."

Rosie took Jamie by the arm and strolled towards the house. She felt unaccountably upset. *Does Daddy think Evans was past it?* He had all kinds of young men from the village doing the rough work already—those that weren't away in the army—and the grounds looked spectacular. She wouldn't ever want Evans hurt, not for anything. She wished everything would stop changing.

"Rosie, why would Evans mind having help?"

"Oh, I think he likes to do things his own way, Jamie, that's all. Nothing for us to worry about. Let's go and read your book."

She switched on the reading lamp in the library as the sun had moved around to the other side of the house by then. The dark panels sucked in whatever light still filtered through the windows.

"Jamie, I want you to look at this word very, very carefully. It says 'could.' Look at the shape it makes. Squeeze your eyes just a little, like this. Had a good look?"

Jamie nodded. "Could." He looked again. "Like could I have some chocolate?"

"Yes, and no you can't! Now, look on this page. Can you find that word again?"

Jamie squinted his eyes again and peered at the page. He poked a word. "There! Did I find it? Did I?"

"That's wonderful, Jamie, yes you did. Now then. You know how to spell out some words, and you know some words by their shape. Perhaps we can read all the way to the end. There might be some more words for you to learn that way, by how they look."

She watched Jamie squirm with pleasure at his success, relieved that her method was working. She'd written to a school friend who taught at a London kindergarten and asked about the best way to teach Jamie to read. Her friend had described the new way they were teaching reading—a mixture of recognition and sounding out, and sent some books. It made sense. Sounding out letters didn't work for many words, and she didn't want Jamie to get discouraged. So far, so good. He enjoyed these books, with text on every even page and a descriptive picture on the odd. She liked the way he looked at the picture to give him a clue when he was stuck. They'd finished the first reader before he went to Blexton, and now they had nearly finished the second. Not bad.

They continued to read and made it to the end by lunch, with only a few cues from Rosie.

"Rosie."

"Yes?"

"I've got to learn to write. Because I've got to write a book."

"A book! That's quite a big job, Jamie. I don't think I could write a book."

"Well, I've got to write down all the things Gran told me. All the big things about good and bad."

"I think she'd like that, Jamie. When you've finished the next reader, we can start working on making your letters."

"Good. You see, lots of people haven't had Grans to tell them what's right and what's wrong. They've got to be told. And I'm going to do it. I know Roy had Gran, but he wouldn't listen. People believe what's in books."

Tears pricked behind her eyes. "That's wonderful, Jamie. Your Gran would be very proud of you."

"I think she's in heaven because she was good. Do you think she can see from up there to down here? Will she see my book?"

"Yes, Jamie, I think she'll see your book."

"Hello, you two," Sir Geoffrey said. They hadn't heard him come in. Rosie saw a softness around his mouth and guessed he'd overheard.

"Hello, Daddy. Did you get through to Sir Ronald?"

"Yes, my dear, I did. I want to tell you both about what happened at Blexton."

"You mean the chocolates, Daddy?"

"Yes. There was something wrong with them. And when that boy—Alan, wasn't it?—stole them and ate them, they made him very ill."

Rosie looked at Jamie, who was frowning at her father. "Wrong with them?" she asked.

"That's a long story, Rosie, and I don't have all the answers. Anyway, I'm afraid Alan died. I thought you ought to know, Jamie."

Jamie found nothing to say. He looked at his hands, clenched on his lap, and shook his head. Sir Geoffrey stood for a moment, clicked his tongue, and left. He wasn't good at emotional moments. Grief had worn him down long ago.

"Jamie, are you very sad about Alan? I know you complained about him, but didn't you like him just a little?" Rosie asked. She hoped Jamie didn't think Daddy was cross. Any threat of a scene made him sound abrupt sometimes.

"No, not even a little. I'm glad he's dead. He was bad. And I hope he's not up in heaven bothering Gran."

"Jamie! That's a terrible thing to say!"

"Well, it's true. He was a very bad boy and made a lot of us unhappy. He hurt people a lot. And he stole my chocolates."

"Jamie, he was just a boy. Do you know that sometimes people behave badly because someone has been very bad to them? Alan didn't have a Gran like yours, I'm sure. Sometimes people have mothers and fathers who are very unkind to them. It can turn a boy bad. Didn't your Gran ever talk about forgiving people?"

"Don't know." He was sullen now.

"Do you know what forgive means?"

"No."

"It's when you say, 'That's all right, I understand. I'm not cross anymore.'"

"Gran said Roy's mum was no good. She said once that she would never forgive her and Roy's dad for what they did. That's the only time I heard her say that word. I think."

"It's important to forgive people. When we hold onto our bad feelings, it hurts us inside. It makes us less good. You've got to let it out. Think about the good things. Do you understand?" What a hypocrite, she certainly hadn't forgiven Robin. Just parroting the Vicar. It was the sort of thing you were supposed to say to those in your charge, wasn't it?

"Think I understand. I can't say it's all right to Alan, though, can I? Dead means he won't come back."

"No. Say it to yourself. Tonight, in bed, before you go to sleep. You'll feel better."

"All right. Suppose so." He didn't sound convinced.

Rosie gazed out of a side window so old its glass made the landscape look like some sort of water world. She felt a little shocked. Sweet Jamie had shown some very sour sentiments. And Gran hadn't been all sweetness and light, either. But who was?

"Let's walk over to the greenhouse."

She took his arm and felt him loosen up as he digested the idea of forgiveness and made it his own.

"Jamie, is there anyone who would want to hurt you?"

"Hurt me? Only Alan hurt me. And Roy used to hit me a lot."

"Roy?"

"My cousin Roy."

"Did he get bombed?"

"No, he went out." She could barely hear his mumble. He usually looked right at her, his guileless eyes fixed on hers; instead, he picked a dandelion clock and blew on it with strange intensity. His face was red. Even his ears were red. *He's lying. Why? So unlike him.*

"Jamie, I think you are keeping a secret. I'm not going to ask you what it is. But think about it. If you want to tell me, then just tell me."

14

George felt very happy to see Jamie, which Jamie could see by his smile. Most other people wouldn't know it for a smile, but Jamie always watched George's face and knew the changes. He probably loved the big windows in the breakfast room where the sun poked its fingers through the mist that usually came after a morning drizzle. He must remember to explain to George why the family always ate tea in the breakfast room. There wasn't a tea room. It was so nice to have George at the Manor. Nice of them to ask him. Nice of Stanton to take Jamie to fetch him.

He gently fed George some cake. It was an important job, taking care of George. He was sure George wouldn't like Sir Geoffrey and Lady Audrey to see him with a mucky face, so he'd better be very careful. He wondered what George thought of the white tablecloth and serviettes. And the pretty flowers in the middle. He turned to Lady Audrey.

"George really likes the cake, Lady Audrey. I know when he likes things."

"I can see you do, Jamie. You are so good at helping him."

Jamie grinned. Lady Audrey looked very nice. She wasn't as old as all that, really. She wore everything green today and had piled all her carroty hair up on top. He'd seen ladies in the mags Gran sometimes brought home that looked like that. She'd put jewels on her fingers too, all nice and sparkly. And pretty white shiny things in her ears. She always stood straight, like when Gran made him walk with books on his head, telling him off when he slouched. He pulled his shoulders back. He never worried about slouching anymore.

Lady Audrey wasn't so pretty as Rosie. Jamie looked across at Rosie and smiled, and she sent him a lovely smile back. White teeth, little ones, not nearly as big as Gran's yellowy ones. And hair that jumped around on her shoulders, always shiny. She must wash it a lot. He loved her freckles. She said once she hated them, but he thought them pretty. Rosie wouldn't be Rosie without her freckles. A grunt from George made him realize he'd stopped giving him the cake.

"Sorry, George, I was thinking. Did you know Alan had died, George?"

George grunted, "Gr'ay, gr'ay, gr'ay . . ."

"I don't know what that means, George. They don't know who did it."

"Gr'ay, gr'ay, gr'ay, mmm . . ." George tried again, his face all squished up now.

After tea, Jamie read the new Peter and Jane book to George and got all the way through on his own. He'd been practicing. It would soon be time to take poor George back to Blexton.

* * *

Rosie got out of the car and watched as Jamie took George's chair out of the boot. He finally got it unfolded with a good deal of pulling and pushing. He told Stanton he could manage on his own, thank you very much. Rosie suggested that Jamie could perhaps go in and get someone to help with George. Jamie hung back as he studied the ground and kicked at the gravel. His body closed up a little and she understood he was afraid. Afraid of being abandoned. He didn't want to enter that place. Rosie went herself and found Graham, who lifted George out of the car and into his chair, none too gently.

George twisted and grunted. *Is he having some sort of fit?* He was very agitated.

"Gr'ay, gr'ay mmm, gr'ay mmm," she heard again. *Trying to say Graham?* Why was he so upset?

"Rosie, this is Graham," said Jamie.

"Yes, I saw him sometimes when I came to visit you," said Rosie. "Good afternoon, Graham."

"Afternoon, miss. Jamie. Hope he's not talking too much for you, miss. He talks his head off, does Jamie." He looked hard at Jamie, who went red again.

"Not at all. We like him very much," said Rosie, annoyed and puzzled by his tone. Jamie didn't answer, just looked at George.

"Well, we must be going," said Rosie.

"Goodbye, George," said Jamie. "It was very nice to see you. Would you like to come back soon?" George more or less nodded and rumbled.

"Goodbye, George, I'm so glad you could come. We'll see you soon, I hope," said Rosie. Clearly exhausted now, he didn't respond. They watched Graham wheel him in through the door. George squealed suddenly. She could have sworn she saw Graham pinch his arm. Perhaps just keeping his arm from knocking against the doorjamb?

"Jamie, did Graham just hurt George?"

"Pinched him. He does that sometimes. Used to do it to me when I was a kid."

"That's terrible! Wait, what do you mean, when you were a kid? You weren't in there that long ago!"

"No, I mean when I was there. No." He was red again. Lying again. *What in the world was going on?* She must have another word with Daddy.

They drove back in silence. They'd just passed through New Milton when the sirens started howling. Almost right away, they heard an appalling crash, followed by the roar of rushing air. They both turned to see what was going on down the road, craning their necks. Jamie knelt on the car seat. All they could see at first was black smoke before flames curled up above the trees. The car sped up and turned off the main road, hurtling through a network of lanes. Jamie and Rosie sat holding onto each other in the back seat, shaking and crying. Their driver focused on the road ahead, stiff and silent until they got back to the Manor.

"You are both safe now," Stanton said. "No need to fret. I've been in the army, you know, fought in the last war. That's nothing compared to what I've seen. Both of you go inside now and have a nice cup of tea. I think I'll visit the kitchen and get one myself."

This was a long speech for Stanton. Rosie noticed his hands shook a little as they uncurled from the wheel. She gave Jamie a squeeze. "Come on."

The two of them sat side-by-side hugging their knees on the sofa in the morning room. Betty bustled in.

"Why, Miss Rosie, whatever's the matter?"

"A bomb, Betty, just after we left the village."

"Oh, dear, I thought we'd be safe here. Oh dear, oh dear." Her odious enjoyment of the drama enraged Rosie. She was about to send her on her way when, surprisingly, Stanton materialized, poked up the fire and tersely instructed Betty to bring hot sweet cocoa to help with the shock. Betty rubbed the back of Jamie's neck. "There, there," she said as she caressed him. Rosie shot her a venomous look. The girl withdrew her hand as if stung and left without another word. Jamie hadn't moved.

They remained there, dozing on and off, until Sir Geoffrey came in hours later, sooty and exhausted. He flopped down in the chair nearest the fire and leaned back, closing his eyes and rubbing his forehead as if to dispel a headache. He'd lost weight recently. With his height, he looked somewhat emaciated.

"Were you there, Daddy?" Rosie asked.

"Yes, my darling, I was. Twenty-four people gone, a cottage—you know the one with the wonderful window boxes—and four shops. In an instant. Bugger! Oh, excuse me, Rosie."

"That's all right, Daddy. It must have been terrible for you."

"Well, a good deal worse for them. Quite a few hurt, too. First time we've been hit that badly down this way."

"I thought we were safe here," said Jamie in a quavering voice.

"That's how it is in a war, Jamie," said Sir Geoffrey. "You've got to put your fear behind you and soldier on. That's the only way to get through it all. So, off to bed, both of you."

Stanton glided in, snifter and brandy bottle on the usual silver tray. "You should be in bed, too, Stanton. But I must say I could do with a brandy."

"As you say, sir. Will that be all?"

"Yes, thank you, Stanton."

"We didn't see any fire and smoke, just a big noise. Was it a bomb? Really?" asked Jamie. "No mistake?"

"It was, Jamie. But if you didn't see it, you have nothing to forget. Put it out of your mind now. Just soldier on, as I said."

"Yes, sir."

"You make it sound easy, Daddy, soldiering on," said Rosie.

"Life is never easy, war or no war. Just keep on going. Keep on going. All we can do."

"Gran soldiered on, you know. She worked ever so hard and wasn't very happy. Do you think it was over in an instant for her?"

"Yes, Jamie, I'm quite sure it was."

15

Lady Audrey and Jamie waited for Rosie in the hallway. They planned a trip to the seaside. Audrey felt a little guilty using scarce petrol for such an outing, but Geoffrey had asked her to see how the new restrictions on beach access were working out, so she supposed it was fair enough. She glanced at Jamie, who was so excited he couldn't stand still. He grinned, shifting from one foot to the other, and curling and uncurling his fingers. Giving Jamie a treat was a treat in itself. He was so unspoiled and hadn't yet learned to expect anything nice from anyone.

If only Rosie were so easily pleased. An underlying streak of discontent seemed to have doused any spark the girl used to have. While Rosie's life wasn't much fun these days, no one else's was, either. *Young people could be so selfish.* Audrey squelched her small flare of annoyance.

Audrey looked up as she heard Rosie's tread on the stairs. She'd put on those slacks again. Audrey couldn't get used to girls wearing slacks. All right for land girls, but people took notice of whatever the McInnises did, and they had certain standards to uphold. The child couldn't see it, though. She made a habit of rejecting her parents' ideas. To be honest, Audrey had behaved the same way at her age. In the twenties, for example, when skirts went above the knees her mother had been scandalized. But slacks?

"Oh, is that what you're wearing out?" She tried to keep her voice neutral, but it didn't come out right.

"Oh, *Mummy*. We're only going for a picnic. Everyone's wearing them!" Rosie frowned, her day's beginning pricked by irritation.

"Yes, dear, but we always seem to run into people we know. People talk." Audrey knew she sounded imperious, but she couldn't help herself. Like her mother before her.

"You're *so* old fashioned." Rosie glowered at her.

Jamie had been looking from one to the other, clearly puzzled. "Why are you both so cross? You look pretty today, Rosie. And Lady Audrey, you look pretty too. But you look a different pretty. Are you supposed to look more the same?"

"How do we look different pretty, Jamie?" Rosie asked, trying to hide an unwilling smile.

"Well, Lady Audrey looks like she spent a long time getting ready. I've seen Gran put her hair up and it took ages. And it wasn't anything like so nice as that when she got finished."

"Don't I look as if I spent a lot of time getting ready?" Rosie asked.

"Well, you look like you made it more easy. You don't bother with a lot of things. Your hair is shiny on its own. You don't have lots of things."

"Things?" Rosie asked.

"Yes, you know. Sparkly things. Ladies look nice with sparkly things, but they don't really need them for pretty. If they are clean and smell nice. If they keep tidy. If they act sweet and kind. You can look at them and see they are pretty ladies. You are both pretty ladies. Just different sorts of pretty ladies. Everybody's different, remember, Rosie? That's a good thing. Mostly."

Jamie puffed a bit after his long speech, and the women laughed as their tiff evaporated.

"You're wiser than both of us, Jamie," said Lady Audrey. "Well, off we go!"

Rosie drove and they let Jamie sit in the front seat next to her. Audrey watched them chat—so comfortable together—as they made their way to Highcliffe. The beach there was sandy, unlike at Barton, which had a stony shoreline that could turn your ankles. And, too, it nestled in a small bay, sheltered by cliffs—perhaps the biggest benefit of Highcliffe's beach from Audrey's point of view, for April breezes were apt to be chilly. As the clouds parted and rejoined, the intermittent sunshine and green-budded trees struck Audrey as almost offensively at odds with the brutality and agony across the water. She found spring and its promise an uplifting time of the year, yet a sliver of sorrow always seemed to lie in wait to puncture her bubble. She had no loved ones at the front, but she couldn't shake off the fear that the front might soon be at their doorstep.

Rosie and Jamie talked about what they might find at the beach.

"You know we can't swim today, Jamie, it's too cold. We have to wait for summer," said Rosie.

"Yes, even in summer, the sea is cold. I put my feet in it once. It made me shiver."

"It's lovely in the hot weather, though," said Rosie. "We'll go again when it gets hot."

"Goody, I love the sea. It's so big and it's like glass that moves."

"We'll find some shells, Jamie, and you can take them home. And I like sea glass."

"The sea has glass?"

"It's glass that fell in the sea, perhaps from a ship, and the water flows across it again and again it until it's all smooth and pretty. No sharp edges left," Rosie explained.

"Ooh, I'd like to find some of that."

Rosie was so good with him and had been really quite unselfish these days.

Audrey could see how Jamie had changed already, how being with decent people had brought him out. His vocabulary had expanded, too, and he'd picked up better grammar. Evans said Jamie was good with plants. And Rosie had taught him to read. Those little successes were good for him, and the treats and knowing they liked him. She wasn't going to let him go back to that place. Geoffrey must fight for him.

Geoffrey should take some time away from all these other concerns and think of his family for a change. Not quite reasonable, considering the situation, but she found her resentment building anyway. Audrey had always been used to plenty of attention. Even Rosie seemed preoccupied these days, and had become very unsympathetic to her migraines, which was so unfair; she couldn't help her headaches. All her little local duties bored her to tears, and the so-called civic dignitaries she had to put up with were unbearably pompous, not to mention their simpering wives. Reading had always been her joy, but she was fed up with being alone so much. She didn't seem to come first with anyone.

Such a pity Rosie had no siblings. Audrey hadn't wanted more children, not after Fiona. God, just thinking the name still cut her. She hadn't meant to have Rosie, it had just happened after a bit too much wine one night. Several nights, actually. She'd left Rosie mostly to her old nanny in the early years, didn't want to risk getting too close. Then it was too late. They were courteous, but not close. Geoffrey had played with Rosie every day, though, had given her the cuddles and kisses her mother couldn't. She regretted it now. She'd never managed to close that distance between them, however smoothly they seemed to carry on. She'd let herself miss the best years.

Jamie, now, he was as good for Rosie as she was good for him. He was a good addition to the household and really no trouble.

* * *

The sea lay quiet today, voicing only a whisper or two as it curled into the shoreline. The sun even presented itself from time to time before sidling back behind the clouds. Audrey had brought a folding chair with her—and had started down the steep trail with it until Jamie insisted on carrying it for her. She'd watched his valiant struggle to balance himself and his load, but both Rosie and she knew better than to offer help. Funny, he couldn't have been taught how to be a gentleman in the East End of all places. He watched Geoffrey all the time, though, so he'd probably picked up the "ladies first" rule from him.

She closed her eyes and huddled into her blanket a little deeper. The smell of rotting seaweed was pungent after the weekend storm had marooned great swathes of it well above the usual high tide mark. She didn't mind, for it carried the memories of carefree childhood and cool waves lapping at hot skin. She and Geoffrey had come here at night once, just before their wedding. She wallowed in her memories and allowed a smile to curve her lips. Deliciously shameful. Sand could be most inconvenient. She shivered and hugged herself, not to ward off the chill, but to hold onto a pleasurable tremor.

She jumped as Jamie called out behind her, "Lady Audrey, look! Look what I've got!"

He had a handful of sea glass. She admired pale green, blue, and a curious citrus shade.

"Look at the sky through it, Jamie, you can see the colors better." She held a piece up and turned it this way and that. "You have a lovely collection. What will you do with it?"

"Oh, I'm going to keep it in my room and look at it every day. It's very special."

"Shall I keep it for you in my pocket? Then you can go and look for more things."

Jamie ran back to Rosie, who was poking a stick around in the rocks near an inlet at the edge of the bay. He was clumsy, not well coordinated. Part of whatever damaged him, no doubt. Perhaps his mother had been a drinker. That could have been Rosie if Geoffrey and Dr. Gibson hadn't stepped in. They said it could do bad things to babies. He was definitely improving, though. Good food, exercise, keeping his mind busy. The dear boy tugged at her heart and he admired her so much. Such a genuine person. He must never go back to that place.

* * *

Back at the Manor, Jamie looked tired, but seemed too wound up to settle down.

"Let's go for a walk, Rosie. Please?"

"Oh, Jamie, I'm so tired. I'm not used to all that fresh air." *Let me be.*

"You're in air all the time, aren't you? When we're in the garden, that's the fresh kind, isn't it?"

"Yes, Jamie, all right, all right. Just a short one."

As much as she liked him, he could be a nuisance with his nagging sometimes. Typical little brother, or so she'd heard from her friends. She wanted to soak in a hot bath before changing for dinner. Not that she was hungry, they'd had a good picnic tea down on the beach, but she needed to relax. Well, she hadn't been to the pond for a few weeks. It wasn't far, just beyond the rose garden.

"All right, let's go and look at the pond. It's got goldfish. At least I think they're still there."

"What's a pond?"

"Like the lake, only much smaller. People keep goldfish in them. They're pretty. Come on."

"Why do you think they might not be there anymore? Fishes can't walk. Or are they special because they're gold?"

Stop asking so many questions! Be nice, he's only a boy. "No, sometimes the water gets too cold in winter and they die."

"That's sad. Poor fishes."

Rosie didn't answer. She'd had a pleasant day, but felt crotchety anyway. That time of the month. Since she wasn't about to explain that particular concept to Jamie, she'd just have to put a good face on it.

They stood at the edge of the pond. The water ran clear and she could just see the outline of the old carp, Archie. He'd been living with the goldfish for years and must be at least a foot long by the looks of it.

"Look, look, a really big one!" Jamie cried out. The carp flicked away.

"Ssh, Jamie, they can hear you and they get scared. His name is Archie. If you keep quite still and quiet, he'll come back. When he gets used to people again, he might let us tickle his back."

Jamie stood still and silent, his arms clamped to his side as he waited. The fish made a languid reappearance and swam towards the surface.

"Hello, Archie," Jamie whispered.

"He's expecting some crumbs, but I forgot to bring any," said Rosie.

"Can we bring him some tomorrow?"

"Yes, why not. Come on, let's go. I want a quick bath before dinner."

"All right."

"There's another pond, a bigger one, way down near the woods. We'll go there tomorrow. It's got big stepping stones all across it. You've got to pay attention, though. It's really mucky if you fall in."

"Is it fun?"

"Oh yes, when I was little, my cousin Julian and I used to go there all the time. Nanny used to get really cross when we fell in." *And we always made sure we did!*

"Who's Nanny?

"The lady who used to take care of me."

"Where was your mum?"

"Here. But in our sort of family, mothers are very busy. They have to go out a lot."

"I see." But he clearly didn't.

She hadn't thought of Julian for years. His mother had left his father and taken Julian with her. Mummy didn't let them come after that because Julian's father was her favorite brother. That wasn't Julian's fault, though. So unfair. It's not as if Julian's father ever bothered to visit. She should try to track him down. He'd been lots of fun in those days.

* * *

She'd saved Jamie from a complete dunking, but one foot had gone smack into the mud. His feet were quite big compared with the rest of him, so she'd asked her father if he had an old pair of shoes to spare. They were only a little on the big side; he'd found Jamie some socks, too. She walked just behind Jamie as they made their way to the vegetable garden and saw that his heels slipped out of the shoes with each step. He might get blisters. She'd better put plasters on his heels.

Evans needed help with the planting because two of his usual boys had just joined up. He had trays of seedlings ready for the beds, which he'd already sectioned with string and markers.

"Now, Jamie, yer goin' to start with proper planting today."

Jamie beamed. "Thank you."

He showed them both how to dig the holes, put a little *nurrishment* in the bottom, then ease the fragile plants in, and tamp the earth down around them. Rosie wondered what his new helper was doing. He never seemed to be around.

"You're a dab hand, Jamie," he said.

"Gran used to like gardening. We hadn't got one, but her

father used to have a nice house. She said they had a lovely garden in the back."

"Where's your Gran, Jamie?"

"She was *bl*-itzed."

"Were you there lad?"

"Well . . . " He blushed and hung his head.

"You're hiding something, Jamie," said Rosie. "You were acting funny when we took George back to Blexton. Stop telling fibs and spill the beans. I'm not going to let you have any tea until you've told."

"I haven't got any beans. Why are you talking about beans?"

Rosie took a deep breath. "It's something we say when we want a person to tell. Now, tell!"

"I promised I wouldn't. But maybe I should tell." And the long dormant story bubbled out as he told them about the fight and all the way through to how he'd used the key to go out and wait for Roy.

Aghast, Rosie and Evans stood and looked at each other.

"She was lying there covered in blood, Jamie? And not moving at all?" asked Rosie.

"Well, yes, but . . ." He stopped talking, clamped his lips, and hung his head.

"Where was your cousin? Roy."

"Dunno."

"What is it, Jamie?"

"I promised not to tell that story, you know. I haven't said it to anyone before. I promised. He'll be so angry. I don't know what he'll do. He'll hurt me."

"Who, Jamie?"

"Mustn't tell."

"Jamie, someone tried to hurt you with the chocolates. You must tell. *Jamie!* Where is Roy?"

"He's in that place. I'm supposed to call him Graham now."

"Stay here with Evans. You're not to go anywhere. I've got to talk to Daddy." *God, he's unbelievably gullible!*

Rosie burst into her father's study, ignoring his inflamed face. He and Sir Ronald were probably discussing important secrets again.

"Rosie, what can you be thinking?"

"Sorry, Daddy, Sir Ronald. I've got to tell you something very serious. I think I know who tried to poison Jamie."

Geoffrey's annoyance soon changed to concern as she related what she had just heard.

"Bring Jamie here at once," he said. "Ronnie, you can use this telephone."

Jamie and Rosie came in a few minutes later. Jamie's face was tense and his eyes fixed on his shoes.

"Jamie, we need to talk to you about Roy," said Sir Geoffrey.

"A promise is a promise. I can't break my promise and tell."

"Some promises are not ours to keep. Because sometimes people make us promise to hide something bad so that they won't get into trouble. This is something that should be told. Do you see?"

"Dunno."

"Jamie, Sir Ronald and I must hear the whole story. Right from the beginning."

Jamie huffed, and started all over again.

"Your cousin Roy shouldn't have locked you and your grandmother in when he saw the Germans were just about carpeting the place. We need to talk to him about it," said Sir Ronald.

"Not carpets. Bombs."

"Never mind. We'll never let him hurt you, you know." The boy looked unconvinced.

The phone rang. "For you, Ronnie."

Ronnie stood with his back to them as he listened and offered no more than monosyllabic grunts, until he barked out, "Murder and attempted murder. Yes, the chocolates. Go and get him. Now." He turned to face them.

"Well, Geoffrey. Remember I mentioned Roy Beck's got form? Lot of West End jobs. A fence in Lymington we raided last month ended up with some of it. That's why they've got the fliers down here. When I get back to my office I'll have my staff track down the air raid wardens in Southwark. Perhaps someone saw something. Perhaps there's still enough left to see if there are any knife marks on the ribs . . . "

"We can discuss that later, Ronnie," Geoffrey broke in, his eyes shifting anxiously to the boy's slumped figure.

"Oh, yes, quite. I'll be off then."

"Rosie, I want you and Jamie to stay in the house today. Off you go."

Sir Geoffrey leaned back in his chair and took a deep breath, puffing it out bit by bit so it blew the hair off his face. He was long overdue for a cut, but he really didn't give a tinker's cuss. Rosie spent her days aimlessly hanging around when she wasn't with Jamie, rotting her life away. Jamie had more misery coming his way. God knows where Audrey had got to. He was just bloody tired. He felt old sorrow creeping over him, familiar and unwelcome.

16

D. I. Falway's blood was up, and so was his driver's. The man screeched around the blind corners of the narrow lanes, oblivious to the possibility of another car coming the other way. Old trees and tall hedges fled by in ribbons of earthy colors. Falway didn't wait for the car to come to a full stop before dashing into the reception area.

"Where's Graham, the attendant?" Two constables panted behind him.

"He didn't come in today. Most irregular," she said, pursing her lips like a corpulent hamster.

"Does he have a room here?"

"Yes, of course." Her eyes flickered over to the constables and back.

"Take me there now."

"I'm not allowed to leave my desk."

Self-righteous cow. "I'm a policeman, madam, I don't give a tuppenny toss what you're not allowed to do."

Her expression didn't change as she walked around her desk and strolled to the stairs.

"Get a move on, woman, it's urgent."

She shifted her heft a little faster.

"Oh, for God's sake, just tell me where."

"Third floor, fourth door on the right."

Falway and the two constables raced up the stairs, out of breath as they burst into Graham's room. Empty, as though no one had ever lived in it. Not so much as a hollow in the eiderdown or pillows, and no personal items left out on any surface.

"All right, you two, do a thorough search. I'm going back down to look for the woman who runs the place."

Falway got back down to the hall, out of breath and patience.

"Take me to the director's office. Quickly!" Her face hadn't lost the hamster look.

They came across Mrs. Clancy in the corridor and the receptionist turned on her heel and sauntered away.

"I'm D. I. Falway. I need to find Graham. We'd better step into your office."

She closed the door and turned to face him, her face set in a sullen reproof. "What is it, Inspector?"

"He's wanted by the police, and we need to find him right away. We believe he was behind the poisoning."

"I simply cannot imagine that he would do a thing like that!"

"It's a long story. We've been up to his room, and he's not there. Do you know where we might find him?"

She frowned a little, patting her wiry little curls before making her way over to the fireplace. Falway breathed through his teeth, trying to rein in his irritation. She lowered herself into a diminutive pink armchair. He cleared his throat in an effort to prompt her as he paced around this horrible cozy den that looked almost like his grandmother's parlor. He passed several ghastly pictures of pretty kitties and the like.

"Well, he does go into town sometimes, but he was supposed to be working today. It's been very difficult because we had to call in one of our other attendants, Bernhardt Visser, and he'd gone out for a long walk. You can't leave these patients alone for a minute, you know."

The poisoning business seemed to bother her less than the inconvenience she'd been caused.

"Any ideas where to start?"

She sighed the sigh of a martyr, put upon by all and sundry.

"Well, he's not one for walks, not like Bernhardt. I think he likes pubs, maybe the Rose and Crown in Barton. I gave him a lift there a couple of weeks ago. But they'd be closed at this time of day. I know he went to Christchurch once, I remember him asking me about the bus. Sorry I can't be more help." She didn't sound sorry, more as if she expected Falway to be sorry for stirring things up.

"We'll have to search the place—start with the house, then move onto the grounds. I'd better call in more help." Surely that bloody villain couldn't have known he'd been rumbled.

"If you must. Try not to upset the patients, they are very difficult to handle if they become agitated."

Her office door burst open. An old man, his craggy face ashen, staggered in and collapsed into a chair that looked too dainty to withstand such a thud. His chest heaved as he tried to bring words to fruition, not quite succeeding.

"Clive, whatever is it? Are you ill?" asked Mrs. Clancy as she rushed to his side.

"Garden shed, near the azalea bed." He started to pant again, his horny hands alternately clutching the chair and his heart.

"Out with it man!" Falway said.

"Dead. Knife in 'is neck. One o' them fellers what works with the inmates."

"Come with me, Mrs. Clancy," Falway said as he made for the door. "Did you touch anything?" he asked Clive over his shoulder.

"Not bloody likely," said Clive, still gasping.

They looked down at Graham's corpse, contorted and petrified by the onslaught, his hands clawing at something long gone. The knife's long thin blade had been thrust between the vertebrae into the side of his neck. A tin of rat poison sat on his chest, its skull and crossbones front and center.

"It's Graham," said Mrs. Clancy, pale and shaky, hand clutched over her mouth before she went back outside. He heard her retching, which did nothing for the state of his own stomach.

Falway crouched by the body, fighting down his own bile. He hadn't seen that many dead bodies and it didn't get better with time like his colleagues said it would. Terrible smell, like the cottage outhouses down by the docks. Shit, piss, and mildew. *Don't think about outhouses now, for God's sake.* He pulled out his handkerchief and clapped it over his mouth.

Falway was no expert, but it looked like a professional job; it couldn't be easy to get the knife in just the right place, especially in this half-light. And the killer knew about the poison. Or had worked it out. He'd left a message. The face looked lopsided, one cheek full and the other caved in. He hadn't noticed it before because of the death grimace. Something poked out of the mouth. Better leave it to the doctor. Cheek pads? He peered at the hair. Dark roots. *No wonder his cousin hadn't recognized him.* He held his breath and gloved his hand with the handkerchief before picking up the rat poison tin between his thumb and middle finger. He doubted there'd be any prints, but you couldn't assume anything. He stood and held the tin up to the meager light. Nothing obvious. He'd wait until the doctor got here before he searched the man's clothing.

Falway walked around the shed, not finding anything he wouldn't expect to. Neat, all the tools hanging or stacked in a box. Shelf full of tins of God-knows-what that gardener uses to keep pests at bay. Only one space with a ring in the dust the size of the rat poison tin he'd found on the corpse. No other dangerous poisons, not that he could tell; anyway, they'd all have to be checked.

They'd need to know roughly when the man died. Perhaps he was killed last night. In total darkness, by torchlight? *Not likely.*

"Mrs. Clancy!" he called.

"Yes, Inspector," she replied in a tremulous voice.

"Please get my constables down from Graham's room. Tell one of them to ring Sir Roland and tell him we found the subject, deceased. Then they're to come here and stand watch until the body is removed."

"Very well."

Wait a minute, hardly any blood. He wasn't killed here. For God's sake, any schoolboy who went to the pictures would have thought of that. Face it; he didn't have much of a cool head when put to the test. He took in a deep breath, forgetting why that wouldn't be a good idea. He couldn't hold it down, gagging and retching in a corner, trying his best to muffle it. He'd say the woman did it. Poor old girl must have been only too glad to get back indoors.

He peered around the shed again. No, not much blood, so he must have been killed somewhere else. They'd have to search the grounds. Maybe he and his killer had had a rendezvous somewhere and it had all gone wrong. Or maybe it was planned. What the devil was going on?

* * *

Next morning, D.I. Falway stood in the Manor's library waiting for Jamie to be sent in. He admired the stately room with its old leather-bound books and high smoky windows. Such deep armchairs that a man would have to be quite agile to haul himself out of one, and the desk, huge and burled and dark, polished a thousand times against the knocks of daily use. The room wouldn't get much sunlight, and the fire laid in its cavernous hearth had not yet been lit. He shivered as he breathed in the musky odor of old paper and heirlooms. Peaceful, yet in some way oppressive.

The butler opened the door with practiced quiet. "Master Jamie, sir."

The boy looked shifty. "Good morning, Jamie. Do you remember me? I'm Detective Inspector Falway. I need to talk to you about your cousin Roy."

The boy's face closed up. He looked better than he had in Blexton, but his eyes had the kind of wary watchful look of one who is vigilant, yet bemused. Rather like a precocious child at a funeral.

"Jamie, when did you know that Graham was Roy?"

"I'm really, really bored of it. And it upsets me. I hate thinking about Roy and Gran and bombs." He looked at Falway, who raised his eyebrows. Jamie sighed, produced an annoyed adolescent shrug, and told his story. All of it, as far as Falway could tell, it certainly took long enough.

Interesting bit about his cousin's interest in Bernhardt's goings on. So where did that foreigner fit into all this? He was the one who had been out for a long walk when Mrs. Clancy was looking for him. He'd better call Sir Ronald. If the fellow were up to no good, they'd better not tip him off.

"Jamie, I have a photograph I'd like you to look at."

The photo was of Roy, taken on the doctor's table. They'd cut his hair almost to the roots and removed his moustache and cheek pads. A sheet covered him to his shoulders.

"That's Roy. Why's he having his picture taken when he's asleep?"

So they hadn't told him. Well, it wasn't up to him to break the news.

"All right, Jamie, that will do for now. You've been very helpful. Thank you."

"Don't mention it." Jamie said, almost prissy as he turned to leave. He turned at the door and said, "If anyone needs me, I'll be in my room."

So, highfaluting ways were rubbing off on him. Well, good luck to him, poor little fellow. He deserved whatever good things came his way.

17

Geoffrey caught up with them on their way to the pond. He'd like to get to know Jamie better. The boy rather got under one's skin. You found you cared for him a great deal before knowing quite how or when it happened.

"Where are you two off to?"

"The pond, Daddy. Jamie loves it."

"I nearly fell in last time and got mucky."

"I know, I lent you my shoes, remember? Rosie and her cousin fell in plenty of times." Geoffrey laughed as he thought of Nanny's outraged admonitions as she stripped off their clothes and plopped them into the bath.

"I like trying to get across. It's like getting across the day."

"What do you mean?" Geoffrey asked.

"Well, I get up and try to keep my feet on the stones. If I fall off, I might get back into the muck, like being back in that Blexton place."

"You won't go back there if I can help it, Jamie," Geoffrey said, taken aback. That was quite an abstract idea for Jamie. Amazing how quickly he'd blossomed here. He hadn't spent much time with the boy, but come to think of it he did sound different now, and Rosie said he was reading quite well. It didn't do to lock people away, lock up their minds. Couldn't grow. Like prep school, ghastly place. Perhaps he should get the boy a tutor. There must be plenty of wounded officers who'd like the job. Be a good role model, too.

"Evans tells me you're a big help to him, Jamie."

"Oh, I love it with Evans. He's been teaching me about flowers and planting seeds and everything. I want to be a gardener like him one day."

"And so you shall, Jamie, so you shall. Here at the Manor."

"Really? *Really* really?"

"Yes, Jamie, I mean it."

"Daddy, you are sweet," said Rosie. "Jamie could be assistant gardener and Evans can teach him everything."

"I'll go and tell Evans right now," said Geoffrey. "Know where he is by any chance?"

"Kitchen garden, I think," said Rosie.

He hadn't been sure how Evans would receive his proposition, but the man had been pleased as Punch. So, young Jamie had captivated the old man, too. He said Jamie understood things about plants you wouldn't expect. Do the boy a world of good in his considered opinion. And yes, he'd watch out for intruders and keep a close eye on the youngsters. The new man looked like a gardener right enough, but didn't want to have much to do with gardening.

Audrey might question the boy being treated as a gardener when he was, *de facto*, one of the family. But when all was said and done, he himself was little more than a farmer. He'd wanted more, but there it was, that's how families like theirs did things. You had to face it, the boy had talents, but he had limitations. Everyone should have the chance to be good at something. Everyone should do his best. Rosie included. It was time for her to get on with doing something useful and not worry too much about marriage and breeding at her age. Plenty of time for all that.

And Audrey. Wouldn't she be happier if she had something to feel impassioned about, or wasn't she capable of that? He treated her with kid gloves, always mindful of her grief. *Shouldn't she be over it by now? Have I enabled her frailty, treating her so gently?* It all got so tiresome. He often found himself wishing for a heartier companion, then immediately feeling guilty and cruel, which led to him treating her with more tenderness than ever. Maybe he should talk to Reggie. Should have talked to Reggie years ago. Come to think of it, Audrey hadn't mentioned her for some time. Run off her feet at that hospital, of course. He'd heard they'd shipped a few casualties over from Southampton. The war chipped away at all of them in one way or another.

* * *

Geoffrey and Audrey sat across from one another in front of the library fireplace. The fire licked gently at the logs as it took the chill off the room. He'd turned the lamps so low that the books lining the walls effaced themselves into the gloom. Geoffrey studied Audrey's face as she gazed into the flames. Still beautiful, she made his breath catch when her eyes caught his with the almost imperceptible glint that signaled she felt ready for lovemaking. She was tender and receptive, but the fireworks had faded long ago. She looked a little too thin; she didn't eat much these days. Well, since Fiona's death, really. Twenty years ago. He avoided thinking of her name as often as he could, but couldn't always manage it.

Most children got over influenza, but not the delicate one-year-old Fiona. As he watched his child fade away, he faded with her, and never fully revived. Then Audrey came down with it, and he thought he would lose her too, as grief and sickness ravaged her. She'd pulled back, but not entirely. The familiar ache he'd suppressed long before flared up again, kindled by Jamie. It was high time they came back, came back all the way.

Jamie managed to endear himself to everyone he came across. Almost everyone. Not that devil of a farmer, nor his cousin Roy. The thought of a gentle soul like Jamie being put through such trials made him seethe. He would have liked Roy Beck to hang for his viciousness. Jamie was one of the innocents. He had to be protected from a world all too ready to chew him up and spit him out. He hadn't been able to save Fiona, but he'd certainly fight to save Jamie.

Jamie wasn't quite the son he'd wished for, but he was a fine soul. And he liked the idea of a brother for Rosie.

"Audrey. I've been thinking."

"What about, dear?"

"Jamie doesn't have anyone at all except us. I think we should do something about it, legally, I mean. I'd like to talk to Chatterton about making him our ward. Or even adopting him."

"I think that's a wonderful idea, Geoffrey. I've been so worried about him." Audrey's hand fluttered to her breast. Jamie's plight must have been weighing on her, too.

"Me too. You know, we've got to explain a few things to him."

"Like what?"

"Well, he's got to know that the chocolates were for him and that the other chap died by mistake. That they think Roy killed his grandmother and set fire to the flat."

"I thought he knew."

"I think he suspects now that his grandmother was already dead when the house burned, but I never spelled it out. There's no absolute proof, of course, but Ronnie tells me there were signs the flat was set on fire, but it was bombed soon after some firemen discovered the body. They found that green toy of Jamie's too and saved it, just in case. It's wonderful how people do these small kindnesses, even when they're afraid for their lives. Anyway, no one had time to do anything about it that night. That was the worst attack on London so far. Hard to imagine there weren't more killed and injured. So many historic buildings gone."

"Yes, I suppose we're relatively lucky down here."

"And he doesn't know his cousin is dead."

"Oh God, I'd forgotten that. Why don't we have Stanton send him into us now, Geoffrey? It may as well be now. And I think it's best if Rosie comes too." She took a deep breath, steeling herself for Jamie's sorrow.

Geoffrey lay back and closed his eyes, vaguely hearing Audrey speaking to Stanton while he tried to think how best to soften the dreadful truth for Jamie. Good news first, of course.

* * *

"Daddy? Stanton said you wanted us."

He sat up with a start. "Oh, yes, Rosie, we have to tell Jamie a few things. But first, Jamie, we would like you to know that we want to talk to our solicitor about you coming to live with us for always. You'd be like our son. Would that be all right with you?"

"Oh! Yes, yes, Sir Geoffrey!" Jamie's smile almost seemed to split his face, and he shuffle-hopped from one foot to the other, not quite knowing what to do with his delight.

"Daddy, Mummy, that's wonderful! Thank you so much." Rosie hugged them in turn with a show of ebullience not seen since she got engaged. "Jamie, you'll be like my brother. I've always wanted a brother!" And she hugged him too.

Geoffrey flushed and he noticed Audrey's eyes were brimming, but with happy tears for a change.

"Now, Jamie, we have some serious things to tell you too. Not quite such nice things, I'm afraid."

His mouth quavered. "I can't stay after all?"

"Yes, of course you can, I just said so. Other things. Jamie, do you understand that your grandmother was already dead before the house was bombed? *Take it slowly.*

"Yes, I've been thinking. When you said that about the blood when I told the story. I never thought. Poor Gran. I might have helped her."

"No, I don't think you could. She died at once. I'm afraid we think Roy hurt her.

"No!" A cry from a chasm of sorrow. "No, no, no!"

Keep your voice level. Gentle. Don't look at Audrey. "He was very angry with her, wasn't he?"

"Yes. She said she'd have to turn him in. He took stuff from people's houses. And he put it in the shed of one of her ladies," Jamie said, the words puffing out of him as his fists opened and clenched. "Of course, it was only us in the house. I should have known."

"He probably did it in a fit of anger, probably didn't really mean to," Geoffrey said, in a softer voice.

"He is bad, bad, bad. Gran said he was no good."

"And we think he wanted to do away with you too, Jamie, with poisoned chocolates. I'm sorry."

"But why? 'Cos I'm slow?"

"No, because he was afraid you'd tell people your story and they'd know what happened."

"He said people would say I was mad if I told the story. I was scared of staying in that place forever. I didn't understand about anything, even Gran being killed not asleep, because I'm slow. I am stupid." Jamie's cry of despair sent him to his knees where Rosie joined him and wrapped her arms around him, resting her cheek on his head.

"You are not stupid, Jamie, you just think the best of everyone, and not everyone is good, you have to understand that. Get up, old chap!" It came out rougher than he intended. Emotional scenes stretched his boundaries and he could only tolerate so much.

"How do you know he wanted to kill me? What's that about the chocolates?" Jamie stood over him now, his body rigid, his stare intense.

"Because the chocolates were sent to you. But Alan took them and ate them. They had something called poison in them, something that made Alan die."

"You mean Alan died for me?"

"Instead of you. But it was not your fault. Roy was the one who put the poison in the chocolates, and Alan was the one who stole them."

"You mean all these bad things they did made bad things happen to them."

"Yes." *Close enough.*

"Is something bad going to happen to Roy? He killed my Gran, and she was kind to him. She took us in when our mums and dads went away and left us. She was very good. He should have something very bad happen to him."

"Something bad already did, Jamie. Roy is dead too."

"Did you kill him for me?"

"Good God no, I don't go around killing people! Someone else did it. The police don't know why. Do you know?"

"No."

"Did he ever talk about anybody?"

"Just some blokes that were after him. Something about a job."

"No names?"

"No, can't remember any names."

They sat for a while; Jamie's breath still ragged as he lowered himself into a chair and closed his eyes. Rosie knelt next to him.

"Gran's in heaven, I know that. But I don't think Roy is good enough for heaven. And he shouldn't be bothering Gran there, either. And not Alan, neither. Those two should be put somewhere together. I don't really want them to go to the bad place, though." Jamie still had his eyes closed; his voice sounded eerie, far away.

"There's a sort of in between place, you know," Geoffrey said, inwardly squirming at his own hypocrisy. He didn't believe in all that mumbo-jumbo.

"Yes, that's where Roy and Alan would be. Not one thing. And not the other."

"Rosie, why don't you both go back upstairs. Jamie's got a lot to think about." Audrey's voice sounded small and tired.

* * *

Jamie cried into his pillow for a bit while Rosie sat on his bed not knowing what to say. He finished snuffling and blew his nose with a big honking sound.

"Ugh," Rosie said, "that's a horrid noise."

"Sorry. Lots of stuff to get out."

"Ugh," Rosie said again. "You're not supposed to say things like that."

"Sorry."

"Listen, Jamie. You're my brother now. Or will be after the parents talk to old Chatterton and get all the boring papers done."

"Can we get married as well?"

"Married! No, you can't marry your sister." Rosie felt panicky. Surely he didn't have those kinds of feelings. *Does he?*

"Oh. I wanted us to get married because that way we could be together always." He pouted.

"But we're brother and sister now, so that means we'll always be in the same family. Always," Rosie said.

Jamie took a breath and blew his nose again, quietly this time. "Well, I suppose that's better, really. Married people sometimes fight. I heard them all the time in the other flats at Gran's."

"Sometimes brothers and sisters fight, but that doesn't mean they don't love each other."

"People fight a lot, don't they?"

"Yes, I'm afraid they do, Jamie. But nice people who care for each other make up and go on being good friends." *Should have been a Sunday school teacher.*

"We'll be nice and good friends, won't we, Rosie?"

"Of course. You'd better go to sleep now. Goodnight." *Sweet child.*

"G'night."

That was a relief. He hadn't a clue about marriage. *Didn't even understand about going to bed with people, thank God. Do people like him get those kinds of feelings?*

Rosie had thought she loved Robin, but he'd tried to force himself on her the evening before she broke the engagement. She'd hated that, realizing that she didn't have those kinds of feelings for him and had been disgusted by his touching her in intimate places. He'd been irresistible at first, the way he scoffed at society's rules. Life in a girls' school had been so narrow, so utterly boring. He'd been absolutely beastly when she told him they were finished. Daddy's spoiled little Lady Muck, he'd called her. It was clear now that he'd coveted the family connection, even as he'd mocked it. She'd been not quite eighteen. She felt older and wiser now—nineteen next month.

She'd been thinking about sex a lot lately, wondering what it would be like, so maybe she was going to have those feelings soon. One of the girls at school had teased her for being "a good girl," always even tempered and never in trouble, never talking about boys and necking. She didn't know anything about the real Rosie. She often felt out of sorts, but almost never showed it. It was especially important to be agreeable at home.

There were undercurrents in this family, tensions and a hint of secrets never aired. It was all about that little Fiona, she supposed, unless there were other secrets she didn't know about. How could one small child have caused so many problems? She'd only been one or so. It's not as if there had been that much time to get used to her. Some parents love too much sometimes.

Mummy hadn't loved her all that much. She couldn't ever remember her reading a book with her or having a cuddle. That had been Nanny's job. Poor old Nanny who'd been shipped off to another family when Rosie went away to school. They hadn't told her. She'd come home for half term and found Nanny gone. She wasn't even allowed to write, and she definitely wasn't allowed to cry. Why was that? Did they blame her for Fiona's death? But they kept her for Rosie. Or had Mummy been jealous because

Rosie had loved Nanny and Daddy best? She'd kissed and hugged Nanny goodbye the day Daddy drove her back to school. She still remembered the reproachful letter from Mummy, even though she'd crumpled it up and thrown it away immediately. She'd forgotten to go up to her room to say goodbye. It hadn't seemed to matter at the time. Anyway, if Daddy could find his way to the front door, surely Mummy could have.

It always seemed best to keep things smooth. She hated seeing Daddy's lips tighten when his eyes squinted with hurt, and she kept well away from Mummy when she was having one of her migraines. She noticed the way they sometimes looked at each other, though. They were still in love, even after all that dead-baby business. Poor Daddy, though, he seemed to feel he should treat Mummy as if she'd break in half at the slightest provocation. That kind of life must be nerve-wracking.

Life was boring, though. She was boring. Who on earth would want to fall in love with such a boring girl?

* * *

Geoffrey watched the moonlight play with the lace curtains. They'd forgotten to do the blackout and turn off the little lamp in the corner. He was head of civil defense in these parts and could square it with his own people, but he'd catch hell if any of Ronnie's chaps caught it. He'd get up in a little while and draw the heavy damask curtains. He hated the smell of those things. They got taken out for a good airing and beating each spring, but mustiness soon permeated them again.

When would this bloody war end? He'd watched a dogfight from the Barton cliffs in September. The little crowd of spectators cheered when one of the Hun planes went down first, then moaned in despair when an R.A.F. chap took a dive. There was no more cheering after that, just the stillness of mute despondency. Youngsters on both sides, all of them heroes. What a waste of young lives.

The light patterned Audrey's closed face, now ghostly, now angelic. She opened her eyes, startling him with a soft kiss on his shoulder. He turned into her and brought her under him as he caressed her and loved her. He always felt she might break if he weren't gentle enough, tender enough.

Later he said, "Audrey."

"What, darling?"

"I've made Jamie assistant gardener."

"That's nice, dear."

Always languid after lovemaking, she didn't sound all that interested. She blew hot and cold, her thoughts unfathomable. Had he ever truly known her?

18

Geoffrey eased his estate car next to the hedge that hemmed the Chief Constable's front garden. Ronnie hadn't wanted to meet at his office. More cloak and dagger stuff? The front door opened almost at once, closely framing Ronnie's wife; she must have heard the car door slam. Unattractive woman. Hairdo like a toilet brush and she always wore shapeless frocks and sensible shoes. Got a face like one of those American presidents on Mount Rushmore he'd seen in a magazine once, all craggy and visionary. Since she hadn't a nation to lead, she focused her considerable energies on the household. No wonder Ronnie had done so well—he wouldn't have dared do otherwise.

"Good morning, Sir Geoffrey." And that was it, save a curt nod and a retreating back that seemed to infer he should follow it. She didn't approve of him, he wasn't sure why.

"Morning, Geoffrey. Do take a pew, old chap." *Oh God, Ronnie is in one of his hearty moods.*

The door closed behind them with a finality that seemed to preclude any offer of hospitality.

"Geoffrey, I'm directed—at the highest levels, you understand—to recruit a few liaisons to act as eyes and ears in case of invasion."

"So, they think we're that badly off, do they?" Of course he knew the situation, but Ronnie didn't know of Geoffrey's meetings and liaisons with the Whitehall faceless. So many secrets.

"Afraid so. The shindig last summer just about knocked the R.A.F. for a loop, you know. Lost a third of them. Those poor chaps rarely lasted more than a couple of weeks flying regular missions. They're beginning to build back up, but it's slow. Stands to reason. I think the training's getting a bit rudimentary, though. Not enough time, you see."

"What a bloody mess. I'll do whatever you need, Ronnie. Glad to do my bit, you know." A sad business, throwing these lads to the wolves. They were only boys, boys who believed themselves invincible, believed they'd beat the odds. Pitiful.

"Good of you. We'll go into the details later." He puffed out his chest. "You'll report directly to me, of course."

"Who else did you get?"

"Can't say. There'll be no contact with the others. Unless we need a bit of sabotage done, of course. We'll cross that bridge if and when we come to it. Not a word, mind. Not even to Audrey. What she doesn't know, she can't tell. Those blighters stop at nothing when they want information."

"God Almighty! Hate to think about it in those terms."

Ronnie stood in front of the unlit fireplace now, rocking back and forth on his heels, enjoying himself immensely. He couldn't quite hide that little half smile under his clipped moustache. *Hasn't anyone told him it was just like Hitler's moustache?* Except Ronnie's was a muddy sandy color, whereas Hitler's looked pitch black in the pictures.

"Yes, well. There you are. And how're your wardens doing? Staying on top of things?"

"Yes, in fact, I got a telling off from one of them the other day. Left my bedroom curtains open and I still had a lamp on. Bit embarrassing. Not a very good example, am I? I wanted to laugh actually. He had such a difficult time coming out with it. But he was respectful, and I apologized, promised not to do it again."

"Heh, heh, caught you with your pants down, did he?"

"Considering I was in bed, you could say that." *Music hall humor, Ronnie, you're showing yourself up.*

"Oh sorry, didn't mean anything by it."

"Quite all right." *Silly ass.*

Ronnie went on to tell Geoffrey what else they'd discovered about Roy Beck's death. A search of Roy's room had turned up some burglary tools, and though there had been a rash of burglaries in the area, they found no sign of any loot. They did find a stockpile of cash, together with a note on his table, in his handwriting, asking for another thousand pounds. Clearly a blackmail note he hadn't delivered yet. They had an idea now who could have done it. The Dutch chap they'd been watching worked at Blexton—Bernhardt Visser. Falway had taken a quiet look at his bank account and found one withdrawal for five hundred pounds. Roy Beck didn't have a bank account; he'd just pried up a loose floorboard. His man at Blexton hadn't noticed anything. Useless, worse than useless, always complaining about the inmates. Not up to the job.

"Is Bernhardt Visser that chap Rosie found wandering on our estate?"

"Most likely, and perhaps Roy Beck found out what he was up to. But we have to keep watching, can't tip our hand yet. The fellow's probably a Nazi invasion liaison and we need to know who his contacts are."

"We haven't asked Jamie about Visser," said Geoffrey.

"I doubt he can tell us anything useful. Too simple to catch on to anything important." That easy dismissal irritated Geoffrey.

"You'd be surprised what Jamie comes out with sometimes. I've taken quite a liking to him. Fine young man, actually. I'm making him my ward. He's had a sad life, and we want to make sure he'll always be taken care of."

"That's very good of you."

"He's good for all of us . . . Any sign of those women?"

"Nothing. Dead ends. We talked to Dr. Gibson. We're not going to bother exhuming the grandmother's body, by the way. Since her killer's dead there doesn't seem to be much point. We're sure he set fire to the flat, though. There were signs of charred newspapers and deep scorching outside her bedroom window. Ground-floor flat, you know."

"Rotten cad!"

"Quite."

* * *

Geoffrey found Jamie in the greenhouse. He watched him for a while as he thinned out seedlings, a frown creasing his whole face. He looked distressed.

"Hello, Jamie."

"Oh, hello, Sir Geoffrey. I'm pinching the little plants out so the others have room to grow."

"I see you are. You look upset."

"I hate this part. It seems so cruel. They could all grow. It's not fair."

"I see what you mean." *The Nazis would thin out the Jamies of this world.* "Jamie, I want to ask you about Bernhardt."

"What about Bernhardt, sir?" Jamie frowned.

"Did Roy ever talk about him?"

"Well, not really. I told him what I saw Bernhardt do once, and he seemed very pleased about it."

Geoffrey went still. "What did you see him do?"

"Who?"

"Bernhardt."

Jamie told him about the door in the ceiling and the stairs that came down. And how he hadn't been seen by Bernhardt but had told Roy about it. Geoffrey allowed himself an unworthy frisson of triumph. *Now see who has nothing important to say, Ronnie!*

"Jamie, I don't want you to go far away from the house. I think Bernhardt may be bad, like Roy. I'll tell Rosie to be careful too."

The boy seemed to crumple a little, crushed by yet another disappointing revelation. People who thought they were better than him, had told him as much, turned out to be bad. Geoffrey hoped Jamie would never sink into world-weariness, would never lose his shining freshness.

"Keep up the good work, Jamie. I'll see you at dinner. I have to ring someone up."

19

Stanton drove them along the Ornamental Drive in the Bentley with a stately solemnity Audrey found amusing. The dear old duck took his position at the Manor with an earnestness the rest of the staff often found irksome. He had to be careful, of course, because the road was crowded with pedestrians, and they weren't looking out for cars because only a lucky few had petrol to spare. The rhododendrons were at their peak—their enormous heads seemed jammed into the branches like bridesmaids' posies. Stanton would drop them off at a good picnic place and run an errand for Geoffrey before coming back for them.

"I thought this was supposed to be a forest," said Jamie. "Some trees are here, but not a lot."

"I know it's called the New Forest, Jamie, but it's part forest and part moorland. Moorland is open space where the animals like to graze. Graze means feed." She was getting used to anticipating misunderstandings.

"What animals?"

"There are many wild ponies, and they eat grass. And in some places where there are lots of oak trees, people can let their pigs out to eat the acorns. Which are the seeds that fall from the oak trees. And, of course, there are rabbits and other small creatures."

"What's creatures? I never heard that word for things in a forest, only for girls who walked around our streets at night. I could see them from my window. 'Nasty, dirty creatures,' Gran used to call them. Roy seemed to like them all right."

Audrey didn't dare look at Rosie, and the back of Stanton's neck had acquired a reddish tinge. She examined her fingernails and said, "Creature is another word for animal. There are deer and foxes and badgers, but we probably won't see any of those. They're too shy."

"Animals get shy like people?"

"They are shy because they have to hide from other animals or people who might hurt them."

"So they have to be careful, too."

"Look, lots of ponies!" said Rosie. "Aren't they simply gorgeous?"

"I think they can hurt people," said Jamie.

"You have to know how to treat them. You mustn't ever feed the ponies here, it makes them turn nasty if people don't give them anything, and then they'll sometimes bite. And look, there are some people riding horses. I used to love riding." Audrey sighed. "But I haven't done it for years."

She leaned back and remembered the feel of the wind rushing past her face as Seeker, her bay gelding, soared across the fields, gliding over the hedgerows, legs tucked under his belly in a neat little package. He wasn't a big horse—not much over fifteen hands—but he'd been stouthearted and nimble. After he died of colic, excruciatingly, she'd felt too brokenhearted to buy a replacement. She used to ride one of Geoffrey's horses when she felt like hacking, but soon gave it up. Rosie had never been interested, unlike most of the other girls in her set. Strange, she didn't seem afraid of horses, just bored by the whole idea. She'd never been sporty.

She wouldn't talk about foxhunting now. Jamie would never understand the idea of chasing a fox until it was cornered and torn to pieces by hounds; it would upset him no end. And it was certainly barbaric. There were other ways to get rid of foxes.

Jamie sat still and quiet, staring down into his lap.

"What is it, Jamie?" Rosie peered at him.

"I don't want to get out of the car. Can we eat in the car? I'm scared of horses."

"You can sit between Mummy and me, we're used to horses. We'll take care of you. Promise. Anyway, they don't usually come where we go."

"All right. I suppose."

They came to a stop by the side of the road. Rosie and Jamie each took a handle and carried the picnic basket between them. Audrey led the way with the rugs tucked under her arm.

"Where are we going?" asked Jamie, his voice fretful.

"To a nice little clearing. It's very pretty there and it has lots of wild flowers. You can pick some if you want to." Rosie smiled at him.

"I wish George could have come. But I think the wheelchair would be too hard to push along here," said Jamie.

"Well, next time we could think about having our picnic in a different place where we could take George," said Audrey. "There are some pretty pubs in the New Forest. They have gardens with tables you can sit at, and sometimes the ponies come into the garden to drink from the fishponds. They have to put special grids over the ponds so the ponies don't suck up the fish along with the water."

"Pubs here have gardens? Well I never. And ponies come into the gardens? I don't know about that. Would they leave us alone?"

"Oh yes, they just wander in and out. And they line up outside the windows of one of the pubs. They sometimes get the leftover beer out of the barrels, and they love that," said Rosie.

"Don't they get drunk? A horse could do horrid things if it got drunk. Like Roy."

"No, horses don't seem to get drunk. And what did Roy do when he got drunk?" asked Rosie.

"Dunno. Don't remember," and he stared ahead as if scanning the horizon.

Poor boy, what else had happened to him? Audrey didn't really want to know; some things are best forgotten if you can. Better change the subject.

"Nearly there. Jamie, will you have tea or orangeade?"

"Cuppa, please! Then orangeade."

They laid out the rugs and tea things and tucked in. Jamie didn't eat much at first; he was too busy peering around as if he expected a monster to jump out of the bushes. The peaceful spot settled him, though, and he began to eat rather more than his fair share. Even so, they pressed more on him. Rosie's compassion for the boy delighted Audrey. Only children were often self-centered, but he had kindled tenderness in both of them, and Geoffrey too. She lay back and gazed up through the canopy.

Geoffrey's concern for Jamie had surprised her. He was a kind and gentle man, but he had never been comfortable with the unfamiliar. She knew he'd hoped for a son, but he never spoke of it. And Jamie was nothing like the sort of son he'd have longed for. What kind of son might that have been? A boy with the right ideas gleaned from the inevitable progression from nanny to prep school to public school to Oxbridge? Sons were good to mothers, easy going. But girls understood their mothers in the end when they came into their own sorrows and disappointments.

Geoffrey had not always been gentle, though. About a year after they got married, he'd found the young son of one of the tenant farmers hiding in a hayloft, his tearstained face buried in his sleeve as he tried to muffle his sobs. His older brother was a drunkard and a lout, much given to starting pub brawls, and in a drunken rage he'd given his young brother a savage beating with his belt. Geoffrey had warned the boy's father about his behavior more than once.

Geoffrey sent a farmhand to bring the drunk and his father to wait for him in the barn. He brought the boy to Audrey, who had been sickened by the bloody welts. She'd been embarrassed to take care of a fourteen-year-old boy's backside, but she'd never seen Geoffrey in such a mood, so she took a deep breath and got on with it.

She left the boy drinking hot cocoa in the kitchen and went out to the barn. She knew Geoffrey wouldn't want her there, but she was curious to see how he'd handle things. She used the back entrance and stood in a dark corner watching as Geoffrey upbraided the smirking unrepentant youth for his cruelty, his color high and a vein in his right temple she'd never noticed before throbbing. Then he horsewhipped him, perspiring as he laid into the boy. Audrey startled a little with each crack, and felt sick again. The young man lost his swagger almost at once and sniveled and groveled like a feeble schoolgirl as the cutting blows cascaded down his back and legs. The father watched in grim silence, his lips squeezed together into a thin line as his jutting jaw pointed at the scene like an accusatory finger—whether at his son or at Geoffrey, she wasn't sure.

"I want you off this farm and far away by eight tomorrow morning." Geoffrey's voice rasped low, but it penetrated the high-beamed space with surprising clarity. "Your brother will stay in the Manor tonight. Mr. Turner!"

"Sir!"

"Your son is never to set foot on our land again—God knows he's had plenty of warnings to mend his ways. If you do not wish to continue your tenancy under the circumstances, you are hereby released. However, you are welcome to remain if you prefer."

"I will stay, thank you kindly, sir. Come along, boy," said the chagrined father. Audrey saw him kick his errant son's rear end through the barn door before she slipped out and returned to the kitchen.

She'd never seen Geoffrey so roused before or since; he'd fallen on her that night like an animal, too, which she had quite enjoyed, although she hadn't liked to say so. They'd had firm ideas about what constituted ladylike behavior in those days—still did—and in his frenzy it seemed he hadn't noticed her enthusiastic response. He kissed her forehead afterwards and said, "Sorry, darling," rolled over, and fell sleep. She'd felt cheated. She'd wanted his arms to wrap her, wanted to tell him his earthy passion was welcome—very welcome—but she was trapped in the pernicious butterfly net of her class.

Geoffrey couldn't tolerate cruelty—and she'd seen it in other small ways. That's what drew him to Jamie and made him determined to keep the boy out of harm's way. She'd never thought to ask Geoffrey if anyone had ever treated him badly. Of course, she'd heard rumors about the things that went on in public schools; the canings, the abuses prefects heaped on the younger boys, and other horrid things only hinted at in whispered euphemisms. She couldn't very well ask him at this late point; it would be intrusive.

"Mummy, wake up!" Rosie shook her shoulder. She must have drifted off. "It's time to go back."

"Lady Audrey, look at all the wildflowers I've got!" Jamie held out his bouquet. "I hope they don't die before we get home. They want water."

"I'll wet a napkin and wrap the stems in it," said Audrey sleepily, his simple excitement warming and lifting her spirit. His terror of marauding ponies seemed to have subsided.

* * *

The next afternoon, Jamie was hoeing the vegetable beds when a long shadow fell across the soil, frightening him. He knew before he turned. Bernhardt. He was all the same sort of colors today, a mixture of dark and pale browns, except his eyes. *What does he want?* Rosie hadn't liked finding him on the grounds last time, and Sir Geoffrey said he might be bad. And he didn't care about Jamie, or any of the boys for that matter.

"Good afternoon, Jamie. How are you today," Bernhardt said with a smile. It wasn't like a real smile, more like when Laddie showed his teeth that other time Bernhardt came.

"I am very well, thank you. Why did you come here?"

"Well, I wanted to tell you that Graham has gone away. I thought you should know."

"Yes. He was really my cousin, only I promised not to tell. And he's gone away in the dead sort of way."

"Ach, so they told you. Graham told me about the chocolates. He tried to kill you. Did you know that?"

"Yes. He was very bad."

"Yes, he was. Did Graham ever talk about me?"

Jamie caught his breath, better be careful. "No, he didn't. He wanted to know if I told people about Gran. I didn't know that he'd killed her. I was too stupid." He wouldn't say he saw Bernhardt go up into the door in the ceiling and told on him. He knew he'd get in trouble for that.

"It was not your fault, Jamie."

Jamie swallowed heavily. "That's what they all say. But I should have known. I just didn't know he could be so wicked."

"There are many people who do wicked things."

"Like Mr. Hitler, he's very wicked. I've heard about him from Gran, and lots of other people too. And I heard Mr. Churchill say it on the wireless once."

"Oh, I do not know about wicked. People just do not know him. They do not understand what he is trying to do. They are all against him here. But there are many people who think he will build a strong Germany and change the world."

"Does the world need to be changed? I don't know much about the world yet. I haven't hardly seen it."

"Oh yes, I would say a lot of changes are necessary."

Jamie got back to his hoeing, hoping Bernhardt would get bored and go away.

"I've been made assistant gardener. Because I'm good at gardening."

"Well, I'm glad you are useful. Everyone should be useful, otherwise they should be dealt with."

"Punished, you mean?"

"Something like that. So, Graham never talked about me?"

"Well, only once. He said you had a toolbox you like to take up in the attic to mend a leak. It made him laugh. I don't know why. He said I was never to tell about it. And I didn't." Bernhardt looked very angry, his eyebrows closing together, nose holes as wide as a horse's, and his teeth and gums showed too. *I should have kept my mouth shut; I never seem to know when to keep my mouth shut. But I only said that Roy said it. Not that I saw it.*

"I see," Bernhardt said between nearly closed teeth. "Well, you must never tell about it. It is our secret."

"But why should mending a leak be a secret?"

"Because I said so. I do very important work up there, and no one must know. I might have to kill you if you tell anyone."

Jamie's breath came in little puffs now and he felt as though he might fall over. *Bernhardt is bad too. Why did bad people have to come to the Manor? They should stay away from good places.* "I won't tell. Not ever. Nobody. Never."

Bernhardt laughed, a nasty sharp sound. "See that you do not." He turned and walked away into the orchard, his brown shirt melting into the trees as if he were one of them.

Jamie's tears rolled. He shouldn't cry, not at his age. *Why can't bad people leave me alone? Why do they always want me? Is there something special in me that bad people like?* He heard footsteps.

"Jamie, where are you?" Rosie, one of the good people. *Dry up on shirtsleeve, all right for once.*

"I'm in the vegetable beds. I'm hoeing." She appeared around the corner of the small hothouse. "It's teatime."

"I have to wash my hands."

"Cook made a seedcake, worst luck! I hate seedcake."

"Why would she use seeds to make a cake? She could grow them."

"They're special seeds called caraway seeds, and they have a particular kind of taste. She just puts some in the cake mixture. There's a bit of Victorian sponge left, though, we can share it if you want. But you ought to try the seedcake. You might like it. Daddy loves it."

"If you don't like it, I'm sure I won't."

"Hey, have you been crying? Your eyes are all red."

"No, I just get earth in them sometimes."

"Come on, race you to the back door!"

The cake did taste funny. Not bad, just funny. He'd finish his slice and then decide. Sir Geoffrey liked it lots, he'd had two slices already. Jamie kept his eye on the last bit of sponge cake. Rosie said she'd share, but you never knew. People sometimes forgot about sharing when it came to cake.

"What did you do today, Jamie?" asked Lady Audrey.

Should I tell? He'd had nothing but trouble with secrets. He could trust these people. They were his friends. He kept on chewing while he thought about it.

"Jamie, Lady Audrey asked you a question." Sir Geoffrey sounded cross.

"Sorry. I had to think. Well, I weeded the perennials, and then this afternoon I hoed the vegetable beds. Then Bernhardt from the place, you know, the Blexton place, came to see me."

"That man, the Dutch one who Laddie chased off that time? What did he want?" Rosie's voice got loud and high. "And why didn't you tell me? And was that why your eyes were red?"

"Well, you were angry with him before. And he told me I must never tell what we talked about. He said he might have to kill me if I told. So I wasn't going to tell. But I was just thinking. When I keep secrets it never turns out right. So now I'm telling."

"I should bloody well think so!"

"Geoffrey!"

"Sorry, darling. Tell me everything he said, Jamie, right now."

The tears wanted to start again; he must keep them from coming down. He told about Bernhardt knowing about the chocolates and about the door in the ceiling, which seemed to be the most important part. He even told what Bernhardt said about Mr. Hitler. Sir Geoffrey said nothing. Was he very angry? He just sat there and finished his cake. Then he got up so suddenly he made them all jump.

"I must ring Sir Ronald," was all he said on his way out.

20

The soldiers' khaki uniforms wound in and out of the shrubbery as they converged on the Blexton Institute, rifles at the ready. Another group had started at the outer edge of the property to contain anyone who might be wandering the grounds. Mrs. Clancy had been instructed to confine the patients to the common rooms after breakfast and to tell everyone there was an air raid warning. She'd not seen Bernhardt yet and thought he was still in his room. Falway suggested that they wait another hour until everyone had settled down, but the two intelligence officers in charge, Cummins and Bretton-Taylor, overruled him.

"Need to get on with it, old boy," said Cummins. *Toffee-nosed bugger.*

The three of them strolled up the path to the front door as if they were casual visitors. The lumpish receptionist sat on her throne as usual.

"Don't get up." She'd made no signs of doing so. Falway waved a document in her face. "We have a search warrant. Stay exactly where you are." Expressionless, she nodded.

"We'll start with his room and search the upper floors. You check the common rooms," Bretton-Taylor told Falway.

"I will." *Yes, sir, three bags full, sir. Arrogant jackass.*

Falway started on the ground floor. A lovely building once—it still displayed some fancy carved wood and stone—but nothing more than a dreary prison now. He moved through hallways that stifled him with their brown and sludge-green paint, cracked linoleum curling up at the corners, and harsh stink of disinfectant. Where did they get that stuff? It wasn't Dettol with its familiar germ-conquering smell most people found reassuring. What a soulless place to spend one's life in.

He opened the door to the boys' common room, just the one attendant whom he'd seen before. He looked harried. No wonder. Most of the boys were quiet, but some muttered incessantly, some stared at nothing, some paced. A burly young man startled him by a sudden arcing of his body to touch his toes, followed by a shrill "Fuck!" That said, he strolled over to the table, picked up a comic, and went to sit and read by the window. He was used to criminals, petty and otherwise, but he couldn't imagine how he'd cope with this unnerving band.

"D.I. Falway. Have you seen Bernhardt?" he asked.

"I remember you. No, he didn't report in. He's supposed to be working in here with these boys. We're short-handed, you know. I even had to give them breakfast on my own. And the wheelchair case is still in bed, no time to see to him." The man sounded aggrieved, whiny.

"So you don't know where he is."

"No. I think I saw him off in the distance on the grounds this morning. He generally takes an early walk. He goes out walking all the time. He's often late, but not this late."

Falway left, relieved when the heavy door clanged shut behind him. He shouldn't feel repulsed, but he did. The common room on the other side of the building was worse. This one was for adult men, most of them probably worse off than when they'd come in, he shouldn't wonder. The stench turned his stomach, and the amalgamated voices formed a dull roar, although there were some whose silence lay deep-sea still. *Thank God Jamie wouldn't have to stay in this place.* The unbidden thought startled him. Would the boy have been reduced to madness here? Most likely. *Nice boy like that—unthinkable.* There was a sweetness about him, and he was too good for this. He took a deep breath, almost gagged, and accelerated his pace.

After a tour of the other two common rooms—for girls and women—Falway hadn't found anyone else who had seen Bernhardt that morning. They'd begun the operation after the start of the first shift, but if Bernhardt had been late for work and walking around the grounds, he might have seen the troops moving in.

He waited in the main hall for the MI5 men. Their suave air of superiority rankled him almost as much as the inmates had. They were the typical upper-class cream of the Oxford and Cambridge crop, accustomed to deference from people like him. He wondered if all that would change after the war. It changed to some extent after the Great War. Trench-seeking mortar had proved a great leveler, and now the bombs. The world had never before seen horror, death, and sacrifice on such a massive scale. Who'd want to kowtow after going through all that?

The men came down the stairs holding a couple of black leather shoulder bags and a cloth packet.

"Under the floorboards," said Cummins. "One of those new compact transmitters and a wad of money. Bretton-Taylor's finishing the search upstairs. Nothing in the attic. Did you find any sign of him?"

"No. The boys' attendant said he'd seen him in the grounds early on and apparently he's often late for his shift. He must have spotted us," said Falway.

"Damn. We should have waited."

"Yes, you should." The man bristled at the implied criticism.

"Any idea where he might have gone? Any favorite haunts?"

"No idea. He wasn't much of a one for pubs, I'm told. The woods, perhaps?" said Falway.

"Woods? Any around here?"

"Many. And you may have heard of the New Forest."

"No need to be sarcastic," said Cummins, his mouth pinched around the corners.

"He doesn't own a car. He'd need transportation. I'll check to see if any stolen cars have been reported."

"Yes, do that, please."

Mrs. Clancy arrived, a little flustered and breathless. "Telephone call for you, Inspector Falway. It's Miss Rosie

McInnis. She's quite distraught and said the station told her to call you here. Jamie is missing."

Falway sprinted up the passage to her office and picked up the phone.

"Falway here. What's happened?"

"It's Jamie. He told me he was going out to the greenhouse before breakfast, but Evans says he never saw him. And he didn't come in for breakfast. I've looked everywhere. And Mummy's car is missing. So's Laddie." *Visser. Transportation.* But what did he want with Jamie and the dog?

"Where's your father?"

"I don't know. He went out and dropped Mummy off at the hospital on his way to a meeting."

He ran back to the hallway and told the men what had happened. "Bernhardt's behind it, mark my words. Let's go."

21

He'd promised Evans he'd water the seedlings in the greenhouse before breakfast. As assistant gardener, he was in charge of things like that. Maybe he'd go out through the kitchen. Cook often passed him something tasty and he'd still got a while to wait until breakfast.

"Mornin', Jamie."

"Good morning. I'm just going to the greenhouse to do some watering. The little plants get thirsty a lot."

"Good boy. Here, take a couple of biscuits with you. They're ginger snaps, just out of the oven. Must keep your strength up, you know!"

"Thank you. I love ginger snaps."

They smelled gingery delicious. He finished the first one and sniffed at the other. As he rounded the stable wall he spotted a figure opening the door where Lady Audrey's car was kept. Wait a minute, he knew that man. *Bernhardt again.* He stood still and watched for a minute. He munched the second biscuit. *What is he doing? He's not allowed in there.* He heard him cranking the car. *Is he going to steal it?* He crept close to the stable, staying close against the wall, and peered in.

Sweat dripped from Bernhardt's forehead as he tried to get the car started. He stopped for a minute, panting as he leant against the dark-green bonnet. Jamie mostly finished chewing and swallowed, but it went down the wrong way, making him cough and splutter. Bernhardt reached him before he could run far. He grabbed the back of his collar, dragged him into the stable, and threw him into the car.

"Spying, are you?"

"You're not allowed to take Lady Audrey's car! That's stealing!" It came out as a mumble, what with his mouth still having some biscuit in it.

"When Germany has conquered England, we will take everything from these people. Now be quiet or I will hurt you. I may have to anyway."

"Are you Mr. Hitler's friend?"

"You could certainly say so." Bernard shoved him over against the door handle. "Get in!"

"Are we going somewhere?" Jamie stumbled as he climbed into the high seat.

"Oh, yes."

Jamie closed his eyes and tried not to cry and make Bernhardt angry. He'd been frightened a lot since this horrid blitz business started, but this man scared him in a different way. Bernhardt had a face that didn't have much showing on it. Roy, so very unkind, liked hurting Jamie and laughed while he did it. But with him it always came to an end, even when he'd hurt him so badly that time with the handle of Gran's hairbrush. Jamie wished he could forget that, but he couldn't ever. He'd thought about telling Gran, but it was something so dirty it had to stay a secret. *Stupid to think about Roy now, gone forever.*

Berhardt swore as he cranked the engine again. He opened his eyes a tiny bit. The man was sweating and very red in the face.

Breathe properly. He felt giddy, couldn't breathe in enough. Jamie cupped his hands over his mouth to keep the cries inside. Breathing got easier. *Think about something else, anything but Bernhardt and Roy.*

Last week he'd come into the kitchen when Cook was getting rabbits ready for cooking. He stood in the doorway, his legs and arms all frozen up. They'd been so pretty once. She'd already taken off their skins. She slit the tummy open of one, cut out his inside bits and threw them in a pail. She was singing a tune, a cheerful pretty one. She stopped when she saw him there.

"Jamie, it's all right. We have to eat. God put these good creatures on the earth to feed us. That's what they're for."

She hadn't felt sorry for the lovely rabbits, her face wasn't sad at all. She was used to it, probably did it all the time. Bernhardt would be like that, only with people. *Why couldn't he think about nice things?*

He opened his eyes when the engine started.

"Well, Jamie. Who did you tell about our little talk?"

"No one. Honest." His heart was going too hard and he wondered if Bernhardt could hear the lie.

"Then why did the army come to Blexton, slinking around the place like hyenas?"

"Don't know." *Mustn't tell. Hy . . . what? Don't ask questions.*

"I need to leave now, earlier than I planned. Your fault, I think. You are lying, too, I think. I will make you talk when . . ."

A ferocious growling and barking interrupted and a black and white blur leapt at Bernhardt. He punched the dog in the chest, and Laddie was thrown against the wall.

"Stop it, you're hurting him, stop!" Laddie lay there panting a little before struggling to his feet. Bernhardt jumped into the car and started to back out.

"What are you going to do?"

"I am going to take you to the forest and leave you there. Then I will go down to the sea and find a boat to take me across to the Isle of Wight. There are people there who will help me."

"You'll leave me there all alone?"

"Who else would be there? You will not care by then." He smiled, but that didn't make Jamie feel better, because it wasn't that kind of smile.

"Of course I'll care. I'll be scared."

Bernhardt didn't reply as he drove slowly along the driveway. Jamie looked out of the back window and saw Laddie limping after them. He lost sight of him when they got out onto the big road.

Jamie didn't feel like crying now. He felt too cold and heavy. His tummy felt funny, too, and the clever things that lived in his head lately had emptied out. He was breathing properly, though. He turned his head to look out of the window. There were pretty things to see. Perhaps this was his last chance to look at pretty things. Cheery flowers, a big old tree that reminded him of Evans. *Would the baby plants die? Would he die? What would it be like?* He'd be glad to see Gran, though he hoped he wouldn't have to see Alan or Roy. *Would it hurt?*

This was the road they'd come on with Lady Audrey, the one with all the great big flowers. The car stopped.

"Get out." Bernhardt didn't sound angry.

He took a bag out of the back seat, grabbed Jamie's arm, and walked fast into the trees. Jamie kept up as best he could, but he couldn't help tripping sometimes, and then Bernhardt would yank him up and hurt his shoulder. The hurting made him want to cry, but he mustn't. He couldn't see the sky any more, too many trees too close together. How could they live so close? They were plants and all plants need space and air and light. Evans said so.

"This is where we say goodbye."

Trying to be brave, Jamie stood up straight and put his shoulders back like a soldier. He looked at Bernhardt's eyes. Not completely cold and mean, they looked back.

"We Nazis believe that people like you should be exterminated like rats. But you are not so useless. You know how to work in a garden. Not so bad. I will leave you here. If they find you in time, you will live. If not, well, that is how it goes. Sit down against that tree."

Jamie sat, feeling the rough bark itch his back. The roots weren't very comfortable. He squirmed to find a softer spot. Bernhardt took some rope and a big knife from the bag and tied his feet, then his hands. He gasped as another rope went round his body and the tree.

"Well, the knife was useful after all, although I did not think of using it for cutting rope." He made a funny sound, like people who are doing a laugh they don't mean. Bernhardt's hand shook a little. He was scared too.

"Don't worry. I think it will be all right." Jamie looked up at him.

"What will be all right?" Bernhardt sounded surprised.

"Everything. You are a spy, aren't you? Sir Geoffrey was telling me about spies at dinner last night. And Cook told me some things too."

"Of course I am a spy."

"They'll hang you if you get caught."

"I suppose they will."

"I don't want them to do that to you." He certainly did want them to do it, and he hoped it would hurt. A lot.

"Thank you. You must not lie now. Did you tell anyone about what we talked of?"

"No, I always try to keep my word." *Will God punish me for that? Some lies are good.* White ones, Rosie told him. It was hard to tell the difference sometimes.

"I think I believe you. If you had said you told, I might have cut your throat." *Definitely a very white lie.*

"Goodbye, Jamie. I hope they find you, but not too soon. Wish me luck."

"Goodbye, Bernhardt. I'll be brave. Thank you for not doing what you said with the knife. Good luck." *May he rot in hell.* Gran said that about Roy's dad once. It sounded nasty.

* * *

Bernhardt went a few paces and stopped. He must be mad, letting such a creature live. And he might have been lying. He should kill him. No worse than butchering hogs like he'd done every year with his father. At least they gave meat. That was their purpose. He opened his bag and took out the knife. He could creep up behind him. He'd only see it at the last moment. A good knife does its work quickly. He fingered its edge, a sharp slicing one. A surgeon would not have a better one.

Graham had only understood in the last few seconds what would happen to him. He had been terrified, could not move. *Coward*, Benhardt thought. He had even looked that way after death, his hands claw-like and his mouth stuck in its unfinished scream. Bernhardt had heard about people who died violent deaths being frozen in their last throes, but he had never seen it before. He had only seen the slackening before the eyes glazed over. He liked looking into eyes that could not look back. He turned back toward Jamie. The boy was shaking, but not crying.

Trying to be brave, just as he had said. Wishing him good luck! Well, what could you expect from an idiot.

No time to waste, I must be on my way. Bernhardt shoved the knife back into the bag and ran to the car. He had parked it behind a wall of tall rhododendrons. *Thank God the damned English rain held off for a few days so the ground is firm.* He tossed the bag in and got out the crank. You would think these people could afford something better, but the Bentley had been low on petrol. This one was nearly full.

It would only take him one hour to reach Lymington, maybe less. The ferries were still running, but he could not run the risk of taking this car onboard. He would have to abandon it. But if he left it too near the dock, they would guess where he was going. He must think of some better way. At least he would be warm and dry on the ferry. Better than the rowing boat that dumped him on Barton Beach in the middle of the night.

Bernhardt needed to put more distance between the Manor and himself, but he should stop soon and change his appearance. Graham had done that quite well. Just a few simple changes made a person look quite different. No need to use silly disguises. He had already put on work clothes. There was not much time. They might be looking for him already.

I should not have let the boy live. What's one more death in the struggle?

He drove up a small lane and parked. He pulled a cloudy old mirror from his bag, the one he stole from the female staff dormitory at the Institute. He taped the sides of his face so his eyes slanted down a little. Not much, but enough to deceive. Cheek pads; Graham had used those too. He had boasted about them, had never known when to keep his mouth shut. There had not been time to change his hair color, but a woolen work cap hid most of it. Must remember to keep his eyes down, magnificent Aryan blue eyes, unusual here. These English had such muddy coloring. *Good enough. Time to get going.*

Maybe he should take the car on the ferry. What else could he do? Nothing would point to him faster than someone finding the car abandoned. The car parks were mostly empty these days, and restaurants and pubs had not opened yet. And if he left the car somewhere, he might have to walk a long way. Time was his enemy. *Scheiss*, he had said Isle of Wight to the boy. The idiot would not remember. Should have killed him.

Have to piss; should have thought of it back there. Well, he was nearly at the turnoff that would take him into the town. He got out and walked a short way down a narrow rutted track. No one about.

His fingers froze as he buttoned up his trousers. What sounded like an army Jeep rushed past what must be the turnoff before coming to a standstill. Voices. He crept out to the end of the lane. The sounds came from around the corner. He could cut through the copse that filled the angle and see what was going on.

An army roadblock. Perhaps for him. Perhaps not. If he turned back, they would not see him. *Verdammt*, he should have planned a better escape route. He ran back to the car and cranked it. The engine came to life at the first try. *God's on my side. And the Fuehrer's side, naturally. Always.* He drove back to the road. *What now? Where to now?* He needed a hostage. Not Jamie, no one would sacrifice capturing a spy for such a one. And if he remembered the Isle of Wight, so much the better.

He smiled as the perfect solution came to him. *Inspired. Brilliant, actually.*

22

It was very, very quiet in the big dark forest. Not all quiet. Wind shook the leaves, little things moved. Thank goodness not big things, nothing big as a horse. Jamie closed his eyes and tried to think about nice things. *Birthday cake.* Gran couldn't make the last one like usual because *bl-itz* came down. And Roy stopped her with a knife. *Stop thinking about knives, nasty cruel things.* He'd think about what he wanted for his next birthday cake. Chocolate icing on top and butter icing in the middle, and the butter icing would have chocolate in it too.

Twigs broke, his eyes snapped open. Better keep his eyes open, best to be ready. He couldn't see much, even though it wasn't nighttime yet; maybe one of those little animals Lady Audrey talked about. Not fierce, just shy. She said that.

He wanted to be proud of himself; he must be brave, all the time brave. He wondered if saying a prayer would help. Gran had taught him one once. It said . . . he couldn't remember; he thought it started out, "Our father." His father was dead though; so many people dead now, and if they didn't find him, he would get dead. Bernhardt said that might happen. *Be proud, think about nice things, and above all don't cry. Does God ever let dead boys come back?*

A little ant crawled up his leg. He'd seen people squish ants and thought that very unkind. He jumped when it bit him; sharp. He shouldn't move, didn't want to get more ants, didn't want to get bitten; it didn't feel nice when that ant bit him. That ant was lucky Jamie couldn't reach to squish him. He'd like to squish him now. Maybe other people had the right idea.

Rosie. He'd close his eyes some more so he could see Rosie in his head. She'd have on that lovely blue dress he liked best. It was quite tight at the top and showed her shape. She'd got a very good girl shape, better than most girls. He wondered what her shape looked like underneath. *Soft and white? Cuddly, probably, like a cushion. It would be nice if Rosie put her arms around me now and let me put my head on the softest part of her shape.* He'd feel better then. Thinking about her often made him feel funny too. *Better not think about Rosie too much, it made all those things happen.*

If only he could marry Rosie. *But brothers aren't allowed to marry sisters. If she married somebody else, we could all live together, though. They'd be a family. It's so nice having a proper family. I'll see them all soon, if they find me.*

Poor Laddie, Bernhardt hurt him. Hope he's better now. That was very mean of Bernhardt. He seems to be as bad as that man Hitler, who had probably squashed loads and loads of ants. And hurt dogs too.

Hungry, never got his breakfast. Thirsty. Will Bernhardt be able to hear me if I shout? Probably far away now.

"Help, help me! I'm Jamie! Come and find me!"

Nothing but rustles and scuffles. No Bernhardt, though.

It was cold in the middle of all the trees. Windy and no sunshine. It smelled moldy, like Roy's room after the upstairs bath leaked down on it. Jamie hoped it wouldn't rain because he'd be cold if he got wet. Catch his death. Gran used to say that, catch a cold, she said it meant. *Catch death? Funny thing to say.*

"Help! Help! Is anyone there?" His voice flew over the trees and away and left a big empty silence.

A crashing noise, a big animal staring at him, shaky and quiet. *Did it hear me call? Could it hear my heart?* His heart kept making big thumps. *Must keep still, must keep quiet, breathe, and be brave.* It had kind eyes and a pretty face. Four stick legs and a little white tail. It was a deer; he remembered it now from a book about the New Forest Lady Audrey had in the library. *Pretty enough to be a girl, must be a girl.* He had to sneeze, couldn't help it.

He scared her with his sneeze and she ran away. She had been good company, and he wanted her back. She had looked sweet and just stood still, watching like an angel.

"Do forests have angels?" he asked out loud. "Is my angel here? Are you watching?" Gran said he had a guardian angel, all white with wings and she sat in a corner looking after him all the time. *Where was she now? Was it even the truth?* Gran sometimes told him funny things to keep him quiet when she was tired or busy.

Another animal, a small one, hopping on the grassy place. A rabbit. Bigger than the rabbits Cook had. He couldn't bear to think about what she did to them. *Put that thought away.* This rabbit had a pretty face, like the big animal. *How could someone eat a creature with a pretty face?* He would never eat a pretty thing. One of his new words. *Creature. Must remember that and use it more often.*

The trees were too close for horses to get through. And there wasn't enough grass for a really big animal to eat. So they wouldn't come anywhere near where he sat.

"Help me, help me, help me!" *Try again and again, keep trying.* Nothing. His throat started to hurt. If he closed his eyes he might sleep. Sleep would make the time go by. He'd think about Gran.

She's coming home from work. In this pretend Roy hasn't been home all day. Gran's walking tired, like she does. Cleaning's hard work. She's got bad legs. She makes herself cheerful for him. Makes a cuppa and puts her feet up before she gets the tea, bacon, and eggs. They only have bacon and eggs for breakfast at the Manor. They have big teas, only they call it dinner. They have lunch when they had dinner at Gran's. All upside down. And their teas are just in between. Tea and little sandwiches and cake. He liked it, though. He liked everything at the Manor. But he'd liked Gran's way too.

She's telling him about her ladies, now. She's not very nice about them. She pretends to talk like them and that makes him laugh. She said once that Mrs. Thomas needs one person to cook for her, one to clean the house, one to wash her knickers, and another one to wipe her bottom. She explained it was only a joke, not really true. So rude. Gran doesn't usually make jokes like that. Sometimes when she makes jokes and laughs a lot it means she is really cross and tired. He thought probably other people do that sometimes. People are all different.

She's cooking bacon and eggs. Fried bread. He's hungry. Lovely smell, makes his mouth water, a good thing, it got too dry. She'd left him a sandwich for lunch; cheese and pickle and a glass of orangeade, but he finished it hours ago. He gets hungry a lot. There's no chocolate to be found nowadays, she tells him. There used to be chocolate. Ought to forget about the poison chocs, but could he? Would it ever taste the same?

He opened his eyes and looked around, closed his eyes again; he'd breathe and wait, and think about that prayer. Gran? Her lovey-dovey voice, he could hear it. *Listen, Jamie, listen and remember*. He must listen. *Listen and remember*, she was saying it for him.

Our Father which art in Heaven
Hallowed be thy name.
Thy Kingdom come . . .

What did that mean? Would God help him? *Will you Gran? Don't leave. I can't hear you anymore. I'll come along soon. If you want . . . forever and ever. Amen.*

* * *

Wake up, Jamie. Stay awake. Come on, boy. Open your eyes. Too dark, but he tried to see. Nothing and no one. Gran had only been in his head. A dream. Nice dream. He panted and panted until he felt dizzy, all upset because no one might find him. He'd be left to die all alone, no one to help, no one to care. Are they even looking for me? *Maybe they think I ran away. Sit up, be proud, and control yourself.*

The panting died down and he felt better. Gran used to cuddle him when he was a little boy. She stopped doing that when he turned twelve. Said he'd be a man soon, and soppy stuff like that wasn't for men. He wished he still had someone to be that close to, especially right now. He'd just have to pretend. Betty would be cuddly. *What on earth made me think about her?*

Gran used to cuddle him till he fell asleep. When he was little. *Say the prayer again.* He thought he could remember all the words now.

* * *

Jamie had to go to the toilet, but how? He had to go, right now. *No hands, all tied up.* Couldn't stand up. He'd just have to think about something else. *Maybe go back to sleep. Think about reading my book. Think what I'll write in my own book.* Everything Gran had taught him about right and wrong. He'd write down that it was for her, so people would always know how good she was. "For Millie Jenkins," he said out loud. Sounded funny, not the same as Gran. "Gran, are you there? I will write it, promise. For Millie Jenkins, my Gran."

* * *

Got to go. Oh dear, oh . . . all wet. He hadn't done that for years and years, but he couldn't help it. They'd think him dirty and smelly. He hoped they wouldn't come too soon, that they'd give him time to dry off. He couldn't help it, he couldn't. It was warm at first. Then it went cold, made him feel cold. A few drops of rain came down. The rain might wash him off. Couldn't help crying. No one to see. *Too many tears. So tired of tears.*

* * *

Raining cats and dogs, Gran used to say that. It felt like needles. Smelled grassy fresh. At least he might get clean now. *Cold. Can't sleep. So cold. Hands hurt; hurts all over, even my throat.* No good calling out and making it feel worse. No one was coming. If they found him dead, he hoped they'd find him washed clean at least.

Dark, black dark. The rain only tickly drizzly now. Shivery, scary dark. He didn't think animals came out in the dark much. Other bad things might. *So cold. The ground all wet and nasty.*

Something coming near, only he couldn't see it yet. *Moving, pushing leaves along with its feet. Not a person. A thing. Maybe coming for him. Did animals in the forest eat people like people eat them?* Coming closer, he couldn't see it, no sun, no moon, no light. Only a big black hole. *Moved off, didn't want him, not tasty enough. So, so tired.* Slept a bit, woke and slept and woke. So tired. But he felt warmer, much warmer now. *Sleep, lovely sleep.* He wanted time to pass by fast, just like the fields and animals he'd seen from the train window.

* * *

He heard poor Gran crying up in Heaven. People were supposed to be happy there. So sad, so sad. *Jamie, listen to me. Listen to me!*

Why is she so unhappy? Wake up, she won't cry if I wake up. Too tired, can't.

* * *

Light again, better than dark, but can't wake up all the way, too sleepy. *Go back to sleep. Not hungry anymore.*

Wake up, Jamie!

Leave me alone, Gran, too tired, coming soon. Terrible sore throat.

Stay awake. Jamie! What about the book, Jamie. The book! Call out, call out! Do it!

He dreamt Laddie's barking woke him up. He closed his eyes again, mustn't lose Gran. Dreamt Laddie's tongue licking, licking. Voices, had they come? Laddie lay right on top of him, warming him up with his thick, furry body. *Lovely dream. Wonderful dogs, the best animals of all. Soft and sweet like cake and Rosie.*

23

Jamie dreamed of Laddie barking, barking, people calling through the fog. He heard, "It's him!" and "We've been looking for you" and "Good boy, Laddie, good boy!" Laddie's soft body warmed him in his dreamy comfort.

Big arms scooped him up, but he didn't know whose. *God's maybe.* He smelled the car's old leather seats, felt its rocking as it went along; this seemed real enough. Hard to tell between real and dreams. *Going home, the aloneness over now? Gran stopped crying, stopped talking.*

They lifted him out of the car and he heard Rosie's voice, "Jamie! I was so worried about you." Soft arms around his neck, big kiss on his cheek. That got his eyes open. Rosie kissed him. Tired as he was, he felt his lips almost stretch to a smile. Then he had to close up again, too tired to do more.

Warm water covered him. Slippery soap all over that smelled like flowers. He opened his eyes a little, but it was too hard. He didn't know who was washing him, who dried him and put on his pajamas. He knew he was in his bed now, a soft, sweet-smelling bed with a cloud pillow. Warm. Would Gran visit soon? Jamie floated between heaven and earth, not sure which way to go. He could always see Gran later. She wasn't going anywhere. *Stay down here, no need to leave so soon. Rosie might need him.*

He woke up a bit at the sound of men's voices.

"Got to get something into him, Geoffrey. Broth would be best."

"Cook made some for him, but we didn't like to wake him."

"Got to. Help me sit him up."

Jamie wanted to sleep some more, but did his best to sit on his own. Sir Geoffrey held him close, and that felt nice. His brown, hairy jacket itched Jamie's cheek in a comfortable sort of way. The other man was that doctor, but he couldn't remember his name. He put his cold metal thing on his chest.

"Breathe in, Jamie. Now out." So hard.

"Try to do what Dr. Gibson says, Jamie."

"I'll try." He made a big breath with a great pushing of shoulders.

"That's better, good chap. Bit of a cough, but he doesn't seem to have pneumonia, at least not yet. We'll have to keep an eye on him. I'll be back in the morning."

He turned his head when Rosie knocked and popped her head in. She'd given him a big kiss when they carried him into the house. He'd been half asleep, but the kiss had woken him up for a while, and he hadn't forgotten, wouldn't ever. She wanted to know how he felt. Had to eat broth, they both said. Didn't feel like it.

Rosie disappeared again and Sir Geoffrey let him lie back down. His bed felt warm and soft, a good place to be. He coughed a few times. *Mustn't get pneumonia again. Try not to cough, got to push the pneumonia down and away.*

"You must eat, you haven't had anything to eat or drink for three days." Sir Geoffrey sounded very far away.

Swallowing hurt. He choked a few times and knew he was dribbling. He couldn't help it and he didn't really care. Rosie came back and wiped his chin. Sir Geoffrey still held him up. He could smell it was him, smoky and his special soap. Back down into the covers. He wanted to sleep for a long, long time now, but not forever, not yet.

* * *

Sun moved through the drizzle and made sparkles on the windows. Sunlight was a wonderful thing; wonderful because it showed everything there was to see. Even bad things were best seen and known. He coughed.

"Good morning, Jamie," Rosie said.

He gasped and turned his head too fast. It was very stiff. "How long have you been there?"

"Since I woke up around eight."

"What's the time now?"

"Nearly nine. I've been watching you."

"Did I snore?"

"No, silly. You looked rather sweet. You look a lot better."

"Where's Laddie? Is he all right?"

"Next to the bed. He's fine. He's been there all night. He must need to go outside pretty badly by now."

Jamie sat up and reached down for the velvety ears he loved to fiddle with. "Laddie's my best friend after you, Rosie. I do feel better. I'm hungry. I think I'll get dressed. Will Lady Audrey be there?"

"No, one of her migraines. She upset herself no end while you were missing. I'll tell Cook you're coming down. You all right to do the stairs?"

"I think so." Jamie swung his legs out of bed and pushed himself up. "Yes, I can manage." He felt wobbly, but he could do it.

He started to dress when Betty knocked on the door and didn't wait before she came in. Jamie had to pull the eiderdown over him.

"Want some help, Master Jamie?" She reached for him.

"No, thank you." He recoiled. *How very rude.* "I can dress myself. I'd like to do it by myself. Thank you."

"You haven't got anything I haven't seen before!" She sniffed and shut the door behind her too hard.

She certainly hadn't seen anything of his before. It almost seemed as if she wanted to see him undressed. He waited a few minutes before he risked getting the rest of his clothes on and done up, every last button.

Jamie took his time going down, holding the banister tightly so he wouldn't stumble. He wanted to see every picture along the stairwell, remember all the faces in case he ever got lost again. He wanted to be able to see everything he liked about the Manor in his mind when he closed his eyes. It was important to practice good memories because they could run away and hide themselves before you knew it. He hurried down the hall when he smelled the bacon.

"I'll fill a plate for you, Jamie," said Rosie.

"Thanks. Lots of everything, please." He slid into his chair and picked up the knife and fork so he'd be ready when she put the plate down. He shoveled the first few mouthfuls in, almost swallowing them without chewing.

"Slowly, Jamie," said Rosie. "You'll make yourself sick. Your tummy has been empty for ages."

"I'm really, really hungry. Still, I suppose it's not polite to eat so fast."

Sir Geoffrey came in, poured himself a cup of tea, and sat with them. "Well, Jamie, much better today, I see."

"Yes, sir. Much better. Very hungry. Oops, sorry, sir, mouth's full."

"All right just for this once. Jamie, I need to ask you some questions about Bernhardt."

Jamie's stomach pinched. He didn't want to think about that man.

"He had a big knife. He said Nazis believe that people like me should be—he said a big word, I think it meant killed—like rats. But he said I am a bit useful, because of the gardening. So he left me there. He said if I'm found in time I would live. If not, I would die. It was very scary, especially in the dark." Jamie watched his fingers twist in his lap. He wasn't hungry any more.

"Jamie, Jamie," said Sir Geoffrey in his gentle voice. "You are a very useful person, and you are good at many things. Bernhardt is just a very bad person who believes very bad things. And when we catch him, we'll put him in prison for a long time, probably forever. We were all extremely worried about you, and we are so happy you are back with us. You do know that, don't you?" Sir Geoffrey kept his voice softer than usual.

Jamie nodded, his stomach getting settled down, his smile coming easier.

"How did Bernhardt find you and take you?"

"I was going to water the seedlings. I saw him stealing Lady Audrey's car. I told him to stop stealing. It wasn't right. Then he made me sit in it and showed me his knife. Laddie tried to save me, but Bernhardt punched him very badly. Laddie tried to run after the car, but he couldn't keep up. He limped a lot." He should have said Bernhardt found him when he choked on biscuit crumbs. But it sounded better this way, more like a hero might do things.

"That was very brave of you, Jamie. I'm proud of you."

"Laddie was brave too. Did Evans understand why I couldn't do the watering?"

"Yes, he did. And, yes, Laddie was very brave. He let us know there was something wrong. He led us to the garage. Then he kept on and on barking, even though he was hurt, poor thing. Laddie helped us search."

* * *

It had taken them a few hours to realize Jamie was missing, and a few more to search the grounds. The vet had given the dog a sedative to help ease the pain of his bruised muscles, and he'd slept in Geoffrey's study most of the day. He'd sat and paced and fretted about Jamie, ignoring Audrey's migraine, quite sure he hadn't run away, knowing he'd been taken. Ronnie couldn't spare any men to search, and Falway's interest lay with the car and Bernhardt. Couldn't blame them, but it angered him just the same. That old helpless feeling haunted him, another life slipping through his fingers, knowing the pressing misery to follow.

He'd watched Laddie waking and stretching in the early evening, still dozy and tottering like an old drunk. When his mind cleared, he'd suddenly pricked up his ears and barked without stopping. It was Laddie who kept trying to force him up the road. Geoffrey had finally put him in the car and driven, stopping every mile or so to let the dog pick up the scent. That had led them to the New Forest, but it was pouring with rain and dark by that time, and they lost the scent.

He didn't mention they'd gone home for the night—not that any of them had slept—but trying to search the forest in the dark would have proved fruitless. At first light he'd dispersed a team of laborers to search in a radial pattern, starting from the place where Laddie had seemed the most agitated. He drove them and himself with a frantic whipping anger; he hadn't missed the sidelong looks from his exhausted men. They'd looked almost mutinous as mealtimes came and went, but he didn't care. If Jamie lay out there, soaking wet and cold, he couldn't last much longer.

Twilight had started to close in when Laddie stopped dead in his tracks, hearing something Geoffrey couldn't, or perhaps catching Jamie's scent on the breeze. Geoffrey sent his companion to round up the others when Laddie ran off, leaving Geoffrey to follow his barking. Close to despair, Geoffrey felt like weeping when he found the dog blanketing Jamie with his body. His emotions almost got the better of him just thinking about it. He'd even welcomed the rank stink of the boy when he lifted him off the oozing forest floor. He hadn't stopped to cut his bindings until they got to the car and its hairy old blanket. Knowing how critical it was that Jamie be warmed up, he'd told one of the men to drive while he chafed the boy's icy limbs all the way back to the Manor.

He passed his hands over his face, massaging his forehead to loosen his taught nerves.

"Sir Geoffrey? Are you all right?"

"Of course, Jamie, just a little tired. What else can you tell me?"

"He wanted to know how the police knew to go to that place where I used to live. He saw the cars. I told him I didn't tell anyone anything. He said he'd have cut my throat if I had. I know he meant it."

"Did he say where he was going?"

"A boat. The isle something."

"The Isle of Wight?" Geoffrey's adrenalin rushed.

"Think so."

"We don't think he made it to the ferry because of the road blocks. But we'll double check. We'll find him, don't you worry. Well, I'd better go and call Sir Ronald." He turned back as he got to the door. "By the way, Jamie, it's all sorted out. You'll be part of our family in a couple of weeks."

The beatific look on Jamie's face as he struggled with words was something he'd always remember, and probably always with a lump in his throat.

"Thank you. Very much," he finally managed.

Rosie ran over to her father and gave him a hug. He felt his face get rather red. He kissed Rosie on the forehead and left the room very quickly, leaving the door ajar.

"Did Sir Geoffrey's eyes have tears?" he heard Jamie ask, sounding worried. He paused around the corner where they couldn't see him.

"No, he's fine," said Rosie.

"I could have sworn his eyes had tears, but I know grownup men don't do crying. I'm still hungry."

"Eat up," said Rosie.

"You never know when you'll have to go without and make do with pretending all the tastes and smells in your head."

Geoffrey pressed his handkerchief to his eyes and hurried to his study.

24

It had been a hazy, muggy day, quite a change from last week's cold snap. The evening's skin-caressing breeze reminded Rosie of the loving moments she'd shared with Robin before he'd shown his complete disrespect for her. What would it be like, going all the way? The girls at school used to talk and giggle about it all the time, but they hadn't a clue, really. Josephine had never joined in their speculation, although she was the most developed of them all and behaved as if she were rather fast. She just frowned and walked away. Perhaps she'd done it and didn't want anyone to know. She and Penny always seemed to be going off somewhere with their arms draped around each other, heads close as if telling secrets. Some of the girls whispered that those two didn't like boys, that they were freaks of nature. Girls could be horribly cruel to anyone who seemed different. Although, looking back, Penny had always had plenty to say on the subject of boys and sex, like she did about everything.

She'd had a crush on the head girl at school once, lots of girls had. Jean Marshal told her that meant she didn't like boys, only girls, and that she was a freak of nature, too, and wouldn't ever get married. She'd dreamed of kissing that girl, holding her tight. Just a phase, she didn't really like girls that way. But it was hard to be sure; it wasn't something you could just try out. Or could you? Maybe if she found an attractive boyfriend, someone she could get close to and see if he made her want to be touched, then she'd know. There weren't too many young men around these days—except maimed ones. Maybe she wasn't patriotic enough, but looking at a stump wasn't going to make her want to do it. Revolting idea. She'd heard a couple of her school friends had lost their brothers. They must be heartbroken, but it was surely better than being left so terribly broken.

Rosie wished she could ask Mummy about sex, but she couldn't talk to her about things like that. Her parents were too old for that sort of thing, anyway. And maybe their generation only did it to get babies and didn't really like it. She got funny feelings sometimes, though, like now, squirmy itchy feelings. She'd just have to wait until the right time came.

She'd left her mother trying to teach Jamie how to play draughts; she'd spent a lot of time with him since he came back. Mummy had never been interested in teaching her own daughter anything. Well, people change as they get older, and she probably had reserves of patience now that she hadn't back then. Jamie was getting the hang of it, slowly. His eyes never left the board and you could see the effort it took to pay such close attention, sweet and heartrending. Why was he that way? What had done that to him? Dr. Gibson might know. She'd ask him next time he came.

She missed Laddie on these walks, but he rarely left Jamie's side now. He feared for the boy. He'd sit at the greenhouse door and watch while he worked with Evans. He wasn't allowed to work without Evans now, although God knows what an old man like that could do against Bernhardt. If only they'd catch that hateful man. Daddy told Jamie he'd probably go to prison forever. True in a way. They'd hang him.

She wasn't allowed out alone either, even in broad daylight. They thought she was in her room. Home felt safe, though; she didn't think he'd dare show his face at this point. He must know half of England was looking for him.

How would it feel to put someone to death? What sort of

person became a hangman? Killing in cold blood. Officially. With society's blessing and plenty of time to think about it. Did they like it, find it exciting, perhaps? Is that why they chose the job? It couldn't be right to encourage that sort of person. Unless they thought it was their religious duty. Jesus would never have done things like that, though.

Rosie had never thought about hanging before. It probably wasn't right. Not something civilized people should approve of. It wasn't like her to think about things like that, Jesus and hangmen. Must be getting dotty like that old tramp who worked the last harvest and prattled on about the Second Coming all the time.

She wished she could walk through the orchard where the last of the apple blossoms were still falling, or close to the lake with its soothing, lapping water. She had strict instructions to keep close to the house, even with company, so she turned into the rose garden.

The gasp died in her throat as a clammy, oily hand clapped over her mouth and an arm clutched her body.

"Do not say a word or I will break your little swan neck."

He dragged her around the back of the house, past the garage and stables, through the orchard to the lane outside the wall. He'd broken the gate. Rosie tried to struggle but only succeeded in pricking her thumb on her brooch. *Drop it.* Like Hansel and Gretel's crumb trail. She managed to unhook it and heard the clink as it hit the stone paving.

She couldn't see him, but knew it was Bernhardt. *Who else?* He gagged her with a filthy tasting piece of cloth and pushed her into the car. He tied her wrists with rope, much too tightly. She could see his profile now as he started the car. His mouth was half open in a sort of desperate breathlessness. The car wasn't one she'd seen around the village.

"The high and mighty Sir Geoffrey McInnis will not let them put his precious daughter in harm's way. He will get me what I want. Keep still and quiet." He showed her his gun.

She didn't know how long they drove, but it seemed like hours. *What will he do with me when he doesn't need me anymore? I'd better cooperate.* He hadn't killed Jamie, after all. *Must keep eyes open.* The car slowed, came to a halt.

Bernhardt came around to her side and pulled her out.

"Walk quietly. We are going to find a boat, and then off to France."

France. God, they'll never find me there. They seemed to be walking along an alley of some kind behind a row of old cottages. The stink of the privies made her forget Bernhardt for a few seconds, until her mind pulled her back to her predicament. They saw no one. *Where are we?* Nowhere she'd been before. She heard and smelled the sea and all the groaning clanking sounds anchored boats made as they rode the swell.

"You scurvy little turd, put that fag out!" a rough voice said.

"Sorry, Sarge."

Bernhardt swore under his breath as he gripped her arm until she cried out, a thin cry.

"What was that?" asked the little turd.

"Nothing, just some seagulls, I expect. Afraid of the dark, are we?"

"No, Sarge. But it's nighttime. No gulls around now."

"A rat then. Keep your eyes open and your mouth shut. I've got the whole bunch of you up and down here to keep an eye on. But I'll be back. If one of those boats starts up, fire first and ask questions later. You know we've got a spy on the loose."

"Yes, Sarge."

Bernhardt and Rosie went back the way they came. Where would he take her now? The salty sea had smelled so free, a happy memory she could hold inside her. Another long bumpy ride and they pulled up outside a stone farmhouse in the middle of nowhere. He pushed her inside and shoved her into an armchair. He took the gag off and she took a deep breath.

"No one lives around here. Get some sleep. I've got some thinking to do."

Sleep? He must be joking. They'll never find me here, either. Where are the owners? She looked around. The door wasn't locked. The windows looked normal. He'd have to untie her hands if she wanted to use the lavatory. Her eyes came around to Bernhardt. He watched her with an arrogant smile.

"Do not even try to escape. You cannot run faster than me. I have a gun. And I know other little tricks to make you come to heel, things you will not like so much."

Bully! "But you need me alive, otherwise you won't get what you want."

"I do not need you alive if you cause me too much trouble. I will not hesitate to get rid of a problem and make my own way. They only need to believe you are still alive."

Her fear was as cold as his eyes. He wouldn't flinch. She didn't want to die; she wanted a life, she wanted to fall in love and have all the feelings that went with it. She mustn't let him see her panic. *You're a lady, show your mettle.* She lifted her chin and met those poisonous eyes again, holding his gaze until he looked away. How odd he'd allowed her that little victory.

Nothing to be done for the moment, at least until he untied her wrists. She closed her eyes. She'd think about home. *Start from the beginning, as far back as you can remember.*

Rosie awoke with a start as Bernhardt pulled her up and out of the back door. She couldn't believe it; only a complete nincompoop could have fallen asleep at a time like this.

"Cars. Someone is coming. Keep your mouth shut, or I will kill you."

Her limbs felt stiff—she must have been asleep for an hour or more—and she stumbled as he dragged her up a small rocky hill and into a thick copse. Once deep inside, he switched on a flashlight and motioned her to sit on a tree stump. It was pitch black when he switched it off. All she could hear was the breeze riffling the treetops. He put a cold piece of metal against her neck.

"I will use this if I have to. So keep quiet. And still. Quite still."

25

Geoffrey paced while Audrey sat, gripping the arms of the chair as if that were the only way to stay grounded. Geoffrey blamed himself. He knew how stubborn she was, he should have checked on her. He hadn't even known she was missing until a couple of hours ago, when Audrey knocked on her door to ask her about some function or other. And where was that bloody gardener guard chap?

They turned in anticipation as Stanton entered with D. I. Falway. Stanton hovered, wringing his hands in agitation, his old face crumpled into crosshatchings of distress.

"Lady Audrey, do you recognize this brooch?" Falway asked.

"Oh, God. Yes, it's Rosie's. Where did you find it?" she asked, lips barely moving.

"Outside the back garden gate. Which was broken."

"It's that devil Visser." Geoffrey fell into a chair.

"Probably, sir. Wants a hostage so he can make demands and make his escape. And we found our man. Dead."

"God, no," whispered Audrey. Geoffrey, too paralyzed by his own feelings, didn't reach out to her.

"We can't let him go, you know."

"What the devil do you mean by that? You'll do whatever it takes to get my daughter back. In one piece."

"Yes, sir, I'm sure we'll all do our best. I'd like to talk to that boy. Jamie. Does he know the girl is missing?"

"No," said Audrey. "We didn't want to upset him. He's devoted to her, you know."

"Well, I'd like to talk to him, just the same."

"I'll fetch him, Sir Geoffrey," said Stanton, not waiting for an answer.

They waited in silence, Geoffrey pacing again, Audrey staring at the Aubusson, Falway shifting from foot to foot.

"What's the matter, Sir Geoffrey?" Jamie asked. "Stanton seems very upset."

"Jamie, I'm afraid I have bad news. Rosie has been kidnapped like you were. We think by Bernhardt. Have you any idea where he might have taken her?"

"Oh, no! Not Rosie, not lovely Rosie!" Jamie's eyes filled and spilled tears down his cheeks. His chest heaved.

"Pull yourself together, boy," Geoffrey said, his tone so sharp it stopped Jamie cold.

"Think back to anything Bernhardt might have said. Not just when he took you, but before, at Blexton, about places he knew. Think! We've got to find her." Geoffrey heard his voice rising. He mustn't show his panic. *Pull yourself together.*

Jamie plopped down onto a footstool and covered his face with his hands.

"You don't remember anything?"

"I'm thinking. This is how I think really hard."

When he at last raised his head, he said, "I did hear one funny thing."

"What? Come on, lad, out with it," Geoffrey shouted.

"When I was still at that place, Rosie came to visit and Mrs. Clancy put us in a room next to her office. There were sort of window things high up on the wall and I heard Bernhardt on the telephone. I don't know if he had permission to go in and use her phone. She would have been quite cross if he didn't have permission."

"Yes, yes, get on with it!" Geoffrey could have shaken him.

"There were a lot of funny words, not like words we say. Then

I heard Bernhardt say, "In Old Ring Copse." I know that place. It's on the farm where Mr. Lake was so unkind to me. It scared me because I wondered if Bernhardt could be Mr. Lake's friend."

"I know the Lake farm," said Falway. "Secluded. Lake's in prison for what he did to this young chap. And he's suspected of doing away with his wife. If Bernhardt's pally with him, he might be using the place as a hideout."

"Let's go!" Geoffrey said, standing, ready to tear into action.

"Sir Geoffrey, this is a job for the army and the police. Let them handle it. I must insist."

Geoffrey looked as if he'd protest, but dropped into his chair again. He sensed Audrey's surprise rather than saw it. He leaned his head back and closed his eyes. Unbearable to sit doing nothing while his child was in danger. He sprang up the moment he heard the front door close behind Falway.

"Stanton!" he roared. "Unlock the gunroom."

26

Clouds ambled across the moon in an untidy parade, sometimes allowing shafts of light to reach through the canopy, sometimes sprawling out and fogging the night. The copse was at the top of an oddly knobby hill, and while a few ancient trees and waist-high thickets of gorse and bracken provided some cover, expanses of low prickly scrub made it difficult to approach on the sly.

Falway, Cummins, and Bretton-Taylor crept up the east side of the hill, flattening themselves when the moonlight searched them out. They'd asked Falway to lead the way since he knew the ground better than them, or because they deemed him more expendable. He didn't know how many troops had been ordered out, but he spotted a few on their bellies and a couple behind the vast oaks, all armed.

He remembered some scandal he'd overheard his mother telling a friend, years ago, something about a fancy little folly amongst the trees up there where, it was rumored, there had been all sorts of wicked unnatural goings on. His mother never let anything ribald pass her lips, so he'd been left to his imagination. Only about eight at the time, he'd thought perhaps people took their clothes off in front of everybody and danced around like that, a titillating thought. Well, he'd probably got it just about right. His adult self smirked. *Concentrate, stop being so bloody flippant.* Whenever things got sticky, his mind tended to scatter into all sorts of odd corners.

He couldn't see any kind of structure, although they should be almost at the edge of the clearing by now. He inched forward, hoping the recent showers had waterlogged the twigs and stems underfoot.

Hissing whispers. He strained for words, but couldn't make them out through the rustling leaves. The breeze whipped itself toward wind, cold for May. He hoped the soldiers weren't trigger happy—the three of them stood between them and their quarry, after all. An odd arrangement, he couldn't see how it could work without catastrophe. They had orders to wait for Cummins's call—*All in!*—but things could easily get out of hand.

He had an old revolver, issued earlier with great solemnity, but he knew himself a rotten shot. All he could hope for was to help flush the fellow out and let the army do the rest. Sir Ronald lurked out there somewhere, no doubt well out of range.

Whispers again, not far. He moved in a little farther.

"You're hurting me, let go!" The girl sounded frightened, poor thing.

"I hear noises, they're coming. Shut up or I will hurt you some more."

They were less than twenty feet from Bernhardt now, at the edge of a clearing much larger than he'd expected. He could just make out a crumbling circular foundation on the other side. That must be the old folly, an Eden for randy old aristocrats.

Damn, the girl was too close to Bernhardt, he held her in what looked like a chokehold. "Hold it, see if Bernhardt will relax a little if he thinks no one's around," he whispered to Cummins. The man looked at him as if he were dirt. "You will follow *our* lead."

"No one's coming up here. Let me go!" Her voice had risen to a little girl's wail.

"I said shut up! You see that bare ground over there?" All the men peered at a gash in the moss to Bernhardt's left, moonlit for a few seconds. "There's a woman under there, a woman who could not keep her mouth shut. Her husband had had enough and I was glad to help him out of his difficulty. You will sleep next to her if you do not behave yourself." Bernhardt shook her arm. "The worms need some fresh meat by now, I think." Rosie sagged and said nothing more.

The farmer's missing wife. Mystery solved. But how did Bernhardt know Tom Lake? At least ten minutes must have passed. Funny how hard it was to keep completely still. His head itched, feet almost numb—God, he wanted to sneeze! He held his nose in a vise-like grip, closing his eyes and counting to twenty. Let the others keep their eyes on the target; it was their show, wasn't it?

Bernhardt stamped his feet now and blew into his hands, even as he clutched his gun. Rosie sat on a tree stump, head bowed. Falway's hands sweated in spite of the chill; he breathed as deeply as he could, a fraying breath, as he watched Cummins raise his pistol. He raised his, too, just in case; Bretton-Taylor pushed his arm back down and shook his head silently.

The report echoed off the trees, startling Falway almost as much as it did Bernhardt. Rosie screamed, then slumped and curled up, whimpering as she clutched her arm. Bernhardt aimed his gun at her head and shouted, "Keep away from me or she dies! I seem to be a much better shot than you!"

Cummins sauntered into the clearing as if he hadn't just participated in the most unbelievable balls-up. Falway muttered to Bretton-Taylor, "What now?" The man neither spoke nor moved. It didn't feel right. He wondered if the army was closing in, although he didn't know what good that would do with so many players in the ring. He feared for the girl. He started to edge away to see if he could get a better aim from farther around the clearing's edge. Bretton-Taylor grabbed his arm, forcing him back. "Keep out of it!"

"Who in the hell are you?" Bernhardt seemed to think himself invincible.

"Never mind that. Let's put an end to this now, Herr Bernhardt Visser. You can't get away. The army is all around us, their guns trained on you. You'll be safer with me, take my word for it. If I'd meant to hit you, you'd be lying in the muck and she'd be running on home to Daddy."

"But I still have the girl. She needs a doctor." A little less sure of himself.

"We can't allow that to get in the way of our work." Cummins's voice oozed like hot runny custard.

"Her father will never allow anything to happen to her. I want a boat and supplies and a car to get me to the docks. She needs a doctor. She can bleed to death if you don't do what I say. I will take her on the boat and take care of her wound."

"We have our orders. It's you we want. Alive. Come now and you won't hang." Falway couldn't see much, but he could wager Cummins was smirking as he watched Bernhardt's new reality sink in. He had no hostage. Rosie was not useful.

Cummins had missed Bernhardt on purpose and Rosie's safety was not a priority. These men wanted information, and they wanted the spy alive. Falway catapulted away from his companion, then walked forward slowly, hands in the air.

"Ach, you." Bernhardt looked him up and down with amused contempt. "Go and tell them what I want."

"Very well. But please, give me the girl!" He knew his request was fruitless, but he had to try.

"Do not be ridiculous."

"Yes, he is ridiculous. He's not one of us," said Cummins, disdain curling his mouth. Falway didn't look at Cummins. He'd have shot him if he'd thought it would do any good.

* * *

Geoffrey had followed Falway and his companions, keeping well back. The soldiers who'd stopped him earlier knew who he was and were unaware that he was not supposed to be involved. "Part of the team, old chap," he muttered several times. He worked his way up the hill behind them and saw them branch off to the east. He would approach from the west. He crawled on a few yards to a clump of gorse. He should keep still for a few minutes and make sure all was quiet. *The fewer men on the move would make for fewer rustles and cracks to alert the bastard.*

He dropped when he heard a shot, his cheek coming to rest on young gorse spikes, the sharp twigs sticking into his cheek a welcome torment. He roused himself when he heard Falway call to an officer about ten feet to his right that the girl was not badly hurt, and to fetch Sir Ronald.

"Psst! Falway, over here!" Falway sank down beside him, revolver pointed awkwardly at a treetop.

"Be careful with that thing. What's going on?"

Falway laid the revolver on the ground, barrel facing away. "You're not supposed to be here. Your daughter's been shot in the arm by Cummins, that MI5 chap. Aiming for the spy and missed. She'll be all right. One of them is trying to talk Visser out. I've got to wait for Sir Ronald."

He must push the panic down; he couldn't afford it, not now. "I'm going on."

"No, stay where you are! Sir Geoffrey!"

"Bugger off!"

Forward, easy does it, keep your wits about you. He crawled on his belly, every sense ticking. *Not too fast, remember your training.* So long ago now, but he could still summon up the immense effort it took to screw up his courage and go over the top at the command, death only yards ahead, the spurious comfort of a quick-mud trench behind him. It was not his life at stake now; he stood to lose a more precious treasure. Whatever it took to save her, he'd do it. He couldn't do otherwise.

He inched along, his breathing normal now, his motions fluid, even his heart staying quiet. Only the hellish abyss of his mind churned, waiting to seize his opportunity.

If only they had set their grief for Fiona aside earlier for Rosie's sake. They should have been grateful to have her. Especially Audrey. She'd barely touched the child in the early years, so selfish in her grief. *What kind of a mother, even a grieving one, doesn't hold her child and make her feel safe and loved?* Long-veiled anger rose like an autumnal fog, clinging and invasive, damp and heavy. *Stop it, stop the blaming and concentrate.*

He crawled on until he reached the clearing behind the ruins. One wall section was high enough to rest his arm on to steady his rifle. Bernhardt stood with his back to him, about fifteen feet away, and another man—Intelligence?—faced Bernhardt on the other side of the clearing. All three of them stood in more or less a straight line, but Geoffrey, well hidden in the shadows, felt himself unlikely to be spotted by either man.

Rosie lay almost facing him, arched like a stillborn lamb. *Open your eyes.* He tried to will the thought across. She thought she was going to die, poor little girl. He raised his weapon; better draw a bead on the target. Rosie lifted her head a little, he thought she'd opened her eyes; just one good moonbeam and she might spot him, then she'd know she was going to be all right. No, she might call out. The wretched man was circling her, muttering some gibberish and pointing his gun at her head. If only the swine would stay still, all he needed was a second or two.

Rosie's pain-filled, five-year-old face filled his mind, a time when he'd had to hold her still for stitches in her arm. He'd withered inside then, held her face into his neck, couldn't look. *Stop that! Focus.*

"We'll keep you safe, Visser, we have a quiet spot to have a little chat, plenty of home comforts." He sounded well bred, should be a good shot.

"I am telling you, Sir Geoffrey will never let his daughter suffer."

"And I keep telling you, Sir Geoffrey is not in charge here, and we ordered him to stay away. I am in charge. And the girl doesn't matter, not to us."

The slimy bastard! They wanted him for their own purposes, and to hell with Rosie. Geoffrey felt a deeper fear then, a bitter fear born of a new understanding of this war.

* * *

Jamie had heard Sir Geoffrey tell Stanton to open the gunroom. That meant he planned to rescue Rosie. Jamie wanted to go, too, but he knew they wouldn't let him. Then Sir Geoffrey yelled from the gunroom to have the estate car brought around. That might be his chance. Jamie waited by the hedge. After the groom had left the keys in the ignition and strolled back to the stables, he crept in the back and hid under the hairy old dog blanket. It smelled like a pig place.

Jamie knew his way around the hill, he'd tried to run away and hide here a few times. Only cold and hunger made him go back to the farmhouse. His eyes were sharp, so he managed to avoid the soldiers on this side of the hill before cutting around to the clearing a bit higher up than D. I. Falway. Bernhardt held

Rosie tight, and, as far as he could see, she felt scared and sad.

The loud noise frightened him, and he was terrified other people had heard his squeal. He saw Rosie fall, too, and hold her arm, crying, hurting. He saw the strange man talking to Bernhardt, and saw the detective leave. They didn't seem to be doing anything. He would have to rescue Rosie; he was in a real adventure now, and he was not a coward.

She lay all in a heap, very sad, clutching her arm. When the moon blinked once he could see dark runny stuff, must be blood, even though it didn't look very red. *Please, God, don't let her lose all her blood.* Bernhardt walked around talking to himself. Got mad maybe. Should he tell Bernhardt to leave her alone?

Jamie could see his gun now, and it looked very big. If he shouted, maybe Bernhardt would shoot the gun at him instead of Rosie. He didn't want to die, didn't want to hurt, even though he didn't want Rosie to die either. Anyway, after shooting him, Bernhardt could always turn around and shoot Rosie some more, and with Jamie dead there'd be nobody to do anything about it.

He spotted a movement on the other side. Sir Geoffrey. He could just about pick out his shape in that nearly dark place, and only then because the moon, going in and out of the clouds all evening, stayed out for a longer time, but he knew it was him. Perhaps he would make things right. He turned his eyes back to Rosie.

Bernhard stood still, feet wide apart and chin down. He lifted the gun up high and pointed it at Rosie's chest. He meant to shoot her and really make her lose all her blood, like Gran did, like what made people die. The other man was still talking.

"No, no," Jamie shouted as he ran at him. "Leave her alone!"

Bernhardt swung around and aimed at Jamie. The shot was shocking, a huge noise, worse than a bomb. So much more dark stuff, had to be blood, clothes wringing wet with it, the ground black with it. *Please not dead, not Rosie.* She looked dead. Bernhardt looked dead too, but how? Jamie couldn't move, couldn't rightly think. He didn't think he was dead. He didn't feel any hurts. Bernhardt must have missed him.

Sir Geoffrey held Rosie to his chest now, like a father should. She cried out, she had pain. *Not dead, not dead.* Lots of people around now. No one held Bernhardt, or talked to him. Jamie sidled over and looked down at his face, ugly now. Empty eyes stared back, mouth open, still shouting, it looked like. Very dead. Finished with hurting. Suddenly, Jamie had to be sick and ran back into the trees; *you had to be private for being sick.*

* * *

Geoffrey thought his heart would seize up when he wondered if he'd hit her, too. When the boy started shouting and running, Bernhardt had grabbed Rosie and turned toward Jamie, trying to pull her up as he went, only she'd been a dead weight. He'd aimed for the man's chest and seemed to have hit his heart, only from the side instead of the back because he'd kept twisting. He'd not so much as nicked Rosie.

Rosie had caught the bullet in her upper arm, but Geoffrey didn't think any bones were hit. *Might still be in there though. Must hurt like the blazes.*

That bastard. Judging from the voice he'd heard, the fellow had been brought up to shoot. There'd be hell to pay.

27

Sir Ronald hunched in the grey drizzle, hands jammed into his pockets as if to prevent his coat from flying off. Geoffrey, a little out of breath after his climb up to Old Ring Copse, stopped by the grave-sized trench two constables were digging. More constables dug in other spots.

"Morning Geoffrey, how's the lass?"

"She'll be in hospital another week or so. Gibson wants to keep an eye on her."

Ronnie paused and bit his lower lip. He seemed unusually diffident, his shoulders tense. "Is she in much pain?" He looked at Geoffrey sideways, as if afraid he might have asked an inappropriate question.

"Not too bad, lodged in her upper arm you know. No bones broken, thank God. He's got her well sedated. Just as well after all she's been through."

"Quite."

Ronnie released his shoulders and turned back to watch the digging. "Look!" He had the avaricious look of a hound, now.

Geoffrey flinched when he saw pink satin blanket borders poking out of the newly turned earth. More digging, careful now, probing around, not through. They lifted the blanket and its contents and laid it on a tarpaulin.

"Open it," Ronnie said. "Gently does it."

The blanket had been swathed so the body—it must be a body—had to be turned and lifted several times as they unwrapped. Geoffrey forced himself to keep looking as Ronnie uncovered the corpse. The odor wafted over, sweetly unpleasant, but not as overwhelming as he'd feared. She was not intact; time and weather, not to mention insects, had taken their toll. A woman's moldy clothing, but it was hard to tell much else. His breath rattled. He'd grown out of asthma, for God's sake don't let it come back now. They'd given him hell at school when he'd had to stop playing rugger because of it. Called him a sissy.

Geoffrey couldn't look away from her ruined head. "Her face, Ronnie. Decay or injury?"

"Massive injuries, a rock I should think. We'll never get her identified that way. Maybe the clothes will help, though they're not in good condition." He picked up her left hand and pried off a wedding ring, most of the skin peeling off with it. He dropped the mess into a paper bag, which he tucked into an inner pocket.

Geoffrey, no stranger to death at the front, and by no means averse to dressing game, felt nauseated by Ronnie's casual handling of this decaying carcass, and a woman at that. He turned his back and walked away until the breeze carried no hints of decay his way. He'd got to get fresh air into his lungs, to flush out death.

He remembered Ronnie had started his career in London, so had certainly seen his share of atrocities; he must have grown emotional calluses after the first few. Ghastly. But then he himself felt strangely devoid of pity for this woman. He hated cruelty of any kind, but she hardly seemed like a person. Wrong-headed, he knew, but she was a thing to him, a repulsive thing. Was there something missing in him, some crucial nexus? He turned around to see what Ronnie was doing now. He didn't want to see, but felt compelled to see it through.

Ronnie poked around some more. "Ah, a brooch." He unpinned it. "We'll see if the daughter can identify these. Then we'll invite Mr. Lake to comment." The brooch joined the ring.

Geoffrey's goose pimples crawled and his bowels loosened

as he watched the body being loaded onto a stretcher. It looked nightmarishly disarticulated, too prone to having pieces fall away. One of the constables looked greenish, the other merely grim as they threw the dirty blanket over it. Her.

"Over here, sir!"

They strode over to see what the man had turned up. A common sack, and inside it two vellum-covered packets wrapped in an old mackintosh. Ronnie undid the vellum and found two small black leather satchels, one about eight inches square and the other slightly longer and narrower. He drew out their contents and laid them out.

"My word, I've heard about these. Falway told me the MI5 chaps found one in Visser's room. They didn't show it to me, though. Beautiful!" He sounded almost rapturous. "A German transmitter, newest model. Three batteries, the set itself, and little Morse tapper, no more than four pounds." He tapped each item as he spoke with a staccato flourish. His chest had puffed out again.

"I can't believe it's so small," said Geoffrey.

"And so efficient. Their chatter is hard to pick up, though we're getting better at it. And you see how portable they are. Their engineers are the tops, hurts me to admit it, but there you are." Ronnie looked crestfallen. "If this is what he was using at Blexton, no wonder we couldn't pick it up. We got glimpses, but could never pinpoint the source. The place is set very far back from the road, you may remember. Clever."

He straightened and shifted from foot to foot, looking awkward.

"I say, Geoffrey. Sorry about Rosie."

"I know. Go easy on Falway. I'm sure he did his best. Were those other fellows from Intelligence?"

"Yes, they were, and I understand they had orders, orders they didn't share with me. Falway wasn't given a choice. They held him back. He went against them in the end, then tried to find me."

"I suppose there'll be trouble for him? If the silly buggers hadn't insisted on playing cloak and dagger . . .well, I would've shot the man anyway. They were willing to sacrifice Rosie. Wouldn't have made any difference." Geoffrey's fury rose again as he thought of the sheer callousness of the plan. His lungs rattled again. Calm down, don't set it off.

"Good thing you all disobeyed orders. Thought it best to keep Falway behind a desk today. He was very shaken up, you know." Ronnie sounded distressed too, not himself, behaving naturally, no pretensions.

"I'm sure he was. He handled that gun as if it were a snake. Don't you train your men?"

"No, Geoffrey, the truth is, we don't. Brass doesn't approve. They're afraid we'll get trigger-happy like the Yanks."

"I can see their point. But still, there is a war on. Perhaps I can bring some pressure to bear, get the army to train them and to leave Falway out of any fuss. If they didn't see fit to let him in on their plans, they could hardly have expected him to cooperate."

"Good idea. Yes," Ronnie said, clearly relieved, "I can't afford to lose manpower with so many coppers called up."

"By the way, I've been meaning to ask. You told me once you had a man placed at Blexton. What happened to him? He didn't seem much help."

Ronnie looked embarrassed again and studied his shoes. "I never told Falway about our plant. He went by the name of Neville Chambers. But I wondered why he'd proved so useless, so one of my men carried out a quiet investigation over the last couple of weeks. It seems he betrayed us and got a little too friendly with Bernhardt, helped him identify suitable houses to rob, helped him fence the stuff and shared in the take. He knew the fellow was suspected of espionage too. It happens. I must say, I'd always thought him pretty feeble, although he came highly recommended. We picked him up early this morning. He'll be a guest of His Majesty for some time. Doubt there's anything more to see here."

The two old soldiers started to walk to the road. Geoffrey was amused how purposefully they marched, gradually falling in step, keeping time to the hard ground crunching under their boots. Would this land ever crunch under the Nazi boot?

"Oh, God!" said Geoffrey, stopping suddenly.

"What?"

"Ronnie, those transmitters must be expensive, precious.

Why would Visser have two?"

"Back up in case one goes wrong?"

"Or for someone else to use. Someone we don't know about yet."

"Bloody hell!"

"Quite."

They started walking again, each lost in private dread.

"Ronnie, you might want to get some of your chaps along to our boathouse. Rosie told me a few days ago she'd noticed some boxes inside that weren't there before. Slipped my mind, I'm afraid. I opened one of them this morning. Could be some of that missing loot." He hadn't uttered the word "loot" since his boyhood, when adventure stories filled his head with fantasies of derring-do.

"I'll get someone round right away."

Geoffrey hadn't tackled the subject of Cummins's cavalier treatment of Rosie. He had to approach the right man, a man who would carry on about the vicissitudes of war, no doubt. They had to take the larger view, he saw that. But he wouldn't forget. He'd find a way to sink that effete little excrescence, however long it took.

28

Falway decided to walk to the station. For once it was a clear morning, apple blossoms spotlighted for now by the testy British sun. He'd expected a good bollocking for interfering with the Intelligence men, but nothing. Sir Ronald had said goodnight when he left as if nothing had happened. Poor kid, he hoped she was on the mend.

"Has a car been laid on?" he asked the desk sergeant.

"Yes, sir, should be around in five minutes or so. Sir Ronald left word that he'll meet you there."

Damn! He might have known the old man would want to be in on the action.

Falway always felt a shifty chill when the prison gate slammed behind him. He could taste the bleakness and smell the seedy existence of the inmates. He signed in at the desk, no sign of Sir Ronald—where the hell was he?—and plodded behind the warden to the interview room, spending those few minutes calming his nerves. Got to get this one right.

Sir Ronald waited outside the door with someone else, a youngish man, not more than forty. Not one of the two from last night, thank God, but a no-name Oxbridge type, sleek and bland, expressionless by trade.

"This is Mr. Chalmering. He'll be sitting in with us."

Chalmering inclined his head, not deigning to speak. Falway afforded him a curt nod in return.

Sir Ronald and Chalmering sat against the wall next to the door, behind Tom Lake; Falway sat across from him at the table. He sat back, arms crossed, and stared at Lake in silence. It didn't take long, as he knew it wouldn't.

"What are you staring at? What's this all about?" Lake shifted in his chair a while longer. "Cat got your tongue?" His voice broke like an adolescent's.

"We've got Bernhardt Visser, Lake. He talked. Told us what we wanted to know." Falway paused, let the man stew for a few minutes. "Told us about your wife. About how you helped him. We found her, by the way. Your daughter identified her wedding ring. And her brooch. It's a hanging matter now."

Lake blanched. "You're lying!"

"We have our ways of making men talk. We've got special people to handle things like that. Don't make me call them in."

Falway didn't look at Chalmering, knew how his lip would have curled upon hearing such trite melodrama. Lake seemed to swallow it, though. Probably never went to the cinema.

"You knew Bernhardt was a spy. Do you need extra encouragement to talk? We have to let them know, give them time to get their gear ready."

Lake started shaking now, his fists clenched on the table top, his head bowed, eyes squeezed shut. Falway stayed silent again. He didn't take his eyes off him.

"I don't believe you. Elsie couldn't have been wearing those things. She threw her wedding ring on the dressing table the night she left me. And I wouldn't let her take her jewelry. I didn't kill her . . . I didn't!" His voice had turned low and shivery and Falway caught a whiff of fresh sweat.

"No, we know Visser did it because you asked him to. And we know what he got in return. A safe haven. Use of the car. A place to hide things. A place to bury things, people. We found plenty of loot from all these burglaries we've been having around here. Was that your doing?"

"No, for God's sake!"

"Oh, I think it was. You're a greedy man, aren't you?"

"Visser was trained to withstand interrogation, he wouldn't have broken under your paltry efforts." Lake bit his lower lip as soon as the words were out of his mouth.

"Now we're getting somewhere. Talk."

Lake heaved a great sigh and gave up. "He needed money to carry out his mission. He had some friend or other who helped him gradually sell things off. He could hardly expect me to support him."

"How did you two meet?"

"Down at the pub, the Feather and Pheasant just after Elsie walked out. I hadn't seen him in there before. He was sitting next to me at the bar and we talked a lot. I told him my troubles—I was damned angry—and he told me some of his. We went back to the farm for a brandy. I invited him to stay." Lake's color had heightened, his voice now stronger and indignant.

"And you talked some more?"

"We talked some more."

"Did you know he had two transmitters, was sending information to the Germans? We found one in his room at Blexton and one buried in the copse near Elsie."

Falway heard Sir Ronald whisper something to Chalmering and glanced over in time to see Chalmering's brief glower. Hadn't wanted that to come out. Those MI5 twits had told him to keep quiet. But he didn't work for them, wouldn't touch their slimy jobs with a barge pole. He turned his attention back to Lake.

"Well?"

"He said so, but I don't see what sorts of things he could have known that were any use. He was just showing off, trying make out he was bigwig spy." Lake looked cocky now.

"He could have reported on coastal defenses, army bases, munitions storage, local leading citizens, food supplies. He could have drawn maps. Useful if the Germans invaded, don't you think?"

"You're exaggerating!"

"And why two transmitters? Was he expecting a friend to join him? Did you see him with anyone else?"

"He didn't tell me his plans." Lake shrugged. "How the hell should I know what he was up to?"

Falway leaned forward and pounded the table with his fist. "Why did you betray your country?" Lake recoiled, scraping his chair back. Sir Ronald had even started a little. "People die because of traitors like you."

"You all betrayed me! Prosecuting me when that little freak caught a cold. I did my bit. I grew food for my country. The country spat on me first!"

"So it's all our fault, is it?"

"Yes, it fucking well is, and that slut of a wife of mine is to blame too! I'm glad she's dead, good riddance! She betrayed me, too. Elsie deserved what she got." He was shouting now. "Yes, Visser did me a favor, and I did him one." He puckered his mouth and a glob of spittle plastered Falway's cheek.

"I think I've heard enough," said Chalmering almost inaudibly as he rose and knocked on the door. Sir Ronald stayed put. Lake sprang for him, or the opening door, Falway couldn't tell which. Chalmering turned and flipped him against the wall with the easy flourish of landing a large salmon. Lake bounced onto his back and lay still. It had taken only seconds and the wardens rushed in to find the prisoner unconscious, a livid bruise already showing on his brow.

"Get him to sick bay," said Sir Ronald, strident now. "I want him alive and well on the scaffold."

Falway watched as they lifted Lake onto a stretcher—none too gently. He wiped his cheek. Disgusting. He dropped his handkerchief into a corner, a necessary sacrifice, even with the shortages. Nasty piece of work.

He'd never watched a hanging. Would he want to? Could he stomach it?

29

Falway sat writing his report on a black market ring they'd just cracked. Boring, very boring. But he'd had more than enough excitement last month. Spies and guns. He shuddered.

A knock on the door and the desk sergeant stuck his head around. "Someone to see you, Guv."

A neat, pale woman stood in the doorway, smoothing her dress with one hand and hanging on to her handbag with such desperation her knuckles showed white. Nondescript at first glance, Falway discerned a certain grace in her features, a face that could prove appealing when at ease.

"Come in, please. What is your name?"

She stayed where she was.

"Elsie Lake, Inspector. Mrs. Elsie Lake."

Falway's mouth hung open like some gormless youth. "We thought you were dead."

"I know, I don't read the papers much, well, not at all actually, but I saw the headlines about the trial at the village shop yesterday evening, so I caught the night train." Her voice trembled.

"Where have you been?"

"Scotland. Just outside Glasgow. I knew my husband would find me at my parents' and find some way to hurt me. He did threaten to kill me, you know, and I think he meant it. I've got an old school friend up there and she helped me find a job. I'm a housekeeper on one of the big estates."

She sounded more self-assured now. Falway sat back and waited.

"And I wrote to my son, although I don't know if he got my letter. Who knows where he is." She sighed, the tension in her shoulders not slipping out with her breath. "I don't suppose he knows about his father. They would have told him about my supposed passing, though. Wouldn't they?"

"I'm sure he was notified. Can't always get the boys back in time, though. Oh, God, I've got to stop the trial!" He dialed with a frantic finger.

"Sir Ronald, please. Urgent. I don't care if he's on his way out. Get him!"

"Sorry, sir, I know the trial's starting in an hour. But you have to stop it." Falway held the phone away from his ear for a moment. "Because I have a visitor here. Mrs. Elsie Lake. Tom Lake's wife." He held the phone out to her. "He wants a word with you."

Falway listened as Elsie gave Sir Ronald the same story she'd given him. He could hear the barking, saw Elsie's mouth harden. A lot of character in that face.

"He was very drunk. He pushed me out of the door and bolted it. He'd forgotten about the bikes. I took one of those and left it at the station. Got myself up to Scotland as soon as I could."

After she hung up, Falway said, "Good heavens, that's more than ten or twelve miles. Must have taken hours."

"I only had one thought in my head. To get as far away from that man as I could before he really hurt me."

Poor woman, married to a brute like that. And the daughter wasn't much better. He'd finally tracked her down in Bournemouth staying with a friend. Got tired of housekeeping and went to stay with the friend of a friend. When he'd asked her to identify her mother's jewelry, telling her it had come off a corpse, she'd just shrugged. Heartless little tart. She kept looking at her watch. Expecting company. The way she was dressed, most likely a paying customer.

She handed back the phone.

"Get that body exhumed."

"Yes, Sir Ronald, right away." So who was the dead woman?

"Mrs. Lake. We found a grave with the body of a woman in it. Wearing your ring and brooch. Do you have any idea who that could have been?"

"No, no idea. I don't think Tom had a girlfriend. He always stayed at home in the evenings, worse luck. Of course, he was always having a go at the land girls, but I don't think they always gave him what he wanted. Most of them just left in a huff."

Falway rose. "Thank you for coming in. You'll have to stay down here. Your parents could put you up?"

"Yes, of course. But I can't stay too long. I wouldn't want to lose my job, I'm very good at it and I'm happy there. Although my boy might turn up, mightn't he? It would be lovely to see him."

"I understand. I'll try to find out your son's whereabouts. But there are matters to be cleared up, so I must insist you stay close by while we conclude our investigation." He hoped he sounded firm.

"Don't try to bully me, Inspector. I've had more than enough of bullying!"

"My apologies, Mrs. Lake. You do know your husband was aiding a German spy?"

She subsided into a chair.

* * *

Falway contemplated the coffin, swaying precariously on its way up from its dank grave, a rip in the carpet of weedy grass. A poor little affair. The parish had tried to do right by her, but they had little money to spare these days. He spotted Elsie Lake watching from a distance. Morbid curiosity driving her to see her *alter ego* disinterred?

The sun shone with a mocking brilliance, illuminating the soil and dust motes. He brushed crumbs of dirt off the brass nameplate.

"Load her up, get her to the morgue."

He'd thought it odd at the time that Sir Ronald hadn't taken it for granted that it was Mrs. Lake they'd found. Wanted a full description of any identifying marks on the body. Canny old sod. Only one other woman had gone missing in the last few months. Now he'd have to visit that poor wreck of a soldier and interview him. No time like the present. He wrapped his scarf tighter, although it wasn't that cold, and walked towards the town.

The man droned on about his faithless wife until he'd just come out and said it.

"Look, a body has been found. It could be someone else, but we need to be certain. Now, what about your wife. Moles? Scars?"

Brutal, he knew, but it stopped the man short. He winced.

"I should never have said those terrible things. Sylvia? Dead? Are you sure?" He'd looked washed out to start with, but had a pronounced pallor now.

"No, as I just said, we're not sure at all. Marks?"

"She had her appendix out when she was about twelve, I think. There was a mole on, er, well."

"Oh, for God's sake! Where?"

"Her bottom."

"Which side?"

"Er, right."

"We'll let you know, sir. Thank you for your help."

He let himself out. The poor fellow could hardly walk.

Falway called in on the soldier again that same evening.

"I'm sorry, sir, I have bad news."

"It was Sylvia?" No emotion this time, mouth set hard. He'd been doing some serious thinking, perhaps.

"Almost certainly. And we obtained some dental records, and they more or less matched up. The scar and the mole were difficult due to de . . . er, due to the time she'd been in the ground, but the doctor was pretty sure of at least the scar."

The young man stared at the wall, his face closed and white. No tears. He knew she hadn't cared about him. Falway had heard the stories when he investigated her disappearance; it seemed just about everyone in their village had heard about her carryings on, and many of the young people in the neighboring ones too.

He didn't blame the boy for his bitterness. Unmissed and unloved while he'd floundered in wet trenches, getting shot at and fearing death every waking moment, and then one operation after the other, lying in pain in hospital while she gallivanted around. She couldn't even be bothered to visit.

He sighed as he let himself out. Bernhardt Visser had needed Tom to trust him and be in his debt. He couldn't find Elsie since she was up in Scotland, so must have looked for a woman who resembled her, at least superficially. Well, she was the type to come to a sticky end. *But why bury her with the jewelry? Visser wouldn't count on her being found. Did he expect Lake to check up on his handiwork?* Probably the sort of thing he'd do himself.

Falway still missed his wife, dead seven years now. Even when the morphine didn't help anymore, he still hadn't truly believed she would die. He'd have liked children, and he knew Ellen blamed herself. They'd been happy, though, except for that one regret, content with their lot. That was more than most people could say, and certainly more than that poor young soldier could say.

Mrs. Lake, now, she had an interesting face. And spirit, too, plenty of gumption. He liked that. He'd spoken to her several times since her first visit. He felt she was warming up to him. She'd been a doormat in the marriage, but she'd found plenty of strength when it mattered most. Besides, she'd had the children to think about.

30

They'd had their first chat in May when Betty's sister, Sarah, came to stay. Rosie and Jamie had gone to visit, not long before Bernhardt left him in the forest. Jamie remembered Lady Audrey had decided to come with them at the last minute, and the sight of her had set Betty in quite a flutter.

Sarah lost a leg in the big December raid in London; the same one Jamie had been caught up in, the horrid blitz business. Poor Sarah, she'd seemed so sad, so breakable, and her low spirits rubbed off onto Jamie.

Jamie had wandered out to the lane and picked at the honeysuckle blossoms, sniffing each one before he flung it to the ground.

"Are you sad, Jamie?" He hadn't heard Betty approach, Jamie been lost in his memories of Gran and teatimes and stories.

"I'm all right. Bet you're glad to have your Sarah home."

"Well, yes and no. Lovely to see her, of course, but you know it's not just Sarah's loss. They were my family too. And Frank doesn't like her. Thinks she looks down on him." Betty watched her thumbs rub against her fingers as if contemplating a tricky problem. "I think she does. He's not quite what my mum had in mind, if you know what I mean."

"Well, now. Are you talking about class? People get funny about that, don't they?"

"Yes, but that's not the only thing. Frank gets cross a lot. He hits me sometimes."

Jamie noticed a bruise on Betty's arm, just about where her rolled up sleeves ended. "Did he do that?" He laid a gentle finger on it. "Why? You're so nice."

"I don't know how much you understand, Master Jamie. Thing is, we don't have a baby. It makes him angry. He wants a son."

"Why's that your fault?"

"Well, he thinks it is."

"You can't make a baby? He can't either?"

"Oh, Jamie, I'll tell you all about it one day, when we have lots of time."

They strolled back to the cottage together to join the others.

He'd only had glimpses of her until about the middle of September when she'd come to his room, ordered by Stanton, to give it a "good clean out," which seemed to involve all kinds of fuss and mess.

He'd sat on his bed and curled his feet under him, settling in for a good chat.

"How are you, Betty?"

"Same."

"Have you got another bruise?"

"Yes." She punished her dusting rag for fingerprints, dust, Frank, and babies.

"You were going to tell me about babies."

Betty stood and, arms akimbo, looked at him like his old kindergarten schoolteacher used to. "I'm not sure you're ready to hear this. You're very young. And . . ."

"Stupid? Slow isn't the same as stupid."

"Didn't say that, wouldn't say that."

"And I'm fifteen, you know. That's big. Tell me."

She plopped down on his desk chair, her big curvy legs spread wide. She rested her elbows on her knees and looked up at him. "People get babies the same way animals do. Didn't you ever see the cows at it? Or the dogs? The sheep?"

"I saw a sheep with horns hurting another sheep. Evans told me it was to get lambs when I asked. That's not it!"

"Oh, yes it is! And they're not hurting them, they like it."

And she'd told him how people did it, mostly, although everyone does it a little different. The main thing is to get this into that. He didn't believe her, it sounded disgusting. But then he remembered what happened sometimes when he dreamed of Rosie.

He'd had a chance to check up on her story a few days later when he came across a couple of stable boys playing cards in the courtyard. He hung back behind the tack-room door and listened in. One of them was telling the other, in great detail, about this girl he'd taken for a picnic. They'd spread the blanket and eaten their sandwiches and had a bit of a cuddle. And then, well, one thing led to another and it happened. First time for him, he didn't know about her. His friend was all ears and wanted all the details. And he got them, and so did Jamie. Took him a while to realize that a *cock* didn't only mean a boy chicken, it was what the boy called his willy. Even Roy hadn't used that word, and he'd never talked to other boys when he lived in London. He must talk to Betty about all this. There were still a few things he didn't understand.

Yesterday was the first chance he'd had to tell her without anyone hearing that he wanted to talk again. "I've got some questions," he said. She whispered she'd try to come up to his room after tea to lay the fire.

A light knock on the door made his heart go fast. She acted as if she was sneaking around. Instead of opening the door flat out, she opened it only half way and slid into his room as best she could, considering she wasn't all that small. Her breasts slapped the door's edge, and Jamie's breath came faster as his eyes came to rest on that big soft pillow of a chest.

"Evening, Master Jamie, just going to lay the fire. These October evenings are drawing in."

Why was she talking loud like that? Someone listening? Better do the same. "Good evening, Betty. I'm glad you came. Was your husband kind today?" he said loudly.

"No need to shout!"

"Sorry, thought you were worried about people hearing things," he whispered through cupped hands.

"No, no, it's all right. No, not kind." She sighed and lifted her skirt and he saw the red stripes across her legs. "Last night."

"Still angry about no baby?"

"Yes, still angry. Doctor told me it's not always the woman, sometimes the man can't make a baby. I didn't dare tell Frank till yesterday, and I only told him then because he started badgering me again and I'd had enough. He was that upset. I shouldn't have told him."

"You mean he can't do, er . . . that thing. You know, what you said. The sex thing."

"No, not that, he does that most every night. Just sometimes the stuff doesn't have enough of the little things in it that swim up inside and make the baby."

Jamie sat back on his bed and thought about this news. *So the stuff is supposed to have little things in it to make babies.* The stable boys had left that part out. Perhaps his didn't have any either. And perhaps they swam too slowly to get anywhere important. Or didn't know how to swim.

He had that feeling down there more often lately, and there it was again with all this sex talk. He pulled the bedspread over his lap to hide it. *You need a wife for those kinds of things.* Unless you were a stable boy or someone like that. Different rules.

"Why did you rumple that bed, Jamie? Here, let me put it straight."

"No, no, I'll do it."

"What are you hiding under there?" She yanked the bedspread off him and looked. Her eyes widened when she saw the bump and she looked as if she wanted to kiss him, her mouth round and soft and rosy now. Her tongue brushed her lips and she stroked his hand, ragged from all the scrubbing, but its rough touch thrilling just the same. Stroking seemed like a fine thing that could definitely be done all over. He could stroke her all over if she ever wanted him to. He felt his cheeks flush as he got bigger and harder.

"Why, Jamie, did me talking about sex make you want to do it?"

"'Course I do. You said all the fellows want to."

"With me, Jamie?"

"You look nice and soft. The good kind of squashy. Yes. And,

Betty, I heard a stable boy talking about his first time with a girl. He called his willy a cock. Is cock a better word?"

"It's a more grownup word. Willy is for children."

"*Cock*. Sounds strong. Cock!"

"Don't keep on saying that, Jamie. Most people don't say it at all. And don't you ever say it in front of anyone in this family!"

"Sorry." He felt ashamed. Perhaps the whole sex thing was shame.

"You know, you could help me, Jamie." She looked at him, her head a little to one side, as if wondering which chicken was plumper. "We could make a baby. Only no one must know. That way, Frank would stop hitting me because we'd have a baby."

She brought her big round face down so their noses were almost touching. Her breath smelled of cheese and pickled onions, like real women who did real work should probably smell.

"Only people like you aren't supposed to make babies. They might send you away, so it would have to be a big secret." She whispered now and her breath warmed his cheek.

"Yes, yes, yes," he whispered, "Let's make a baby. I want to do that now!" His fingernails scratched at the sheets in anticipation.

"Not now, Jamie. We mustn't get caught." She stood up and folded her hands across her tummy. She looked quite cross with her lips all scrunched up.

"Why are you cross? I didn't say the wrong thing, did I?" It wasn't so hard now, but it felt terribly uncomfortable.

"I'm just a bit, you know, anxious. It's a big step. I've got to think how we can get away where no one will find us out."

"Well, who knows you're here now? Now would be nice." The thought was a tingly one.

"Cook knows." She paused and looked down at him, hands on hips, her strong arms pushing her blouse tight. "But your first time wouldn't take long, you're too excited. But you know, it has to happen often to make sure, so we'll still have to find a place."

"Will you take your clothes off?"

"There's no time, just my knickers. Get your things off."

"In front of you? Oh my goodness." He wasn't sure any more. She might laugh.

"Yes, in front of me! Come on, I'll help you."

Jamie sat against the pillow, his legs spread out in front

and let her undo the buttons and pull his trousers off. He felt silly, and scared now, too. He didn't know what it would be like. Maybe he wouldn't like it after all. Maybe it would be a nasty sort of thing to do.

His white pants gaped at the front and out it popped for all to see. He kept his head down but peered up at Betty under his eyebrows to see if she was going to make fun of him. Her face was half serious, half happy. Not laughing.

"Ooh, now, Master Jamie, very nice. Very nice."

"Is it?" He took a good look at that piece of him he'd always thought of as not clean, not to be touched, not to be discussed, certainly not nice. "What's nice about it?"

"It's a good strong big one and it's going to feel nice inside me, Jamie. Women like sex too, not just menfolk. It feels lovely. Sex makes people have babies because they like to do it. Nature's way, you see." She slipped his underpants off. "Only sometimes, like with Frank and me, it doesn't work out. So we need help."

She took her knickers off and pulled up her skirt as she sat on him. He caught a faint whiff of fish. He didn't like fish much, but coming off her it seemed exciting for some reason.

"Will you kiss me, like a man-woman kiss? I've seen them outside a pub, and I saw it in a film once."

"All right, Jamie, you've got a pretty mouth, I'll say that." Her lips closed over his and seemed to suck them in. Her tongue touched his and he remembered an electric shock he got from a wrong wire once, only this was a good shock, traveled all the way down, just right.

Betty lifted herself onto his cock and it went deep inside a warm, soft space, slippery with whatever women have there to make it slide. She moved up and down so it felt sort of happy painful, not quite easy, but ready to be set free quite soon. He felt dreamy, not really in his room anymore, or anywhere he knew. But in a funny way, his mind had cleared, too; he felt clever.

She moved faster and started making funny little sounds, almost like a whining child. She'd said the stuff should come out inside her and he knew it would, very soon. He wanted to explode, felt it in a different way from when he was alone. A hand wasn't as good as Betty's insides, soft and warm and lovely as she was. Her neck had a gentle farm smell: horses and hay and butter and milk. A faint sweat stink from her armpits rose as she moved and he felt drunk like when Roy would give him beer for a laugh. This felt so much better, and probably wouldn't give him a headache, either.

Wonderful and wide, her bottom spread over his legs, and she opened her blouse so her breasts nuzzled his face, their nipples dark and hard looking. Her arms had muscles like a man's and when she pinned him down by his shoulders, he saw only swinging flesh, and plenty of it.

He floated up, almost to the sky, and he pushed himself further into her as the great gush came. They both panted and clutched each other for a few minutes, him still inside although he could feel it slipping down.

Suddenly, there she was on her feet again, pulling on her knickers as if she had a bus to catch.

"Get your things on, Master Jamie. I've been gone a good ten minutes and I'll be missed."

She didn't seem so loving anymore, like she'd finished one job and gone onto the next. Jamie pulled on his pants and trousers, feeling more comfortable now, but disappointed too. A cuddle afterwards would have been nice, and perhaps what people ought to do after nice close times like that. But she was right, they mustn't get caught.

She finished laying his fire, working quickly. "Remember, Jamie, big secret. I'll think about our next time. Do you still want to help?"

"Oh yes! I like helping people. At any time."

"Bye, bye, then," and she blew him a little kiss before rushing out.

Jamie finished buttoning his slacks and lay back, blowing a little air out of his lips as he cupped his hands behind his head. So, he might make a baby for Betty and she wouldn't get hit anymore. Soon, perhaps. Not too soon, that would mean not having to do the making part anymore. He liked the making part.

He'd be a father, a thought that made him sit up, startled out of happy thoughts. No, not really. It was his stuff that made it, but it wouldn't be in his home, he wouldn't be bringing it up or loving it. So he wouldn't be a real father. He wasn't old enough, anyhow. He might be able to see it sometimes and be nice to it.

He might love it anyway, though, even if he wasn't its real father and he wouldn't see it very often. Maybe he wouldn't be able to help loving it. He was good at loving, it came easy.

Then, a horrid thought. Suppose it wasn't right, got born slow like he had. Would Frank start hitting Betty again and the baby too? Frank wasn't the sort to love anyone slow. Oh, God, just supposing. Jamie stuck the heels of his hands into his eyes, pulled his knees up and rocked. Oh, God, oh, God, a slow baby that wasn't loved. *Fiddle-faddle, fiddle-faddle.* But Betty wasn't slow. Jamie's parents? Gran never said.

Gran almost never talked about his mother and father. She'd said a long time ago they were trouble, always trouble, and they'd had to go away for a long time, might never be back. She told him later that wasn't true, they'd been killed in a train crash; she'd wanted to spare his feelings. Jamie didn't know how being trouble and having to go away forever was better than being killed in a train crash, but he looked at her teary eyes and kept quiet. Jamie's father was her son, so she was allowed to be sad, was supposed to be, even if he was trouble.

She'd said something he hadn't understood to Roy a long time ago, he thought it was just after the Christmas before last when he was still only fourteen. The memory nagged, what was it? The picture opened up like a slow dream: Jamie hunched on the floor in a corner, crying, and Roy and Gran sitting at the table. He remembered the breadboard still out with half a loaf, a lump of butter, and a small wedge of cheddar. Gran was telling Roy off for being unkind. He'd kept calling Jamie that word. "Idiot." Horrid, mean word.

"Tell me, Gran, what you think made Jamie an idiot? In the family is it?"

"Don't call him that! You see how you've made him cry? His name is Jamie. He's a little slow, that's all."

"All right, all right, it's not as though he knows the meaning of the word. But anyway, didn't you ask the doc? Didn't he say nothing?"

"Said he thought it was the drink, he's seen it before, especially round these parts. Mother drinks too much when she's expecting the baby and it damages them." Gran sighed and looked old all of a sudden. "She drank from morning till night, Jamie's mum did. Well, God knows drink's bedeviled this family, so you watch yourself!"

Roy hadn't answered, just shrugged his bony shoulders and laughed. Jamie didn't miss that laugh. Not much like a person laugh, more like a fierce animal of a sort Jamie hadn't ever seen, one that would eat you bit by bit, cackling while he did it.

He hadn't understood at the time. People drink all the time, he'd thought then. Water, orangeade if they're lucky. Tea. Funny if that made babies slow. Now, since coming to the Manor, he realized that when people talk about drink, they often mean something that could get you drunk. So his mother got drunk all the time. And that had made Jamie slow while he was still inside her tummy.

Babies coming out of a mother's tummy was another thing he hadn't understood then, not until Betty told him. Jamie hated drunk people. Roy used to hurt him more when he was drunk—if Gran was out, that is. Sometimes he did disgusting things that hurt a lot. Nothing that felt nice, and nothing he'd tell about, *not ever*. And Betty said Frank was usually drunk when he beat her.

He'd ask Betty about the drinking. He would ask her not to drink. He didn't think she did, but still.

Jamie had a dim memory of another thing Gran said not long ago, something about not knowing where her son was. She'd said gone away first, then dead in a train crash, and then he could have sworn she said in the forest she wanted Jamie to find her son. He couldn't quite remember. Another dream, he supposed.

Would Rosie do sex after she was married? He didn't think so. Rosie was more like a pretty pink flower, like her name. Betty was more like . . . well, he wasn't sure what she was more like. More from the earth, perhaps, more part of a farm than a Manor. He liked both kinds of ladies, but in different ways. Like tea at Gran's and tea at the Manor. Gran's teas filled you up fast, Manor teas satisfied you in another way—you had to pay attention to the more special tastes.

But as far as he understood things, sex was the only way to get babies. Rosie would have to do it a few times when she got married, then. But she wouldn't be keen on it like Betty. Too ladylike.

Lots to tell his friend George. But would he understand? Did he get feelings like that? Maybe it would upset him. Maybe not say a word to anybody, like Betty said. He wanted to see George again. It had been too long since he visited at Blexton. He'd ask Rosie. But there was so much happening these days. He'd been busy.

* * *

This time had been best of all. Betty had come to his room a few times. But now they lay on a blanket in the boathouse. He didn't know what she'd told her husband. Jamie told Rosie he wanted to go for a walk. On his own. To think about his book. Rosie had said, "All right then," in a hurt little voice and stomped off. He'd felt guilty for a little while. Not for long, though.

Betty had brought a candle so he could see her bare body, all of her skin, not just parts here and there. He wanted to get a peek at where he went inside her, too, but he thought he'd better not tell her that. He'd explained how he wanted to be stroked all over, and how he wanted to stroke her too, and how he wanted them to lie down together without any clothes on at all. She said she thought that was sweet, just so long as it didn't take too long.

The stroking had been beautiful, like climbing up to heaven, one cloud at a time. And he had managed to take a look down there, at that strange looking part like some sort of fat flower. Pretty, in its own way. Had its own smell, sharp and fishy, quite different from how the rest of her smelled.

He gazed at her body, creamy in the candlelight. Cat lazy, she stretched out on her back, one leg bent across the other, arms all the way out behind her head. Her breasts stood high, very large, very nice to bury your face in, and good to suck on once she'd taught him how. When they'd come to the last part, the magic part, he'd been the one on top, been the master, given her his seeds.

He'd find a way to see the baby, to teach it some of what Gran had taught him. To make the baby understand someone would look after him if things went wrong. He was a man now. A man must do what's right. Even keep this secret, although he'd sworn he'd never do secrets again. This one was different—it was a right kind of secret.

If he told George, it wasn't as if he could turn around and tell anyone else. But perhaps he wouldn't approve. Did he get awfully lonely without any friends to visit? He must ask Lady Audrey if he could go for a visit. It was important, and he didn't have to tell George anything about anything.

And she'd promised not to drink.

31

Jamie frowned as he formed his words, slowly, painfully, mostly staying on the lines, but not always.

"I'll never write my book. I'm learning too slowly. I'm too slow."

"Now, Jamie, it took me a few years to learn how to write properly, you'll get it. Be patient."

Rosie felt far from patient. A friend from school was coming to stay and bringing her brother. She seemed to remember he was rather dishy. He'd been wounded, but was on the mend, apparently, nothing missing. For New Year's Eve she'd get the servants to push the living room furniture back and they could play records and dance.

Nearly 1942 already, she felt life passing her by. Heartily sick of this war, she wanted music and dancing and romance. She didn't want to hear about "Our boys at the front," any more, either. Christmas had been really boring, everyone so serious and brooding. They might have made an effort to cheer up. They never had been that merry at Christmas. Probably mooning over that Fiona. Even Jamie had been quiet, although intrigued by the idea of a dressed up tree and presents wrapped in pretty paper carefully saved from the year before. He'd been thrilled when Mummy opened the box of paper and let Jamie choose some for his own wrapping. Daddy had given him some pocket money and taken him shopping for presents, too. So sweet.

Jamie visited Sarah at the cottage from time to time. Betty wouldn't be able to work at the Manor much longer now that her pregnancy was becoming obvious. Mummy was old-fashioned that way. At least Betty would be able to keep her sister company so Rosie wouldn't feel obliged to go down there so often. Sarah was so damned stoical. Lost her family, lost her leg, you'd think she'd whine or cry occasionally. She'd just about grown a halo. She did a little sewing for the Manor these days in return for extra rations. No reason why she shouldn't. Her hands worked all right, although she wasn't that good at it. She'd sewn up a hem of Rosie's and the stitches were much too big. Funny how she had more brains and refinement than Betty, almost as if she came from a different family.

Rosie knew her annoyance was unreasonable but, these days, everything was annoying.

"Rosie. It's my birthday tomorrow."

"Cook's managing a cake, I think." Rationing was tighter than ever now.

"It's just a year since . . . well, everything."

"I know, Jamie. Are you sad, then?" *God, not more of this.*

"No, I've finished with that, except for sometimes at night. No, it's my book."

"What book?"

"How could you forget? The one I want to write about how people should live right."

"Oh, that. Yes, I remember. But it's hard writing a book. You're not ready yet."

"But I'll be sixteen tomorrow. When?"

"What's the hurry?"

"Well, I sort of promised Gran when she came to me in the forest." Jamie studied his lap, cheeks getting pink now.

"You never told me that." Rosie was surprised, and a little offended he'd kept it back.

"I haven't told anyone except you just now. It's really a private sort of thing, don't you think?"

"Yes. I suppose so." She took a deep breath. Patience. This went deep with him.

"I've got an idea. Sarah doesn't have enough to do. Why don't we ask her to work with you on your reading and writing? You'd be helping her feel better."

"You don't want to do it anymore, do you? You're bored with me." He looked her straight on, no tears, and no quivering chin. He sensed how she felt, but she'd have to lie.

"Of course I'm not bored with you, you're my brother." She patted his shoulder, but he shrugged off her hand. Feeling startled and annoyed and guilty, she slapped her palms on the desk and said in her brightest voice, "Tell you what. We'll make a list of things you want to talk about. Then, when you're ready, Sarah can help you can fill them in with the details. You know, like chapters." Good thought, get this out of his head and off her back for a while.

"That's a wonderful idea. That would mean I've at least made a start before a new year starts." Happy again, so easy to please.

"All right. One word ideas to write about when you can."

Jamie drew the pad towards her. She didn't fancy his pencil, chewed soggy on the end, and rummaged around in the desk drawer for another.

"I might not get them in the right order."

"That's fine, we can switch them around later. Just get started."

"Here goes: Christmas. I never knew Christmas was done this way, so lovely, so quiet and happy. I dreamed of Gran on Christmas Eve, you know, so she wasn't left out."

Rosie's impatience died as she watched his bright face and wide honest eyes.

"I'm glad you are happy here, Jamie, very glad you are my brother now."

"Now, let me see." He chewed on his thumb as he thought.

"I know what should come next. Being honest. Did you get that?" Rosie nodded. "Being kind. Then only keeping right secrets."

"Is that the end, Jamie?"

Jamie turned his big eyes on her and smiled like a cherub.

"Just one more. Making babies."

"What? You can't put that in your book! What do you know about making babies?" *What the dickens is this about?*

"Oh, you've gone all pink. I saw some sheep once, and Evans told me what they were doing and why they were doing it. It's important to make babies."

"And it's important not to talk about it. People don't, not in polite society. I'm not writing that down."

"But my book isn't only for polite society. It's for all the other ones, too."

When did he get so stubborn? "Well, I'm not writing it down!"

"Then I suppose I'll just have to wait for Sarah. I'll be in my room if you need me."

He was walking out on her, having a little tantrum. *What cheek!*

* * *

Jamie snuggled under his blankets and thought about his book. Funny how Rosie didn't like the baby part. But no, now he thought about it, he'd realized before she wouldn't like anything to do with that sort of thing. Anyway, it was his book, and Sarah was different, he could tell. He'd noticed her watching her visitors, as if she wasn't part of anything going on around her. She had suffered a lot, and she had lost family like him. She had lost a leg and he had lost his cleverness before he was even born. All that losing made people think about things in a different way. Their important things were different from other people's important things.

He had a good idea for the book. He'd think of one person to fit each bit—chapter Rosie called it—and talk about them and how they behaved. Some would be there because they'd got it right, and some because they hadn't.

He mustn't write anything to make people know about him and Betty. Better stick to the sheep. Mustn't write anything bad about people still alive. Could make pretend names for them.

Rosie, now. The kindness chapter? She was very kind to him, but sometimes impatient and cross. Got bored easily, especially with him these days, and that made him sad. She used to want to be with him all the time, but not anymore. She was always complaining about the war too. The soldiers had the hardest job, and she didn't have any hard things to do. And she liked a lot of things that don't really matter. But she was mostly kind, and he loved her. His sister.

Wickedness, he only just thought of that. That was Hitler— no need to say *Mister* Hitler. He was even worse than Roy and Bernhardt. Jamie sometimes listened to Mr. Churchill when the family gathered around the wireless in the evenings. In the best talk, Mr. Churchill called Hitler a "monster of wickedness" and said he was a "bloodthirsty guttersnipe." He'd had to practice that last one to remember for later. It sounded super. Hitler had gone to war in Russia when he'd promised Mr. Stalin he wouldn't. And he'd done it without telling him first, which was against the rules. So he'd broken a serious promise and broken big rules. And made people die all the time. Hitler liked to paint pictures, though. He'd heard Lady Audrey mention it to Sir Geoffrey, who'd made a rude noise.

He should write about George, too. He'd have to think of another word for George. Silence? He made noises, though. Goodness? Yes, as far as Jamie knew. Who knew what he really thought about things, all locked up in that twisty body.

Friend. That was not a word for Jamie. He'd abandoned George, and that had to stop as soon as the holidays were over. He could come to his lessons with Sarah. And eat cake when there was any. There'd be cake tomorrow. He'd ask Sir Geoffrey about getting George over here for his birthday. Stop putting him off, stop leaving him until last. Would George be cross or sad? Jamie had not been a good friend.

Honesty. Sir Geoffrey. But he was always in his office talking secrets, or at least that's what Rosie said. He'd acted honest with Jamie, though. A very good man. And *honesty* was not Jamie.

He leaned over the side of his bed and pulled a handkerchief out of the space between the two mattresses. He uncurled it and gazed at the lovely shining ring. He slipped it on his finger and held it this way and that so it picked up the light from his lamp. He'd left the little girl's necklace back at the farm and he missed playing with that sparkly bracelet Gran had given him. Had anyone found it under his bed? Did another boy or girl play with it now?

Biffy's secret sparkly bear heart must stay a secret, just in case. Roy stole it from Gran and Jamie stole it—no, took it—from Roy. No one to remember that brooch anymore. He'd been very good, though, done nothing until Lady Audrey left this ring in the downstairs cloakroom. After washing her hands, probably. She hadn't mentioned it, not that he'd heard.

He couldn't keep it. There was no safe place to hide it. And what would happen to him if they found it in his room? They turned the mattresses every now and then. No, he would have to drop it somewhere. Maybe in the garden. No, in her car. No, behind the toilet in the cloakroom. Yes, then she'd remember taking it off there and it might have rolled across the floor. He couldn't have Sir Geoffrey and all of them looking at him with disappointed faces.

He couldn't keep it. Mustn't keep it. Put it back tomorrow.

A little of this and a little of that. That's people. Perhaps he should wait to write his book, spend another year getting more clever.

He jumped as Betty knocked and barged in and almost dropped the ring as he shoved it back in its place. He loved to feel her bump, and the best thing was when the baby moved. She said it kicked, but how did she know it was a foot and not a hand? Perhaps it wanted to say hello, even to shake hands.

"Got a nice cup of tea for you, dear. I'll start your fire too."

"Betty, I miss you, I miss all of that . . . you know. You are so big and lovely and soft."

"I'll need another baby later, Jamie. You'll just have to wait for a year."

"But I can't wait that long."

"Well, I suppose we can have a little cuddle and see what happens."

She heaved herself onto the bed and took him in her arms. Soon, he found himself drowning again, or was it more like flying? Best to stop thinking at times like these. Even clever people have to stop thinking sometimes, only feel and do.

Just knowing that is clever.

CPSIA information can be obtained
at www.ICGtesting.com
Printed in the USA
BVHW03s2151270218
509283BV00001B/9/P